SUPERIOR
JUSTICE
A Lake Superior Mystery

by

TOM HILPERT

SPRING CREEK

Nashville, TN

For Audrey Christison

CHAPTER 1

Daniel Spooner died on a Tuesday in early May, just as the lunch hour was ending in Grand Lake. He died in custody, just in front of the courthouse. He died because his heart was broken into three pieces by a single .30-caliber bullet. Later, some called it a crime. Many more called it justice. For me, once Spooner's killer told me his real alibi, it became a royal pain in the neck.

Two hours after Spooner was shot, I was sitting in my office, drinking smooth afternoon decaf and parsing Greek verbs. Bach played quietly in the background. I vaguely remembered that listening to classical music could actually make you more intelligent. That was good, because Greek verbs make me feel stupid. Even so, I was actually eager to study. Back in the day, I could never have imagined that feeling.

The phone beeped and the speaker crackled. It was my part-time secretary, Julie.

"Chief Jensen on line one."

I grabbed the handset. "Julie, why do people say 'back in the day?'"

"I prefer the expression, 'time was,' myself."

"Time was, back in the day, you could use 'em both at once."

"I hope Chief Jensen enjoys talking with you as much I have," said Julie, and broke the connection.

I punched the button for line one. "Borden," I said.

"Jonah, it's Dan Jensen." Jensen was the chief of the Grand Lake police.

"Hi, Dan, what can I do for you?" I sipped some more coffee. Surely God gave us coffee to show that he wants us to enjoy life.

"Well, somebody popped Daniel Spooner."

"Spooner? The guy who confessed to killing Missy Norstad?"

"That's him."

"Wow," I said. It's a useful word when you're waiting for people to give you more information, like why they really want to talk to you. There was a pause. I could tell it wasn't comfortable for Jensen.

"Well, we don't really know anything right now, of course, but our main suspect is Doug Norstad."

"Missy's dad," I said. I waited while silence filled up the line.

"Come on, Jonah. You're supposed to be the perceptive and intuitive guy here." There was a plaintive quality to his voice.

"Okay," I said. "I intuit and perceive that you need to pick up Norstad for questioning, and you want me to go along to smooth things over." I sipped some coffee. "You Minnesota Norwegians really have a hard time just asking for something, don't you?"

"I'm a Swede," said Dan stiffly. Then, after a moment, he added "Isn't 'intuit' some kind of Eskimo?"

"Sorry about that. I'm sure you're right about the Swede, of course. I think you're wrong about the Eskimo though."

"So, you gonna help me with Norstad? I mean, you are the police chaplain."

"When do you want to do it?"

"Can I pick you up in fifteen minutes?"

"Sure," I said. "Give me time for one more cup of coffee."

CHAPTER 2

Jensen pulled into the church parking lot in a white unmarked
SUV. I was a bit amused by the notion of an unmarked Grand Lake
police car. Everyone in town knew it on sight, which, if Bach had
sufficiently boosted my intelligence to understand correctly,
destroyed the purpose of an unmarked vehicle.

I climbed in next to the chief. Dan Jensen was in his late
thirties. He was tall and a bit heavy, but with a big frame that hid
the extra weight well. His hair was blond, thin and short, peppered
with almost indistinguishable spots of light gray. His wide
Scandinavian face was clean shaved, and his most prominent
feature was a pair of piercingly blue eyes. The impression of
intelligence and acuity given by those eyes was backed up in reality
by a fine brain.

"Hey, Dan," I said, and shook his hand, then climbed into the
front seat next to him.

"Jonah," he returned.

"Whaddya got?" I asked.

He looked at me sideways.

"Hey, come on, like you said, I'm the police chaplain. That
makes me part of the force. What do you think I'll do, taint the
evidence?"

"Department," said Jensen.

"What's that?" I asked.

"It makes you part of the police *department*. We don't really have a 'force.' We have a department."

"I'd rather be part of a 'force'—it sounds so much more exciting than 'department.'"

"May the force be with you then," said Dan.

"You gonna tell me about this or not?" I said.

He sighed. "Okay. But don't think that means I won't throw your rear-end in the slammer if you share evidence in an on-going investigation."

"Hey, do what you think is best," I said. "Part of my job is keeping sensitive information confidential."

"I have a feeling we'll want you in on this one," said Dan after a minute. "Here's what we know: They were moving Spooner to the courthouse over the lunch hour. He was out in the open, and someone shot him, probably with a thirty-thirty." Dan picked up a can of Coke from a cup holder and sipped it.

"You get ballistics back already?"

Jensen nodded his approval of the question. "Not yet. We found a weapon. May be the murder weapon."

"That ought to make it a bit easier."

"Not necessarily. We think this guy was smart. There were a few people around—you know, the press, some rubberneckers, and of course, the cops who moved him. Most everyone we questioned thought the shot came from across the street, maybe up high."

"Remind me, what's across the street?"

"Tommy's café is in the bottom floor. Top two floors are empty. We went over there, and up on the roof, behind the false front, we found the rifle and scope."

"Shoot," I said, "all you have to do is track it down."

"*Shoot?*" asked Jensen incredulously.

"Hey whaddya expect?" I said, "I'm a pastor, after all. You think I'll start cussing a blue streak?"

"I am deeply disappointed in you," said Jensen.

"Get used to it," I said. "It's what I do best, disappoint people. Heck, even my mother wanted me to be cop, not a pastor."

"*Heck?*" said Jensen.

"All right, we just covered my linguistic habits. Now, you got the gun. What's the problem?"

"Jonah, it's a thirty-thirty, an ordinary deer gun. You know how many un-registered deer rifles there are in this state?"

"No idea."

"Neither does anyone else. You don't have to register them. They're bought and sold through papers, garage sales, you name it."

"Shoot," I said.

Jensen glared at me. I returned his look with wide-eyed innocence. A man must have his fun somehow.

"That's not all," he said finally. "He filed off the serial number—probably wouldnta had to, cause we don't track 'em, like I said. He also ran a rat-tail file down the barrel. If he did that after he fired, ballistics won't match."

"What about the brass?" I asked.

Jensen looked at me sharply. I shrugged "My dad was a cop," I said.

"It was only one shot. He didn't leave the brass. Probably at the bottom of Lake Superior right now."

"Anything else at the scene?" I asked.

"Oh yeah. It gets better. He left his clothes."

I envisioned a naked vigilante superhero, racing like a white wad of blubber through Grand Lake. "Anyone see a streaker about that time?"

"Very funny. These still had the Goodwill store smell on them. He probably wore them over the top of his other clothes to prevent powder residue."

"Smart guy," I commented. "I'm assuming then, no prints on the gun, or the area?"

"Nothing," said Jensen.

I digested this for a minute. "Now, Dan, not to be contentious, but why Norstad?"

"Come on, Jonah, Spooner raped and murdered his daughter."

"So, motive. Didn't Missy have a boyfriend? How about him?"

"I'm so glad we have you to help us. Maybe we should promote you to chaplain-detective."

"Sorry. You checked, of course."

"In school," said Jensen.

"So Doug had a motive, I'll give him that. But if Johann Sebastian has adequately restored my memory, I recall that Spooner molested at least three other minors. What about their families?"

"Those were all out of state. We're checking, of course, reverend-detective, but Norstad is closer."

"Hey, Doug is a part of my church. I'm helping you, but I wanna help him too, if I can. I have a right to ask why you're after him."

"We're not after him. But he had motive." He took another sip of Coke, and turned north on Highway 61. "What about his guns? You ever hunt with him?"

I sighed. "Okay, so Doug Norstad uses a thirty-thirty. So do half the men in Superior County, and about a third of the women. So do I, for that matter."

"Doesn't matter that much, I guess," said Jensen. "Whoever this was he's smart. He will have bought the gun from the paper or at a flea market or something. It won't be his regular gun. But it will be one he's comfortable with." He slurped his soda again. I looked out the window at the lake to our right.

"It was a pretty fair shot," said Jensen. "Norstad any good?"

"I don't really like this, Chief."

"Welcome to police work, pastor," said Jensen. "Was he a good shot?"

"Dan, everyone up here hunts. You probably coulda made that shot. Heck, *I* probably coulda made it."

"And so could Norstad. So we got motive, we got method, and you and I are going to find out if we got opportunity."

"Motive, method and opportunity are all pretty circumstantial," I said.

"So far, it looks like that's all we'll have. Doesn't look like we'll have any physical evidence we can use." He sipped his Coke and glanced at me. "Look, Jonah, Spooner was already a convicted rapist and pedophile. He confessed to killing Melissa Norstad. If Doug Norstad gets the right jury, he may even get off altogether."

"You really want that, Dan? A killer gets off scot-free?"

"I don't know what I want on this one. The whole thing stinks. Spooner deserved to die. If Norstad pulled the trigger, he did us all a favor." Jensen grimaced and readjusted his Grand Lake PD ball cap.

"But you don't like anyone taking the law into their own

hands," I said.

"Do you?"

"No. I believe in due process."

"Yeah. It's a lousy system, but it's better than the alternatives."

The car swooped up and down the hills. I glanced at the rocky, pine-clad hill crests to the left, and then turned to gaze again at the great sweep of Lake Superior to our right. I never tired of looking at that timeless horizon and the broad carpet of perfect blue beneath it. But I did turn left to look longingly upstream as we crossed the bubbling, clear water of the Blue River. I could almost feel my rod shudder as I imagined a big steelhead trout stripping line from my reel.

I turned back to Jensen. "Dan, I've spent a lot time with the Norstads over the past six months. First, Melissa disappears. Then, they find the body. Finally, Spooner's confession. That family has been through hell, and they don't need this right now."

"I know it," said Jensen. "That's why I brought you along."

We were silent for a few more minutes.

"Did your mom really want you to be a cop?" he asked.

"*Heck* yeah," I said.

CHAPTER 3

The Lake Superior coastline of Minnesota is known throughout the region as the "North Shore," though in fact the coast here runs from the southwest toward the northeast, and neither the shoreline, nor the lake are really north of one another. The water is sky-clear, colder than a Scandinavian fjord, and nearly as rocky. It plunges quickly towards depths of over 1000 feet, and from a distance the lake appears achingly blue and pristine. Up close it is much the same, rather like a cold Aegean sea. It is not, however, a popular place to swim.

In spite of the chill, the North Shore is the Riviera of Minnesota and northwest Wisconsin. People come here year round to look at the lake to the east and south, and to hike and ski in what native Minnesotans consider to be the mountains that border the coastline. I come from the West, so I can hardly be expected to call them mountains, but they're pretty enough, and bigger than most Minnesota hills.

Years ago the people cut timber and mined the hills for iron ore. The big timber, the money trees are all gone now, and the iron industry is suffering too. And so Highway 61 is the lifeblood of the North Shore, bringing tourists and their money to the resorts and cabins that sprout along the coast like dandelions in springtime.

Some of the resorts are world-class hotels and condos. There are many others too, much like the one belonging to Doug Norstad and his family. Named appropriately, if not imaginatively, "Norstad's North Shore Cabins," Doug and his wife presided over about three acres of rocky shoreline, in which were crowded some ten, rather dilapidated cabins.

Dan Jensen pulled the unmarked police Blazer up to the little cabin that served as the resort office. Resort was probably too strong a word. "Camp" might have been closer.

No one was at the little counter when we walked in. The place smelled of wood smoke, and cigarettes too. Lucy Norstad had started smoking again when her daughter Missy went missing. A door behind the counter hung ajar, and from the room beyond came the melancholy sounds of a daytime soap opera.

Dan looked at me. The man probably had trained to deal with hostile people armed with knives and automatic weapons, but he was scared to talk to a mild mannered Scandinavian who might have killed his daughter's murderer. I didn't blame him.

"Hello?" I called. "Doug? Lucy?" For good measure I banged the little bell that sat on the counter next to a pile of rental forms.

A chair scraped and Lucy Norstad came to the door. Her hair, a lustrous brown a year ago, now hung in straggling gray knots. She had on a pair of big glasses, with hexagonal plastic frames. A half-smoked cigarette hung from her mouth, and her plain dress was wrinkled and spotted.

"Hi, Lucy," I said.

She looked at me with dead eyes. "Hello, Pastor."

Her gaze shifted to Jensen. She looked back at me and shook her head.

"No," she said. "No, no." She started backing away. "I don't know what it is, but I can't take it. Don't tell me anything else. I don't want to know."

I could feel Jensen's Scandinavian temperament floundering behind me. "It's okay, Lucy," I said. "We were just looking for Doug."

"Why?" She was still shaking her head. "Why are you looking for him?"

Jensen was reading the rental forms with avid interest. I was on my own.

"Lucy," I said, "why don't you sit down."

"I don't want to sit down. I don't want to know. Please just go away." She gave a little sob, and I could almost see Jensen shriveling into himself.

"Okay. It's okay. Chief Jensen is here with me because someone killed Daniel Spooner this afternoon."

A little life sparked behind her dull gray eyes. "Daniel Spooner is dead?"

"Shot through the heart," I said. Very pastoral.

She nodded quickly. "Good. I know it's wrong, Pastor, but I still say good." Her voice broke and now the tears started in earnest. I looked around the room for a box of Kleenex, but there wasn't one. I let her cry. I thought maybe pretty soon Jensen would start blubbering too, from sheer embarrassment.

After a while I said, "Lucy, we need to talk to Doug. Is he around?"

She shook her head and wiped her nose on her rumpled sleeve. "He went to the Cities this morning." I felt Jensen stiffen behind me.

"Do you know where he went? We'd like to get a hold of him."

She nodded. The poor woman probably thought we just wanted

to tell him the news.

"He goes down there every Tuesday to see his dad." She shrugged as if I'd asked another question. "Doug's dad and I don't get along very well. In fact, neither did he and Doug until about six months ago, when Doug started going down real regular."

"Is there a number we can call to reach him?"

Lucy looked around at the shabby, dusty little office. "We don't have a cell phone," she said. "You could try his dad's place. I'll get you the number." She started rummaging around below the counter. Muttering under her breath she left the room. A few moments later she returned with a scrap of paper and a phone number.

"When will he be back?" I asked, taking the number.

"He usually stays overnight there, picks up anything special we need for the resort, and comes back Wednesday afternoons."

Jensen seemed to come out of his shell. "Did anyone go with him today?"

Lucy Norstad looked at him as if seeing him for the first time.

"Why do you want to know that?" she whispered. "Why does it matter?"

"We just want to talk to him," I said, shooting Jensen a warning glance.

She kept staring at the Chief. "You think he did it," she accused him. "You think he shot Daniel Spooner." She whirled and pierced me with blazing eyes.

"Lucy," I said, "Chief Jensen just wants to talk with Doug. There aren't any warrants out for his arrest or anything." I fervently hoped that was still true. "The Chief here will just call your father-in-law, and he'll tell him that Doug's been there all day, and then they'll start looking for the person who killed Daniel Spooner."

"But what if he wasn't there? What if he hadn't got there yet? What if he stopped for lunch or something, and he wasn't there when—that scumbag—was killed."

"Mrs Norstad, if he stopped for gas, or for lunch, or anything, there'll be people who saw him, and receipts for food and stuff like that. If that's the case, there'll be no problem." Jensen was getting braver.

"All right, Lucy," I said. "I'll keep in touch. Do you want me to call someone to come out here and sit with you awhile?"

She shook her head, her eyes tearing up again. "I'll be fine," she said. "Doug will come soon, and I'll be fine."

CHAPTER 4

Wednesday morning, I was at Lorraine's Café, eating Lorraine's Superior Breakfast Skillet and drinking coffee by the quart. The skillet was, in truth, Superior. It came in a real, live, cast-iron skillet and consisted of hash browns, onions, peppers, mushrooms, chorizo sausage and two eggs (over-easy, in my case) topped with Hollandaise sauce and mozzarella cheese. Two plate-sized pancakes came with it.

I had eaten one of the pancakes and about two-thirds of the hash browns and eggs when Dan Jensen walked in with another cop. He looked around and I waved at him. He nodded to a few of the patrons as he and the other cop came over.

"Morning, Jonah," he said.

"It is, now that I'm drinking coffee," I said. I looked at Jensen's companion. He was medium height, with salt and pepper hair. Maybe 45, I thought. He wore big square glasses with plastic rims, the kind that were fashionable back in the 1970s, when everyone was on drugs. He had one of those thick mustaches that hid his upper lip. Between the facial hair and the glasses, it would be hard to read this man's expression. Probably a good thing for a cop.

"Jonah, this is Rex Burton, relatively new with the sheriff's department. Rex, Jonah Borden, pastor of Harbor Lutheran."

"Nice to meet you, Rex," I said politely.

"Father," said Burton.

"Have a seat." I gestured to the empty bench across from me in the booth. As they were sliding in, I said to Rex, "By the way, you don't have to call me 'Father.' I'm a Lutheran, and we don't really do that. You can call me pastor, if you want, but my name is Jonah, and that works fine too."

Burton grunted noncommittally.

"Rex came from the Chicago PD about six months ago," said Jensen. "He's still getting used to life out here in the boondocks."

"You must have got here right about the time the Missy Norstad business started up," I said. "Murder, rape. Probably made you feel right at home."

"I don't like to discuss police business with civilians, Father," said Burton.

"Hey, relax," I said. "Just making conversation. But don't call me 'Father.'"

"What are we doing here?" Burton asked Jensen, as if I wasn't there. I sipped some coffee.

"Lorraine's got the best hash and pancakes in the county," said Dan. He gave me an apologetic shrug.

"So what brought you to the North Shore of Minnesota, Rex?" I asked.

"Look," said Burton. "I'm here 'cause Chief Jensen dragged me along for the food. I don't like religious people. I think they are interfering, ignorant idiots. Religion is for pansies, and I don't need it, and I'm not interested in making nice with a priest."

There's one thing that really yanks my chain and Rex Burton had just done it. I can't stand being stereotyped and judged just because I am a pastor. I mean, if religious people are going to be blamed for all the intolerance, then non-religious people simply have no right to be intolerant themselves. "You're sitting in my booth," I said. "Feel free to leave any time." I could feel my face starting to get hot. I looked at Jensen. "I could perform an exorcism on him, if you like. Is that why you brought him?"

Jensen glared at me, and then turned to Burton. "Look. Rex, Pastor Borden is a stand-up guy. He's the chaplain for the city PD, and the sheriff's department too. You wanna work this town, you might need him someday. You got a thing against ministers, leave it at home."

"I am what I am," said Burton. "And I am not a choir-boy, priest-lover, religious bigot. I can get it done without him."

"For Pete's sake Burton, the man's sitting in front of you. At least keep it to yourself, will you?"

"Yeah," I said. "Shut up, or get out of my booth. Better yet, do both."

Burton looked at me with narrowed eyes.

"That's right, I'm serious," I said. "You probably never heard a minister talk like that. Probably makes you think we're all hypocrites or something. I don't care. Go someplace else and think about it."

I met his gaze with a cold-fish stare I had learned years ago. Finally he stood up.

"You're full of crap, Father," he said.

"Like looking in the mirror, isn't it?" I said.

He spun on his heel and walked out.

Jensen blew out his breath. "What the heck was that?"

"Heck?" I inquired mildly.

"You are an unhealthy influence on me," said Jensen.

"Never mind," I said. "The cuss words will come back to you

someday."

"But what about Burton? What bit him?"

"I don't know," I said. "Some people are like that—clergy haters. Could have been abused, or known someone who was abused by a priest or pastor or rabbi."

"He got under your skin, didn't he?" said Jensen.

"Yeah. I shouldn't be so easily riled. But I'm very intolerant of jerks."

"Take it easy, Jonah. I had no idea he'd react that way."

"It's my magnetic personality. Some folks just can't handle the charisma."

"Sometimes that could be true, you know, though 'charisma' isn't exactly the word I would have used."

I grinned, then sipped some more coffee. "Any word on Doug Norstad?"

"No," said Jensen seriously. "How about you?"

"Nothing," I said.

~

Jensen left, and as I finished my breakfast, I called the church from my cell phone. Julie, the part-time secretary answered.

"Hey," I said. "What's up?"

"They teach you that at seminary?" she asked.

"Yeah," I said, "but in Greek. Anything I need to know about?"

"Well, it would help if you knew something about the Bible, or maybe if you had some people skills."

"Nobody's perfect," I said. "I mean right now. Anything that can't wait until I come in this evening?"

She was silent for moment.

"It's okay," I said. "You can't have a snappy comeback for

every single situation."

"But it's what I do."

"I know, and you're good at it. I take it there's nothing urgent."

"Well, the ladies downstairs at the quilting circle may get out of control and call a stripper or something."

"You're pushing too hard," I said. "You've got my cell number. Otherwise I'll see you tonight at choir."

I paid for my meal and stepped outside. It was just after eight, and the air was fresh, clear, and, for the northern realms, deliciously warm. I stretched and then got into my black Jetta.

I lost no time heading for the Tamarack. My waders and my rod were already in the trunk. I went south on 61, taking the faster, four-lane version when it split off north of Duluth. In downtown Duluth I took the bridge across the harbor to Wisconsin and east, toward the Tamarack.

Virtually all of the rivers and streams on the North Shore of Minnesota flow hard and fast through steep hills, dropping in numerous waterfalls down to the Great Lake. Most of them bear trout, even if only the small native brookies, but almost all of the big fish are confined within the last mile or so between the Lake and wherever the first big waterfall was. Because of that, decent trout fishing is spotty, depending on weather and steelhead migration patterns.

The Wisconsin shoreline is different. It runs almost due east-west and the hills are smaller. Most of the rivers flowing into Lake Superior have no waterfalls at all, and the rapids are easily negotiable by trout and Great Lakes salmon. The German immigrants to Wisconsin in the 1870s had brought with them brown trout, and the state subsequently maintained an aggressive stocking program in many waters. Of course, it is the pride of Wisconsin to say that many rivers now produce a healthy population of wild brown trout in addition to the stockings and the native brook trout. This is true, and makes it worth buying the out-of-state license and trout stamp. Seasonal salmon migrations were the icing on the cake.

The road in Wisconsin wandered several miles from the Great Lake. After about fifteen miles, I turned left off of Highway 13 and followed the Tamarack north, back toward Lake Superior. I pulled in to a small dirt parking lot and got out, stretching again. The air was still clear, with that strangely unmistakable appearance of a sky that looks down on a huge body of water nearby. Here, several miles from the coast, the chilling lake-effect was absent, and the air was soft and mild.

I popped the trunk and slipped on my neoprene waders, then shrugged into my vest. Scooping up my rod, I started into the pine forest, working my way down a steep bluff toward the river.

The water flowed like liquid diamonds over round golden stones. The pines towered above their stately reflections, and the birds chirped out a song of joy that my heart echoed. Stepping into the water was like the first taste of a juicy steak when you haven't eaten all day. I sighed, braced myself against the current and lost myself in the pursuit of brown trout.

CHAPTER 5

Friday night, I went to a bar. It was not just any bar. It was Wally's Walleye Bar & Grill, known locally as the "Double W" for short. Some called it the "WW," and after the Internet boom finally hit Grand Lake a few of the younger folks, noting all the Ws, started referring to it as "the dot com." During the elections of 2004 a few people called it the President's Place, but the politics were a bit touchy in the town and it never stuck. The "WW" was probably more accurate than the full name of the place. Wally Helson had opened the business in 1952, but he hadn't been the owner for 30 years. There wasn't much of a grill either. But the WW did sell Walleye fingers, along with cheese sticks, fries, and a kind of potato appetizer that consisted of the skin of several potatoes filled up with pure cholesterol and saturated fat. I had never dared try the burgers, but they had a decent seafood chowder too.

I got there at about 8:15, and slid into my usual high-backed booth, facing the door. I took off my coat, turned over the ashtray, and went up to the bar.

"What'll it be, Pastor?" asked Henry, the middle-aged bartender.

"The usual," I said.

He grinned and got me a Coke. On the rocks.

"Also, send me some chowder when you get a chance," I said.

"You got it," he said. He cocked his finger and fired at me.

The WW was busy, as it usually was on Friday nights. Most of the folks were regulars. I liked to fancy myself a regular too—I came two or three Fridays a month. Heck, I went to that bar more often than a lot of "regulars" came to church.

I turned back to my booth. Allison, one of the waitresses, was there talking to a middle-aged couple who were standing next to the booth. I saw the man shrug and steer his lady away.

"I saw the ashtray turned over," Allison said to me, "so I told them it was reserved."

"Thanks, Ally," I said.

She smiled, put her hand on my shoulder and let it trail across my back as she left.

I sat down with my Coke and took a few sips while I looked around the room. I noticed a few people I'd never seen at the WW before. Within about five minutes, John Dorland slid into the booth opposite me, holding a beer.

"Hey," he said.

"John," I said, "how's it going?"

He nodded like I'd asked a yes-or-no question. He glanced around the room a bit and then looked back at me. "Actually, Jonah, things aren't so hot for me right now."

I sipped my Coke. "Why, what's going on?"

He nodded again, and smiled without humor. "Well, Kelly and me aren't getting along so well."

I was quiet. I took another gulp of soda.

"She says she wants to leave me."

"She left yet?" I asked.

"I don't know," said John. "I haven't been home yet since I went to work this morning. I'm scared there'll be no one there when I get home."

"So you don't want to lose her," I said.

"Hell, no," said John. "Kelly's the best thing that ever happened to me."

"Do you know why she wants to leave?"

John looked down. "I'm not the greatest guy in the world, you know?"

"No," I said, "I don't."

He looked over at a pair of young women at the bar. "I'm not a saint, okay? I'm just a guy. I can't be Superman."

"You think Kelly wants you to be Superman?" I asked.

"Nah. It's just . . ." He seemed to be out of words. "I guess I don't really know what she wants."

"John," I said, "You're here every Friday, right?"

"Yeah," he said, "pretty much."

"I've only met Kelly once." I said. "And that's the only time I've ever seen her here. How come she doesn't come?"

"Well, someone's gotta stay home with the kid."

"Why don't you both stay home sometimes?" I asked.

He stared at me like I'd just suggested he take all his clothes off, right there in the WW.

"Whaddya mean?"

"How often do you come here?" I asked.

"Not that much," said John looking around the room. "Maybe three, four nights a week."

"All right," I said. "What if, three nights a week, Kelly went out with her girlfriends. Say she goes to places where there'll be plenty of alcohol and plenty of good-looking guys. And when she goes, you gotta stay home with your child."

"Hey, Pastor," said John, waving his forefinger at me, "I'm not fooling around on her. Serious, I'm not that kind of guy."

"I didn't say you were," I said. "I just asked you how you would feel if Kelly did what you do."

John was quiet for a bit. "I think I see what you mean. It kinda looks like I care more about having fun at the WW than hanging out with her."

I wanted to slam the table with my fist, stand up, and shout "E'gad, the kid's got it." I restrained myself.

"Why don't you go on home right now?" I asked Dorland. "Surprise her. Get some flowers on the way."

He shrunk back into himself. "What if she's not there?" he asked.

"If she is still there, the sooner you see her, the better," I said. He nodded.

"Next Friday, get a babysitter and bring her here," I said. The three of us can sit and talk about stuff. I don't think she wants a Superman. I think she wants you to really listen to her, and spend more time with her."

Dorland's face brightened. "She likes you. She might go for that."

He stood up and shook my hand. "Thanks, Pastor." He turned, grabbed his coat and left the WW.

My Coke was gone. Within thirty seconds of John Dorland leaving my booth, Ally, the waitress, brought me another drink and plopped down opposite me.

"Got a minute?" she asked.

I looked around. "Got nothing else going on," I said.

Ally was in her mid-thirties, trim, blond and petite. She was a single mom, and there was trouble with her teenage son, Zack. I'd heard some of it before, but she shared the latest installment with me. I listened carefully, offered a few words of encouragement, and held her hand while the tears welled up from her eyes. When she was done, she leaned over and kissed me on the cheek. My spine tingled.

"My break's over and I gotta go," she said. "Just having someone to tell these things to and get a bit of advice is so much help. Thanks, Jonah."

She got up and went back to the bar for an order.

After that, two more people came, one at a time, and shared my booth and their troubles for a little while. So far, none of them had ever come to church. I figured it was the least I could do to bring church to them.

At about ten, I had a break in the action. The WW was noisy and crowded, and I sat and looked around the room for a bit.

At the bar was a gorgeous woman, maybe twenty-five or twenty-six. She had dark, lustrous hair that fell in thick waves past her shoulders, a bit like Jaclyn Smith in the old *Charlie's Angels*. She turned to say something to someone at the bar and I caught the flash of animated dark eyes against smooth, olive-tinged skin. She looked like maybe one of her parents or grandparents had been Asian or Native American.

She caught my glance and smiled directly at me. The effect was stunning. I smiled back at her. I felt weak-kneed, and it was a good thing I was sitting down She turned back to the bar to say something else, and I realized my heart had started pounding. I looked at the empty booth across from me. When I looked back at the bar, she was coming toward me, carrying her drink. She had on tight, low rider jeans with a fitted red blouse that occasionally bared a bit of smooth tan belly as she moved. Her features were even and she had curves in all the right places. Several men turned to look at her as she walked by.

Now she was standing in front of me. Wow.

"Hi," she said. "Is this seat taken?"

I retained my professional decorum with effort. "It is now," I said, "by you."

She smiled again. Her teeth were white and even. I could smell a faint, enticing perfume. Yipes!

"I'm Leyla," she said.

"Jonah," I said. We didn't shake hands, but she slid gracefully into the seat opposite of me with a slight hint of a wiggle.

We were quiet for minute. For some strange reason it wasn't awkward.

"All right," she said, looking me in the eye, "I'm interested in whatever it is you got."

"I'm sorry," I said. "What do you mean?"

"All night long people have been coming over here, sitting across from you and talking very earnestly, and then leaving. I don't see anything changing hands. What are you doing here? Selling real estate? Used cars? You don't look like a dope peddler or a pimp. I'm very curious."

"You mean you weren't drawn here magnetically by my athletic physique and rugged good looks?"

A faint touch of red crawled up her cheeks and she lowered her eyes demurely. "That may have played a role," she said.

I looked at her closely. It was easy to do. She was gorgeous, and yet also almost familiar, as if I had met her somewhere before.

I was pretty sure, however, I would have remembered meeting someone like Leyla very clearly.

"Well," I said, "about now people are probably wondering what sort of personal problem you are having."

She looked up at me and knitted together her smooth dark eyebrows in an endearing, puzzly expression. "I beg your pardon?"

"Well, people come over here to tell me their problems. I listen, and offer some advice if I have it, which sometimes I don't."

"What are you, a shrink?"

"Think of me as the bar chaplain."

"Chaplain? Are you a priest?" She looked shocked.

I nodded. "A pastor."

Her face cleared. "I see." She was smiling now. "So tell me about the Lord, Father."

I smiled back. "You don't believe me."

"Well, would you?"

"Maybe not." A statuesque blonde walked by, and I turned my head to admire her.

"There! See?" said Leyla. "You're not a minister."

"Because I looked at a beautiful woman?" I asked.

"Yeah. Lustful thoughts and all that."

"I'm looking at you right now," I said.

"Are you having lustful thoughts?" she asked.

"Not yet," I said. "Maybe later."

"So," she said, tossing her hair. "Seriously, what are you doing in this booth?"

"I really am a pastor," I said.

She shook her head, her hair flying slowly back and forth around her face and shoulders, a twinkling smile shining through.

"We're done with that, Mr. Jonah."

"Let me tell you about men looking at women, Miss Leyla," I said. "If you read the book of Genesis, do you know what it says about God's creation?" She shook her head again, mutely, but her eyes were speculative.

I went on. "God made the earth. He made the sea life and plant life and then moved on to animals. He kept on, making life more and more complex and wonderful as he went. The very last thing He made, the ultimate crowning piece of his creation, was woman. Not man. Woman."

Leyla put her chin on her hand and looked at me. Her eyes sparkled. "Go on," she said.

"Don't you see? Women are God's masterpiece. He made them to be beautiful. When they show their beauty—appropriately, of course—then it's like watching God at work. It's like looking at beautiful scenery. I am *supposed* to look, to be amazed, to be attracted even, to God's beauty shining through women. All men are."

"You are a fascinating man," said Leyla.

I nodded. "Women want me, fish fear me."

Just to prove my earlier point, I admired her beauty for a moment. Then she said, "But what about lust and all that? I'm sure that's in the Bible somewhere."

"Yes, it is. If I go beyond admiring God's beauty shining through a woman, if I take her to bed either in my thoughts or in reality, then I'm sinning. Unless I'm married to her. Then it's something beautiful again."

Leyla's brows were knitted together again. "You're starting to sound like a minister now. And if you are, then you can't get married. That doesn't seem fair."

"Why can't I get married?" I asked.

"You know, your vows and everything."

"I'm a Lutheran. My only vow is to drink a lot of coffee."

She put her hands down on the table and tilted her head at me. "Really?"

"Well, I guess there's more to it than that," I said. "But I can get married. In fact, I was married, for four years."

She leaned forward. "'Was?' What happened?"

"She died," I said shortly.

Leyla reached out and put a slim hand on my arm. "I'm so sorry," she said.

"It was five years ago now," I said.

There was a silence. It wasn't awkward.

"So you really are a pastor?" she said.

"Absolutely."

"But you can go out on dates and everything?" she asked.

"I'll prove it to you," I said. "Want to have dinner with me on Sunday night?"

She smiled widely. She had, I noticed for the first time, very cute dimples. "Okay."

"Six o'clock," I said. "Where should I pick you up?"

She frowned. "Actually, I live in Duluth. Can I meet you somewhere?"

I thought quickly. It had been a long time since I'd done anything like this. "How about the breakwater down by the lighthouse. You know where that is?"

She nodded. "I think so. I can find out anyway."

"Let's meet there. We can walk out on the breakwater and look at the lake, and then go back to my place."

She looked a bit startled.

"I am," I said, "a halfway decent cook. I'll make you dinner."

She laughed. The sound made my toes tingle.

"It's a date," she said.

CHAPTER 6

The next day was Saturday. I woke up to the smell of fresh-brewed vanilla-hazelnut coffee. Automatic, timer-set coffee makers made all the horrors of modern civilization seem worthwhile. Yawning and stretching, I stumbled out of my bedroom into the kitchen and poured myself a steaming black mug. I took it through the big, A-frame living room, out my patio doors and onto the deck. It was still chilly, but in my bathrobe and thick wool socks I was comfortable. I sipped my coffee and stared at the empty blue of the lake.

My cabin sits up on the ridge, a few miles south of the town of Grand Lake. The living room with its two-story windows, the mezzanine above the living room, and the deck outside the living room, all face the incredible, clear, icy waters of Superior, a mile or two down the slope. There were better ways to wake up, perhaps, but the only one I could think of off-hand involved marriage, at least in my moral code, and I wasn't married at the moment.

By the time my coffee was finished I was feeling vaguely functional, and I walked back through the pine-paneled living room into the open kitchen which faced it. In the fridge were some fresh brown eggs. One of the farm families at church kept me well supplied. The milk was straight from their cow too. Someday maybe I'd learn how to churn my own butter, and then I could pretend to be a pioneer, living at the edge of the wilderness, drinking gourmet coffee and browsing on the Internet for sermon illustration material.

I walked over to the stereo and flipped on a Fleetwood Mac album, then returned to the kitchen to fry eggs and sausage. After breakfast, I poured another cup of black elixir and then called the church number and punched in my voice-mail code. Saturday was not a day off, but I typically did a lot of work from my home-office in my pajamas. Later in the afternoon I had a youth ball game to attend.

The first two messages were mundane and easily dealt with. The third was from Julie, left at about eight last night.

"Hey," said Julie's recorded voice, "I forgot to tell you that Channel 13 from Duluth called. I told them you would be available for an interview at the church, at eleven on Saturday morning. I figured that would usually work out, but if it doesn't, you might want to call them." There was a pause. "Don't forget the Little League game on Saturday afternoon."

I had done a few brief interviews with newspapers when Missy Norstad first disappeared. I imagined that the TV crew wanted to talk to me about recent developments. I finished my coffee while I put the finishing touches on my sermon. Then I called the Channel 13 number.

"Hello?" said the voice of a middle-aged man. The voice was high and nasal and the enunciation was overdone, almost feminine.

"Yes, this is Pastor Borden, from Harbor Lutheran in Grand Lake" I said. "I was scheduled for an interview this morning, here in Grand Lake."

"Just a minute," he said, and apparently covered the mouthpiece while he spoke to someone else.

"Okay," he said after a moment. "Yes, Reverend Borden. We have you down for eleven this morning at Harbor Lutheran Church in Grand Lake."

I thought for a moment. "So what is this?" I asked. "The angle where the good religious father gets judgmental and goes around shooting people?" My experience with the TV media was not universally positive.

The man from Channel 13 gave a fake chuckle. "Reverend Borden, we wouldn't do that. We've discovered that you've been working with the family all throughout this crisis, and we're interested in your perspective."

I had been thinking while he talked. Doug Norstad had been missing for almost a week. Maybe I had an opportunity here. "Will this be live or taped?" I asked.

"It will be taped," he said. "We have to edit it, and fit it into the time window and so on."

"I'll make you a deal," I said. "I'll give you the interview. But you have to give me thirty seconds to make an on-camera appeal to Doug, for him to turn himself in. You can't edit my thirty seconds."

"Reverend Borden, that's really not the way we do things around here, I'm afraid."

"That's fine," I said. "I'm sure you can come up with another one of those scintillating stories about the zebra mussel."

"Hey, that's important stuff," he said. There was a pause. I waited. The man from Channel 13 waited.

"Okay, Reverend Borden," he said finally. That was getting on my nerves. "I can try to get you your thirty seconds. But I can't promise you anything. I don't make the final decisions on these things. I'm just the scheduler."

"I'll tell you what," I said. "Talk to the person who *does* make the final decision, and have them call me back. Whoever it is can call my cell." He started to protest, but I relentlessly gave him the number. "Have a great day," I added, and hung up. I could hear him still protesting as I clicked off.

Ten minutes later my cell phone rang. It was a Duluth number.

"Borden," I said.

"Pastor Borden?" said a pleasant, older female voice. "This is Erika Hahn, from Channel 13. I hear you've been giving poor Evan fits."

"Poor Evan," I agreed. "Did he tell you what I said?"

"Yes. You can have your unedited thirty seconds and that will be fine." She paused, and then continued on in a weighty tone. "You should know, however, we don't usually do that sort thing. We're making a big exception for you."

"I'll be sure to mention it to God, next time we talk. Or is He your station manager?"

Ms. Hahn laughed. It sounded genuine. "No, that's me. I'm sorry, we do take ourselves a bit too seriously in the television business sometimes. I must say, your own profession has a bad reputation for that too. It's refreshing to meet a clergyman with a sense of humor."

"Some folks in my congregation might argue that point with you, Ms. Hahn," I said.

"Erika," she said.

"Thanks, Erika. And you can call me the Very Reverend Pastor Jonah Borden, if you wish."

She laughed again.

"Seriously," I said, "Jonah is fine."

"Well, thank you, Jonah. So it is on for eleven?"

"It's ten already. It usually takes about an hour and a half from Duluth."

"No, we have someone up there already, Jonah. We sent them up yesterday afternoon."

"Okay then, I'll meet them at the church, at eleven o'clock."

We hung up.

I showered and shaved and put on a pair of khaki Dockers and a navy-blue Eddie Bauer button up cotton shirt. I was going to be on TV, so I inspected myself carefully in a mirror. I looked more or less like an accurate representation of myself. Primetime Pastor. I winked at the mirror and shot my finger at my reflection.

Perhaps I'd been living alone too long.

After putting on my hiking boots and shrugging into my polar fleece jacket, I left my cabin and turned into a trail that ran into the pine woods from my front yard. It was a bit more than two miles through the forest to the church. This direction it was almost all level or downhill, so I had plenty of time.

A half-mile from my place I stopped at the overlook. The lake was intensely blue, like a giant ruffled carpet out in front of me. Along the shore in either direction I could see hills and small cliffs.

Ah, God, you did it again.

I made it to the church by ten-thirty. For a change, there didn't seem to be anyone around. I opened up the building and went into my office and straightened up for a few moments.

At about eleven I heard a vehicle pull up, and I came out of my office. A min-van was in the lot. A woman got out and started unloading camera equipment. She looked somewhat familiar. I walked out of the building towards her. Her back was turned, but I could see that she had lustrous dark hair, and was very well put together.

"Can I give you a hand?" I asked.

She turned. It was Leyla.

My mouth dropped open, and so did hers. Then she smiled.

"So you're Pastor Borden. You never told me your last name, Jonah."

"Sorry," I said. "You work for Channel 13?"

"Weekend reporter. I take it you haven't seen me?"

Smooth move, Borden.

"Actually, I thought you looked familiar last night, but I couldn't place where I'd met you. I realize now I must have seen you once or twice on TV."

She smiled again. It was something I could get used to looking at. I made a mental note to watch more news on the weekends.

"Actually, I wasn't sure you were telling the truth last night," she said. "About being a minister, I mean."

"I'm probably pretty weird for a pastor," I said. "Don't let your misconceptions go just yet."

I looked around. "Where's the rest of the team?"

She laughed. "Let me introduce you," she said. She hefted the camera. "This is our camerawoman, Leyla Bennett." She put it down. "This is our makeup lady, Leyla Bennett." She made a small bow. "Our lighting person, Leyla Bennett, and our on-site producer, Leyla Bennett." She turned and grinned at me. "And not least, our intrepid reporter, Leyla Bennett."

"Intrepid is right," I said. "But I might have said 'lovely.'"

She tossed her hair. "That would be sexist."

"So," I said, as I helped her lug her gear into the building, "you do all this on your own? I thought you guys went around in crews with producers and camera people and so on."

"They do, in larger cities. But this is Duluth, Minnesota. News on a budget."

After inspecting my office, she decided to shoot the interview there.

"Is there a little girls' room here?" she asked.

When she came back, her face was made up a bit more than was attractive. She must have seen my look.

"It looks ghastly in person—way overdone—but it really shows up better on TV."

I thought for a moment. "I think I read somewhere that Richard Nixon lost the 1960 presidential election because he wouldn't wear makeup for the TV debates."

"That's probably true," she said. "Although, I didn't know he ran for president in 1960."

"Yeah. But he wasn't elected until 1968."

"That's probably because he started wearing makeup," said Leyla.

After looking at my office more closely, she said, "Why don't you sit there, behind your desk." She fussed around some more with lighting. Then she did some test shots to make sure the camera was set at the right angle. Finally everything was ready.

Leyla's normally expressive face focused into a sober, businesslike expression, and she began asking me questions about the Norstad family, the crime that had taken Missy's life and then about Doug Norstad in particular.

"Now," she said finally, with a touch of drama for the camera, "do you have something you'd like to say on-camera to Doug

Norstad?"

I looked directly at the lens. "Doug," I said, "it's time to come home. I don't believe you shot Daniel Spooner. Your family needs you. The police will want to talk you, yes, but you didn't do it, so there's nothing to fear. It's been a terrible and difficult time for you and your family, and you aren't helping by staying away. I believe justice will be served, Doug. The police and the courts will straighten this out. I'll help too. Come on in. It will be okay. Come home, Doug."

She said, "That wasn't thirty seconds."

"I might have needed all thirty," I said. "It's like a gun. Better to have it and not need it, than need it and not have it."

She opened her mouth as if to argue, and then closed it. "Well, it was a surprise to see you here, but I think you did very well on-camera. I've got to run down to Duluth and edit this—but not your time at the end," she added hastily. She offered me her hand.

I took her hand. The shake was firm, but it felt awkward to me. "See you tomorrow afternoon then," I said.

"Yes," she said softly, letting me have the full effect of her dimples. With a breeze of faint perfume, she was gone.

CHAPTER 7

Sunday Morning I preached a brilliant sermon, as always. Only half-a-dozen or so people fell asleep. I never quite understood the concept of sleeping in church. It always seemed to me sort of like buying a ticket to a ball game you had no intention of watching. What was the point? Wouldn't their own beds be more comfortable? Did they think God didn't know? Did they think *I* didn't know?

Actually, I wasn't really *sure* they were asleep. It's hard to tell sometimes, especially with Scandinavian Lutherans. A Scandinavian Lutheran who is asleep looks pretty much the same as one who is dancing. Not that they ever dance, of course.

In any case, a few people did in fact seem interested, and, as usual, some even commented afterwards. Some of the comments were even positive.

By one o'clock I was back up in my cabin overlooking Lake Superior, wearing jeans and a gray sweatshirt, listening to the Twins game on WCCO radio. I got a bottle of Woodchuck's Hard Apple Cider from the fridge and took a long swig. I took out two steaks and sprinkled oregano, pepper and garlic on both sides of them. Then I slipped them into a Ziploc plastic bag, added some soy sauce, and put them back in the fridge to marinate.

Grabbing some slivered almonds from the cupboard, I put them in a little frying pan with sugar and poured in some juice from a can of mandarin oranges. After the sugar dissolved and coated the almonds, I set them aside and made a sweet mint vinaigrette dressing. The Twins were losing. I didn't mind. Baseball on the radio was just ambiance, a Sunday afternoon spring sound.

Eating a turkey and Swiss sandwich out on the deck, I finished the cider. When I was done with the sandwich I put up my feet and closed my eyes and drifted into the stillness of the warm afternoon.

~

At five, I got into my Jetta and drove down the hills until I reached Highway 61. Turning north, I went all the way into Grand Lake and then right toward the waterfront. The North Shore had not been ignored by developers, and there was a plethora of beautifully planned resort complexes up and down Lake Superior. Though I hadn't had much occasion to visit too many of these, the ones I had seen took full advantage of the awesome and pristine scenery offered by Superior's rocky cliffs and achingly blue water.

The towns, by and large, were a different story. They had grown up on the logging boom and matured during the iron boom. Water, to the town planners, had been merely convenient transportation. Some still hadn't caught on to the tourist boom. I was often surprised to find, in the towns of the North Shore, how little use had been made of the shoreline by restaurants or other tourist merchants. In fact, few of the towns even had a waterfront park.

Grand Lake was an exception to all that. Sometime during the past forty years, some very wise city planners had anticipated the rise of North Shore tourism. They had purchased a tract of waterfront, developing part of it into a beautiful park, and creating a waterfront street with the rest, lined with shops and restaurants on the side across from the park. It looked like an oceanside park in L.A., with the absence of palm trees, and, for that matter, the temperatures that climbed regularly above 65.

Even so, the city planners had been right. The strip of tourist waterfront was wildly successful, in part because no other North Shore towns, other than Duluth, had such a thing. To the north and east of the park, connected by a walking trail, was the old breakwater than protected Grand Lake Harbor, and at its end, a harbor light. The harbor itself wasn't all that much—a few huge, old, ore boat wharves, and several boat ramps for private pleasure craft. About ten years ago some enterprising developer had added a marina which leased slips to larger yachts. I had been told by a wealthy member of the church that North Shore slips were hard to come by. Grand Lake Marina was always full, at any rate.

I parked across the street from the shops, on the park side, near the breakwater. As I got out of the car and looked across the water, my hands began to itch. It was very difficult to be alone by a body of water without trying to catch fish. For that matter, it was difficult even if I wasn't alone. Truth was, I reminded myself, Superior is cold and sterile, and I was very unlikely to catch much of anything off the shore or even the breakwater. The salmon and lake trout liked to stay deep most of the year, as did most of the other fish. It wasn't like a regular lake where I might amuse myself for twenty minutes fly-casting for sunfish or the occasional bass. Even so, I had a rod in the car, and a few spoons and spinners.

Breathe deep. Think about Leyla.

After I thought about Leyla for a bit, I decided maybe I should think about fishing again. It isn't hard to find someone to be attracted to. But I hadn't been *interested* in anyone since Robyn had died, five years ago. And of course, I hadn't been interested in anyone but Robyn for about five years before that. Ten years was a long time, and I was bit nervous.

On the other hand, if I were a fish, I would be nervous of me. There didn't seem to be much further for me to go along that line of thought either. It was a mistake to come here so early. I decided to think about my sermons—maybe I could bore myself.

Actually, one of the reasons I was a pastor was because sermons—particularly my own—did not usually bore me at all. I was interested in that stuff. For instance, there was a little text I was often tempted to preach on: *Judas went out and hanged himself.* It was a great text. That was the kind of Bible verse that would wake you up. That was the kind of verse that would make people sit up, Scandinavian or not, and say, *what will he say about that?* And the thing is, I *did* have something to say about it.

The time passed more quickly as I strode around the park, thinking about Judas and Peter and the other disciples and that amazing night of triumph and tragedy that has dominated the Western world for two thousand years since.

When I looked up, there was Leyla, stepping toward me with a graceful swing to her hips. She was wearing a pleated khaki skirt that stopped just above her knees, and a tight, dark-blue long-sleeved pullover. Her legs were sensibly covered by dark blue tights that ended in dark brown boots that came midway up her calves. Her makeup was understated but expert, and from her ears dangled complicated, very feminine, silver earrings. My heart skipped a bit. Judas be hanged, she was something to look at.

"Hi," I said.

"Hi," she returned.

It wasn't a bit awkward. There wasn't a need for a joke or a whole bunch of words.

"Would you like to walk for a bit?" I asked.

"Yes," she said. "I like to walk and talk."

"Me too. Somehow I think better when my feet are moving."

We walked along the trail just above the sea wall in the park.

After a minute she said, "I just want you to know, I don't usually pick up men in bars."

"So it's official?" I asked. "I've been picked up?"

She made an embarrassed little gesture with her hand.

I smiled widely. "I don't usually get picked up in bars either," I said.

"Actually, I was there in the course of my job. I was trying to see if I could learn anything more about the Spooner shooting or the Norstad story."

"Strange," I said. "I was there in the course of my job too."

"So we met at work?" She looked at me slyly.

"Definitely," I said.

"My mother will like that better than a bar," she said.

We walked from the far end of the park out toward the breakwater, which thrust three quarters of a mile out into the cold depths of the harbor. The water was calm, but the wind was cool. Leyla would have had cold legs without the tights. A good number of other people were about. A mild Sunday afternoon in May, in any part of Minnesota, is never ignored. We continued talking as we went. She told me about her brief career in the world of television news. I told her about my life growing up in the Pacific Northwest.

Walking slowly, we reached the end of the breakwater and

leaned side by side on the railing, looking out to sea while the golden evening flowed around us.

"So," she said, turning to look at me directly, "you were married for four years. Are you attached now?"

"You mean romantically?" I asked. Years as a pastor had made me very astute.

"Yes."

"No," I said, very clearly.

She held my eyes. "I'm not either," she said. "There was a guy in college, but it didn't work out once we started our separate careers."

"Where is he now?" I asked. Just to be polite, I told myself.

"Omaha."

"That's good," I said. "I mean—"

She laughed and turned the full weight of her dimples on me.

I gave it up. "Okay, to be honest, I am glad he's in Omaha. Makes it easier for me."

"You wouldn't have to worry, even if he were in Duluth," she said.

"Also good," I said. We both looked out at the azure waves.

"I haven't done this for a very long time," I said after a while.

She looked at me from beneath long eyelashes. "Don't worry," she said, "I'll help you."

"How about dinner?" I asked.

"I'm hungry," she said. We turned from the rail, and she slipped her slim hand into mine, interlocking our fingers. She swung our arms playfully. "Remember this?"

"I do," I said. "It's good." I felt somehow that she had taken control of the situation. It wasn't an entirely bad feeling.

"Yes," she said, "it is." She stopped swinging our arms, but didn't let go of my hand. I was glad. I think I needed the support.

When we reached the cars, I said, "Why don't you ride with me, and later I can bring you back here?"

"Okay," she said. "Just let me get my purse from the car."

I opened the Jetta door for her when we got there. Then I climbed into the driver's seat and started the car. As we pulled out of the parking lot, her brow had a cute little wrinkle in it.

"Fleetwood Mac?" she said. "That doesn't seem very pastoral."

"This isn't their reunion stuff," I said. "This is from back in the day. It's got passion to it."

"They're saying 'damn,'" she observed.

"Singing," I corrected. "They're singing it."

"Okay, but it's still a swear word."

"Feel the pain and loss of their lives apart from God," I said. She didn't know if I was serious.

"I don't know," I added. "Maybe I'm whitewashing it just 'cause I like the music, but there's something in this song that's real and raw. I think it's about loss."

"Never break the chain? Sounds like co-dependence to me."

"Hey, I said, 'real' not 'right.'"

"Is this the whole album?"

"No," I said, "I download stuff from the Internet. There's a song about sugar daddies on that album. I find no redeeming value in that song, so why buy a whole album and get a song I don't like?"

"You're really ruining the whole pastor-thing for me."

I shrugged. "Misconceptions are comfortable. But don't get me wrong, I'm serious about my faith and about being a pastor. I'm just not serious about conforming to everyone else's expectations of how pastors are."

"How does your church like that?" she asked. Smart. And quick.

"I'm a good preacher," I said. "Funny how much people will appreciate you, and how much slack you get if only you won't bore them for a half-hour on Sunday mornings.

"They don't really know you, do they?" She was even smarter than I thought.

"I suppose many of them would be shocked to hear some of the music I listen to. And maybe some other things about my life would surprise them. But I don't go around pretending to be like I'm not. I don't hide behind the pastoral mask or anything. On the other hand, I don't feel the need to say, from the pulpit, 'Just in case you ever wondered, I sometimes listen to hard rock. Oh, and I hate your perfume, Mrs. Denton.'"

Leyla laughed. "Fair enough," she said. "Is there a real Mrs. Denton?"

"Indeed, there is," I said.

"And her perfume?"

"Could probably be used as a method of birth control."

CHAPTER 8

When we stepped into my cabin, she stopped for a moment. "This is where you live?"

"Yes," I said.

"You own this?" she asked.

"Be it ever so humble," I said.

"Wow," she said. "This is incredible." She bent to take her boots off and then walked into the vaulted living room. "Look at the view!"

The long Minnesota twilight still had a ways to go before dark. The pine-clad slope below and the awesome, endless lake were still clearly visible.

"Let me throw the steaks on the grill, and then I'll give you the tour."

Leyla was gratifyingly charmed with my Northwoods, light-pine home. She entered each room as if she were unwrapping a Christmas present, and showed a great deal of interest in seemingly every picture, knick-knack and book. As we entered my office, she stopped short.

"Did you kill that?" she asked.

"Yes, I did," I said proudly. "It's a fourteen-point whitetail buck."

"He looks sad," she said.

"His eyes are glass," I said. "They can't look sad."

"What about those fish?"

"That's another story," I said. "That one is a 25-pound Atlantic salmon I caught down in Wisconsin. The other is an eight-pound brown trout, also in Wisconsin. As far as I know, they're both still swimming free."

"They look to me," she said, "as if they're both hanging on your wall."

"When I caught them I measured them, weighed them, and took careful digital pictures. Then I let them go and sent my pictures and measurements to a company in Duluth. They made these replicas."

"So you kill mammals and release fish," she said.

"I am what I am," I said. A sudden thought occurred to me. "You're not a vegetarian are you?"

She smiled mischievously. "And what if I am?"

"You might be a bit hungry tonight. We're having steak Borden."

She shook her head, still smiling. "No, I'm not. Actually, I love steak once in a while."

We returned to the living room. Leyla sat on a stool at the counter between the kitchen and living room, while I bustled around, putting the meal together.

"Would you like some wine?" I asked. "It's Riesling. I know it doesn't go with steak, but I like it, and I don't really care."

"That's how I am too," said Leyla. "I'll have a glass."

When everything was ready, we sat down. "Mind if I bless the food?" I asked. She shook her head.

She was suitably impressed with my bachelor cookery. The steaks, the mandarin orange lettuce salad with candied almonds, my buttered new red potatoes all seemed to go down well.

After we'd been eating a while she took a sip of wine and looked at me seriously. "I need to tell you something," she said. "I just think it's good to be honest and get things out in the open before—well, before a misunderstanding would get really painful."

"Okay," I said.

"I don't know quite how to say this. I guess, maybe, I just want you to know where I'm at with religion and everything. I mean, it seems pretty important to you."

"Religion, no. Faith, yes," I said.

"That's what I meant," she said. "I guess the best way to put it is that I'm sort of a retired Catholic." She looked at me, searching my eyes for something. "I don't know," she went on after a moment. "It's hard to put into words."

I waited while she struggled for a moment, and then I said, "Would you like me to take a stab at it?"

She relaxed against her chair. "Okay," she said.

"You were raised in the church." She nodded. "Your parents were very faithful taking you to Sunday school and church." She nodded again. "Did you go to Catholic school?"

Her eyes were unreadable. "Yes, until eighth grade."

"Okay, so you were a faithful Catholic girl. But something changed for you. You probably can't lay a finger on exactly what it was. You got disillusioned with the church. When you went away to college, you quit going." I held up my hand to forestall her explanations. "Let me try a little more, and then you can tell me if I'm right."

I took a sip of wine and went on. "You haven't really been back to the church since then, not regularly. But you still believe in God. You still believe most of that stuff you learned. You might still believe in Jesus too."

"Yes," she said firmly.

"But even so, you can't seem to make yourself go back to the Catholic Church. And yet, at the same time you don't feel right about going to any other kind of church either."

Her eyes now sparkled. "Go on," she said.

"You don't feel right about this. You know you should be connected to a church. You want to be, even. But this dilemma holds you back from both the Catholic Church as well as any protestant congregations. You'd like to resolve it, but you don't know quite how, and you've been focused on other things for a few years now. You don't really want to give up on it all, but you don't know what to do."

She was staring at me. "How did you do that? How did you know all that about me?"

"I am," I said, "good at what I do. Plus, I've known a few retired Catholics."

"Are you saying there are lots of people like me?"

"I'm pretty sure there is no one in the world quite like you, Leyla," I said. "But, yes, there are lots of people who have had experiences with faith and church like yours."

"What do they do?"

"Depends on the person, I guess. Some of them just keep drifting away, and eventually they don't really care that much about God anymore. Others brace themselves and go back to the Catholic Church, and probably end up happy there. Some folks overcome their inhibitions and try out other kinds of churches, and even become quite comfortable there."

She toyed with a chunk of red potato.

"But you know," I added, "I really don't think it's about where you go to church. Church is a part of it, an important part. But the main thing is your relationship with Jesus. Get that straight, and the rest usually works its way out."

"I've never heard any of the priests say something like that."

I shrugged. I don't like to criticize other denominations if I can help it.

"So," she said, looking at me and smiling winsomely. "Are you okay with that? With where I'm at?"

"Are you?"

"Well, no," she said slowly. "You got it right when you said I still believe. I do. I don't want to retire from Jesus and all that—the church has been my problem."

"Leyla Bennett," I said, "You're more than okay with me."

She smiled and our eyes locked for a moment. Wow.

"Let me tell you where I'm at," I said, "and don't worry, I'm not gonna preach."

"Okay."

"I'm not really into religion," I said. She looked startled. They always do. "What I mean is, I'm not into doing things just to do them, or because that's what's always been done. I'm not big on rituals and traditions."

"Isn't that a bit odd for a pastor?" she asked.

"Doesn't bother me," I said. "Anyway, but I *am* into faith."

Leyla frowned. Even her frowns were cute. I was getting it bad. "Isn't that more or less the same thing?" she said.

"Not in my book. Faith isn't about rituals or traditions—though those things do aid some people in their faith. But faith is really about *relationship*. Through faith, I have a relationship with God.

He's very real to me. He is, and always will be, the most important person in my life." People sometimes get uncomfortable when I start talking like this."

Leyla seemed fine. Her head was tilted slightly and her smooth dark hair fell to one side.

"He's been important to me for a long time," I said. "But when Robyn died—well, He was all I had left. It was just Him and me. He was a very real comfort, a very real friend." I looked out into the darkness beyond my deck. "I guess what I'm saying is this: I'm not married to the church—I never will be. I always put Robyn before church—in the short time we had. But God is different than church, separate. And He'll always be number one in my life. That doesn't mean there's no room for anyone else, but I suppose it may bother some folks."

"It doesn't bother me," she said softly. Our eyes locked again. "Jonah Borden," she said smiling, "You're more than okay with me."

CHAPTER 9

The next morning was Monday, my one full day off. In my considered and well-educated opinion, there is no better way to spend a Monday in May than thigh-deep in the Tamarack River, fishing for brown trout or the occasional steelhead.

I left early, around five-thirty, to beat the traffic in Duluth, although traffic was not a notorious problem in that Athens of the Far North. Just outside of Grand Lake a sheriff's car snapped on its lights and pulled me over. It was Rex Burton.

He walked up slowly to my window, which I lowered.

"Thought it was you," he said. "Where you off to in such a hurry, Father?"

I sighed. "Every Monday morning between April and October I go fishing down in Wisconsin"

"Meeting somebody?" he asked.

"Fishing." I said firmly. "I only want to meet fish. What's the problem here?"

"Every Monday?" he asked.

"And Tuesday mornings, sometimes," I said. "What's it to you? I'd go Wednesday, Thursday, Friday, and Saturday if I could; any time I can swing it. Do you have something to say to me, because I want to get going."

"You were going awfully fast, just now. The fish will wait for you."

"Cut the crap," I said. "I know you don't like me, not that you're very subtle about it. You gonna ticket me for that?"

"No," he said. His face behind his large glasses and thick mustache was, as I had suspected, unreadable. "I'm gonna ticket you for doing seventy in a forty-five zone."

"We both know I was doing forty-three," I said. His face remained impassive.

"Why not make it one-hundred-and-seventy?" I asked. "Why not just charge me for murder while you're at it?"

Burton continued silently writing the ticket.

"Burton," I said. "I don't know what your problem is, but I know it's got nothing to do with me personally. Lay off, why don't ya, or so help me, I will bury you at the bottom of Lake Superior."

"Gonna send my soul to hell, Father?" he asked, ripping off the ticket and handing it to me.

"You're doing that all by yourself, apparently," I said.

"But I won't go alone," he said, and for a moment his expressionless face almost cracked. "I will take plenty of company along with me." He flipped his ticket book up and turned away.

"I'll see you there, Father," he said, and walked back to his car.

CHAPTER 10

I pulled into the SuperAmerica about a quarter of a mile from where Burton ticketed me. This particular SA sold very good coffee.

"Morning pastor," said the attendant at the counter as I walked in.

"I'm having an extra one this morning, Rich," I said to him as I walked to the counter with my coffee and three glazed donuts. "Need to celebrate my ticket."

"I saw that," said Rich. "What did he pull you over for? You sure weren't speeding."

"You don't think I was doing seventy?" I asked.

He gaped at me. "No way," he said, shaking his head. "I saw it. You weren't speeding at all."

I nodded. "You're right. But I have a ticket for seventy anyway."

"That ain't right," he said, still shaking his head. "Who was it?"

"Rex Burton."

"Never heard of him," said Rich. "If you need me as a witness, I'm there."

"Thanks, man," I said. "I appreciate it. If you're serious, I'll probably take you up on that."

"I'm serious," he said. "That ain't right."

I thanked him again, paid and left.

~

The ticket had me in a somewhat foul mood, but I find it is

impossible to remain upset when I am driving south along the
Superior shore on a bright May morning, the sun rising gloriously
over the indigo waters, headed toward great fishing while sipping
coffee and nibbling on a donut. Ticket or no ticket, all was well
with the world.

An hour and a half later, the Tamarack welcomed me into its
cold clear bosom, and I began to wade upstream, casting ahead of
me to reach current breaks and subtle edges where the brown trout
like to hide, waiting for prey.

It was a glorious day. The sun struggled from the grasp of some
fleeting clouds and raised the temperature to a comfortable sixty
degrees. I heard the hope-filled songs of the birds that had been
away in the south for the past six months. An otter glided smoothly
away from me at a turn in the river, and I scattered three does about
a half mile further on.

The first fish struck on the fourth cast. My heart leaped, and
my spirit sang with the birds. The short rod bucked in my hands,
and the world was forgotten as I slowly coaxed in a twelve-inch
brown. I put my hand into the water and held her, belly up, still in
the stream, as I carefully removed the hook. After pausing to
admire her bright colors, I released the trout.

That was the first of many. Fish after fish struck at the lure.
Many of them missed, of course, but I could see them clearly in the
tea-colored water, through my polarized sunglasses. And I did
manage to hook a good percentage of them.

After I'd been fishing for a couple hours, I turned a corner and
came to a quickly flowing, nondescript stretch of water. The
current slipped over a little riffle and the banks ran parallel for a
hundred yards or so. I dropped my spinner neatly beside the roots

of a big Norway Pine that held in the bank. The water exploded. The rod bent, bobbed, then settled then into a taut arch as the line started to strip. This fish was swimming against a fast current, and yet it was still strong enough to pull out line against the drag setting on my reel. Oh boy!

On cue with my thoughts, the line went slack.

"No, no, no, NO!" I shouted. I cranked the real furiously.

And then suddenly the fish was on again. It had turned downstream, and was now swimming toward me. I saw him dart past, and the adrenaline burst into my veins. This trout was big; big and fat. There was no time, my line was taut again. The pull of the current, combined with the pull of the fish, threatened to snap the line or tear the hook out if I tried to muscle the trout back to me. With a fish this size, I had to get downstream of it to have a hope of landing it.

I raced, slipping over rocks, plunging precariously into waist-deep holes, praying desperately that I would neither lose the fish nor my balance. We went tearing around a sharp corner where the stream dropped into a deep slow hole and an eddy swirled the current backwards near the bank. The fish dove for the bottom of the hole just as I, coming downstream, hit the upstream eddy. Spray erupted, and the bottom dropped out beneath my moving right foot. Off balance, carried by my momentum, I titled forward, and water began to pour over the top of my chest waders. I gasped in shock— the Tamarack was no more than fifty degrees in May—and began to fight desperately free of the water, flailing both arms wildly. I snapped the fishing line with my windmilling, and heaved myself, gasping and on hands and knees, up to the bank.

I was still breathing heavily from the cold water that had

flowed into my waders. It was theoretically possible that my waders could have filled up too quickly, their weight pulling me to the bottom of the pool and drowning me before I could escape. Water as cold as this shocked the system, slowing down the body and making it hard to move. Downstream, Lake Superior was even colder, somewhere near forty degrees in the summer, and even good swimmers drowned there regularly because of the crippling cold.

I warmed up quickly, however, because my waders are neoprene and, even with water in them, functioned more or less like a wetsuit to keep me warm. Even so, it wasn't comfortable being that wet. I stripped them off and sat on the bank in the sun to dry.

I munched on some nuts and dried fruit, and took a nap. When I woke up my clothes were reasonably dry, and the inside of my waders had settled into a cold damp. I was willing to make great sacrifices for fish.

I wondered if I should keep a few, and drop them off for Leyla on my way back through Duluth. I could say, "Here, baby, have some dead raw fish. Remember to cut off the heads and tails before you eat them!" One slick Romeo, that was me. I decided to let the fish keep swimming.

By early afternoon I was back on Highway 13, heading west toward Superior and Duluth. I wondered whether I should call Leyla and offer to grace her with my presence on the way. I felt like I was back in high school: Will she be offended if I don't call? Will she feel pressured if I do? I decided to forget the whole thing—didn't need the distraction anyway.

My phone rang.

I waited. It kept ringing. I picked it up.

"Borden."

"Jonah." It was Chief Jensen. I was somehow disappointed.

"Hail to the chief," I said.

"Doug Norstad came in today," he said. "They've got him down at county."

"Dan, you really think he did it?" I said.

"I don't know what to think, Jonah," he said. "Why'd he run, if he didn't do it?"

"Why'd he come back, if he did?" I said.

"You really don't know?" he asked.

"What are you talking about?" I said.

"Jonah, you told him to come back. You and that cute little reporter. You told Doug Norstad to come home, right there on primetime TV."

CHAPTER 11

The county jail was in downtown Grand Lake, near the Superior
Justice Center, which held the courthouse and various county
offices. It was Tuesday morning, and as I walked in, I passed Eric
Berg, the assistant district attorney. Berg was tall and distinguished,
with an intelligent forehead and Minnesota-blue eyes. His hair was
receding slightly but in that curiously attractive way that some
lucky balding men experienced. It made him look more sensitive or
something. He wore a smartly tailored gray suit. Word was, Berg
had the Democratic Party okay to run for congress in this district in
the next election. To bolster his run, he had an outstanding
conviction record. In the past six months especially, it seemed like
he won every case. He was well-known, urbane, and
overwhelmingly upwardly mobile. His family had money. I didn't
like him very much.

"Jonah!" he said, coming toward me with his hand
outstretched, a politician to the core. "Good to see you," he said,
gripping my hand firmly, and bending slightly toward me. "A
terrible business about Doug Norstad. He was a member of our
church, wasn't he?"

Berg undoubtedly knew very well that he was. "He still is,
Eric," I said.

He was a bit taken back. "Yes. Of course."

"Did they book him?" I asked.

"Of course," said Berg.

"Murder one?"

Berg looked as though he smelled something faintly unpleasant. "I believe that's so, Jonah. I need to get going. It's been so nice to see you."

I was surprised he didn't say "Come again soon." I reached out my hand as he turned away.

"Eric!"

He turned back, his eyebrows raised smoothly.

"Surely, you don't really think it was him? All you have is circumstantial."

"He ran, Jonah. We don't want him to get away again. We'll sort it all out in court, don't worry." He patted my hand and left hurriedly.

I made my way down to the visiting area and told the guard who I was. After about half an hour I was ushered into a little room that contained five booth-like separating walls. Each booth looked through a glass panel into another booth on the opposite side. There were phones for speaking through the wall between prisoners and visitors.

I sat down in a booth and shortly Doug Norstad appeared opposite me.

"Hey, Doug," I said into the phone. Profound words of pastoral wisdom.

"Hi, Pastor," he said.

"You being taken care of okay?" I asked.

"I guess," he said. "No one's hurt me or nothing."

I tried to meet his eyes through the glass wall and through the thick lenses of his glasses. His face was gray and unshaven.

"Listen, Doug," I began. "I'm your pastor. That means—by law—you can tell me anything, and as long as it is not a crime you are intending to commit, I don't have to tell anyone."

He sat there, silently.

"What I mean is, you can tell me if you killed Daniel Spooner. And the court can't force me to tell anyone. This is what we call 'privileged information.' What we say to each other doesn't get said anywhere else."

"You think I did it?" he asked dully. "On TV, you said you knew I wasn't guilty."

"I don't know, Doug. I don't know why you didn't come home that day. What I'm saying is, if you *did* do it, tell me. Murder is a sin—even the murder of a scumbag like Spooner. If you did it, get it off your chest now. God forgives even murder."

Something flickered in his eyes. "You think God forgave Spooner for killing my little girl?"

Way to go, Borden. A-1 pastor. Come to me, and I'll screw you up worse.

I took a breath, and got help.

"That's all between Spooner and God now," I said. "My point is, let me help you deal with what's between *you* and God, if there is anything."

"I didn't do it." Norstad's voice was flat and unemotional. I looked at him carefully. I knew I would have been capable of murder, in his shoes. "Doug, this is serious stuff—I mean, spiritually. Think about it. You know me, Doug. I've been with you. I haven't held anything back from you. You can trust me. You really didn't do it?"

Something animated his face at last. His eyes crinkled, welled up, and then his whole face crumpled and he began to cry. I reached out and impotently touched the glass.

"The world knows I wanted to," said Doug. "I still hate that man, really hate him, down deep. But I didn't do it, Pastor. I really didn't." He looked up and met my eyes.

"I believe you," I said. I did.

I waited while he regained his composure, wiping his nose with the sleeve of his jail fatigues.

"You need to tell them why you didn't come home last week," I said when he was done. "They think you're guilty 'cause you ran."

"I heard it on the news that afternoon on the radio. I was on my way home. I knew they'd think it was me. I was scared, so I didn't come home."

"Why were you scared? All you had to do was tell them you'd been with your dad. They would have called and checked, and then let you go. Now you've got a whole week to explain. I assume you didn't hide out with your dad? I know they checked there first."

He shook his head. "No, I wasn't there."

Something clicked in the back of my head. Something wasn't right. I couldn't quite put my finger on it. I shook my head irritably. Our thirty minutes was almost up.

"Hey, Doug, let's pray before they kick me out, okay?"

He nodded and bowed his head.

After we were done, I went back to the waiting room and walked up to the guard who sat in a chair directing the traffic in and out of the visiting booths.

"Is there anyone here who hasn't had a visitor in a while?" I asked him. Might as well keep doing my job while I was in the building.

He checked his list. "Yeah," he said after a moment. "There's a guy by the name of Robert Crow, hasn't had a visitor in more than a month."

"I'll talk with him, if you like," I said.

"Sure thing, Pastor," said the guard. "Just give me a minute to get him down here."

Five minutes later I was back in a booth. A medium-sized black man walked into the booth on the other side of the glass, looked at me, and then glanced around. He shrugged, sat down, and picked up the phone.

"Who you?" he said.

"I'm Jonah," I said. "I visit folks in jail or prison from time to time. Something about it in the Bible, I think."

He shrugged. "I ain't got much religion."

I shrugged. "Doesn't matter. I heard you hadn't had a visitor in a while. So I thought I'd see if you want to talk, if you need anything, you know."

A gleam came into his eyes. "We don't have much of nothing in here," he said. "I ain't got nobody lives nearby to bring me stuff. To deposit money in my account, you know."

"Sorry, man," I said. "I need to clarify. I don't do that. I'm not here to give you stuff. I'm here to talk, to listen. You doing okay? Got anything on your mind?"

He shrugged again. "Got no big complaints. I did my crime, now I'll do my time."

"What's your name?" I said. I had already heard it from the guard, but sometimes you got to do heavy lifting to get a conversation started.

"My name's Bob Crow," he said. "Mostly folks call me Bronco."

"All right, Bronco," I said, "do you like to fish?"

As it turns out, he did. We talked for the next twenty minutes about fishing and the Vikings and the NFL in general. When he left, Bronco seemed to have more spring in his step. I felt a little energized too. It seems there's always a payoff for doing something nice for no particular reason.

~

I left the building and drove up Highway 61 to the church. Julie usually didn't come in until after lunch on Tuesdays, and usually I had the building to myself until one or two. I went into my office and flicked on the lights and computer, and then went back out to the main office and started making coffee.

I thought through the sequence. Doug Norstad had been at his father's when Daniel Spooner was shot. On his way home, he heard about it on the radio. He was afraid they would arrest him, so he stayed away. It didn't make sense. Doug was not well educated, but that didn't mean he was dumb. All he had to do was tell the police where he'd been, and then wait for them to corroborate the story with his dad. Surely he knew that. Why, then, did he run away?

Unless . . .

I went back into my office and grabbed the phone. I punched in a number.

"Grand Lake Police," said a female voice on the other end.

"Chief Jensen, please," I said. "This is Jonah Borden."

"Please hold." There was a pause and I waited.

"Chief here," said Jensen.

"Dan," I said. "Jonah here. Listen, do you know if Norstad's story checked out?"

"Sheriff's department is on it for the most part, Jonah," said Jensen.

"Come on, Dan," I said. "You gotta know."

"Listen," said Jensen. "I know you think he didn't do it. But he wasn't at his dad's that day like Lucy said. He gave us the same story when we pulled him in."

"What did the dad say?" I asked.

"Jonah, I'm so sorry. That family's been through hell, and now there's this. But we gotta uphold the law."

"I believe in justice too," I said. "And that's why I'm concerned here. Norstad didn't do it. What did his dad say? If there's a discrepancy between their stories I'm sure there's an explanation."

"Jonah," said Jensen firmly, "listen to me. Doug Norstad's father has been dead for two years."

CHAPTER 12

After I hung up, I went back into the main office to get coffee. I was looking forward to a few hours of quiet study. A young couple, hand in hand, walked through the door.

"Hi, Pastor," said the woman. "I know we're a bit early. We can wait if you need to finish something up."

I didn't smack my head with the palm of my hand. "Greg and Cindy," I said slowly. "Pre-marriage counseling, eleven o' clock, Tuesday."

Greg's brow furrowed. "You didn't forget, did you?"

It is important for pastors never to lie. I didn't. I merely said, "I'm here, aren't I?"

His brow cleared, all except a small line in the middle. I knew he was suspicious. But I was here, wasn't I?

"Hold on for just a few moments," I said to them. "Let me get a few things squared away, and then we'll sit down. Do you want some coffee?"

Cindy accepted and Greg declined. I seated them in some chairs in the main office, and went back into my private office with a cup of my own. I took out two premarital questionnaires and some writing implements. I sat down for a minute to talk to God, and then to listen back. At five to eleven I came back out.

"All right," I said. "Why don't you two come into my office now."

An hour or so later they left, happy and with an upbeat outlook at their future marriage. I had seen a lot in just six years as a pastor, but on the whole I tended to agree with their positive assessment.

The phone rang. I left it alone. Julie could deal with messages when she came in. If it was important, she'd tell me right away. I straightened up my office, and then pulled my Greek New Testament from the shelf, along with a lexicon and Reinecker & Rogers' *Linguistic Key to the New Testament*. Reinecker and Rogers was a small thick book with a clean matte finish on the cover that made me want to just sit and run my fingers over it. Maybe I could absorb Greek through my fingertips. I slipped Bach into the CD drive of my computer and sat down to study.

Thoughts about Doug Norstad kept invading the inflected verbs. I had been so convinced that he was telling the truth. Actually, I had been half-convinced even before I went to see him that he was innocent. It made me mad to fall so completely for a lie. If I was honest with myself, I knew that a good portion of the anger was at my own lack of judgment. I'd seen enough as a pastor, and from just living, to spot most lies fairly easily. How could I have missed this one?

Reinecker and Rogers didn't care. I kept stolidly at my study, but in the background my mind was still gnawing at the Norstad problem.

Julie came in at two. She stood in the partly open door of my office and tapped the jamb with her knuckles. I looked up at her.

"Hey Julie," I said. "How 'bout I answer the phone for a while and you parse verbs?"

She shrugged. "It's all Greek to me," she said casually.

"I knew that was coming as soon as the words were out of my

mouth."

"You gotta take 'em when they're handed to you," she said. "How was Esther Newman?"

There was a pause, and we were both silent.

She looked at me closely. "You forgot, didn't you?"

Confession cleanses the soul. "Yes, I did," I said.

"Maybe we shouldn't schedule you for anything before I'm around to remind you."

"Maybe we shouldn't let one slip rearrange our schedules."

"Maybe we should have you checked for Alzheimer's."

"Hi, I'm Jonah Borden," I said.

"I think it's your delivery," said Julie. "It's off." She put a finger to her mouth and looked up at the ceiling. "Or maybe it's your material." She looked quickly back at me. "What about the engaged couple? Did you remember their premarital counseling today?"

"Have a little faith in me," I said. "We had a good session."

"They came in and you just happened to be here, didn't you?" said Julie.

"Julie, if I remembered all this stuff, what would you have to do? I want you to feel important. Necessary even."

"No fear," she said. "I guess you could still see Esther. It's not like she'll be out on the town somewhere."

"I guess that's one advantage of being a shut-in. People could come by anytime and you'd be home."

"Let me check the messages first, then you can go," said Julie.

"Whatever you say, boss," I said.

She stuck her tongue out at me and left. There were no messages that Julie couldn't take care of, so I packed my stuff and went visiting for the rest of the afternoon.

Esther Newman was, in fact, a little upset that I hadn't come at the appointed time, but she forgave me anyway.

CHAPTER 13

On Thursday afternoon, Julie beeped me on the intercom. "We have a collect call from the county jail."

"Probably Doug Norstad," I said. "Take it."

"Okay. Line one in just a sec."

I picked it up.

"Pastor?" said Doug. There was a lot of noise in the background. "It's Doug Norstad."

"Hi, Doug," I said. "What can I do for you?"

"Listen, can you come see me?"

I had seen him two days ago. "What's going on, Doug? Has something happened?"

"I don't wanna talk about it on the phone. Can you come?"

"Sure," I said.

"Thanks," he said. "When will you be here?"

"I'm not exactly sure," I said. "I've got a few appointments yet today. And some other things to finish up."

"It's really important," he said.

Of course it was. He was sitting in jail with nothing else to think about.

"You know what you said the other day, about making a confession?"

"Yeah," I said. Now this was more interesting.

"I want to talk about that."

"Okay, Doug," I said. "I'll see what I can do."

"Thanks, Pastor Jonah," he said.

We hung up.

I beeped Julie. "I've got to go out for a bit."

"No, you don't," she said. "You haven't finished your notes for the bulletin, and the Cramers are coming in ten minutes."

Sometimes it was a handicap, being unable to use profanity. I opted to sigh instead.

"I know what that sigh means," said Julie. "Don't use that language around me."

"Anything after the Cramers?" I asked.

"There's the bulletin," she said.

"I'll finish that later." I said. Now it was her turn to sigh.

"Watch your mouth, young lady," I said.

She laughed. It was a pleasant, everyday sound.

~

Robert and Rachel Cramer had been married seven years. Things weren't going so well for them. Mostly it was a matter of self-centeredness on the part of both of them, and a little bit of blindness on the part of Robert. A lot of people didn't realize that love had to be tended, like a flower garden. And most people never considered that love always involves a certain amount of work, and not all of that work comes naturally. And of course, there were always those folks—most often men, though a fair number of women too—who didn't have a clue how to go about the work of love, even if they would do it willingly enough.

The Cramers had come to me talking about divorce. A lot of couples did. But most people thought their marriages were worse and more hopeless than they really were. If people were willing to do the work involved in loving each other, all that remained was learning what to do, and how. It wasn't normally rocket science.

The Cramers were coming along well. They set another appointment when they were done, but I suspected that if they followed my recommendations, it would be the last one they felt the need for, for a while anyway.

After they left, I straightened out my office and went down to the jail. Nowadays everyone called them "correctional facilities," but that name was almost the opposite of the truth. Jail-time removed the menace of the criminal from the street, but it never corrected anybody.

After about half an hour, I was able to see Doug Norstad. He looked agitated. Once we were greeted and seated, he said, "Tell me what you said the other day, about confessing to you."

"Well, I think for some sins it is particularly important to confess them not only to God but to someone else. Just knowing someone else knows and hearing them tell you that you're forgiven, can change your life."

Norstad nodded. "And you said you can't tell anyone what I say to you in confession?"

"That's right. No one—not even the court—can compel me to tell what you say to me in a confession; as long as it is not about a crime you intend to commit in the future. I don't even have to tell about a crime you may have committed in the past."

"What about a sin I might commit in the future?"

I laughed. "We all have those. If it's not a crime, why not just wait and see whether you really do it or not."

"But you don't have to tell anyone?"

"You mean, if you have some sort of ongoing struggle with a

particular sin?"

He nodded eagerly.

"No," I said. "I don't have to tell anyone, as long as I don't think you're going to commit a crime in the future."

"Okay," he said, drawing a deep breath. He looked around him. "I have an alibi for the murder of Daniel Spooner."

"Not the one you already told me?"

He shook his head. "This is the real one."

"Why didn't you tell the police the real one?"

"You'll understand when you hear it."

"Let me get this straight—you want to tell me your *alibi* in confession?"

He nodded quickly.

"And you don't want me to tell anyone *your alibi*—the thing that could clear you from this crime."

"That's right," he said.

I thought I could guess what sort of alibi he had.

He took another deep breath and told me.

CHAPTER 14

As I left the jail, I noticed a small crowd by the front of the Justice
Center. Eric Berg stood on the steps, looking serious and saying
something. People had microphones thrust toward him, and I could
see news trucks and cameras.

I saw Leyla's Channel 13 minivan, and my heart leaped. I
walked over to the little crowd. Berg finished before I could get
close enough to hear what he was saying. I moved to where Leyla
was standing in front of the camera, doing some sort of wrap-up
report.

"Back to you," she said at last. She stepped around to the back
of the camera and turned it off. Next to her, a tall man from the
KSTP-5 truck said something to her. She replied and they both
laughed.

I walked over to Leyla and reached out to give her a one armed
hug. She flinched and then returned it awkwardly. When we broke
apart her eyes were flat.

"Hello, Jonah." Her voice was warmer than the lake, but only
slightly.

I am a pastor. My highly honed perceptive skills can tell me
when something is wrong. Plus, I was married once, for five years.

I looked at her. Not just coldness and anger. Hurt. Ah, yes. No
phone call.

"Leyla," I said. "I didn't call you. I . . ."

She cut me off. "I don't have time to talk right now, Jonah. They need me."

"Actually," said the tall man, "I think we're good for now. We'll call you if we need anything." He shook Leyla's hand. "It was nice to see you again."

Leyla turned to glare at him, but he was already getting into the news van. She whirled back to face me.

"Thanks a lot," she said. "Now the Minneapolis station thinks I'm in the middle of relationship problems. With a pastor."

"Don't say it like it's a dirty word," I said. "After all, I've got a crush on a reporter."

She looked at me levelly for a minute, and then tossed her hair. "Everyone gets crushes on TV stars."

"Yes," I said, "but I know what this one is really like. She's not just a pretty face." I paused. "She has a gorgeous body too."

A faint smile tugged at her mouth. "And her personality?"

"I think that's beautiful too. And forgiving. Very forgiving."

Her dimples appeared. I wanted to pump my fist and shout "Yes!" but I would have hit Leyla in the stomach. I settled for smiling back.

"I'm sorry I hadn't called you yet. I don't understand why. I've thought about you every day."

"A girl likes to be told, you know," she said.

"I'll make a note of it," I said. "Wanna go for a walk?"

"Okay," she said.

We set off toward the waterfront, three blocks away. For the first few minutes we were silent, walking so closely that our shoulders touched. The silence was not awkward. I think that was one of the things that struck me as so special about her.

After a while I said, "Do you want to hear the real reason I didn't call you?"

"Yes," she said, looking up at me and meeting my eyes as we walked.

I glanced forward, then grabbed her hand and pulled her away from walking into a lamp post. She laughed, then twined her fingers into mine and held them firmly.

"I think I was scared."

She didn't say anything, but just looked at me.

"I feel like we really connected last weekend, and it scared me. I was processing through whether or not I was ready for this. In all that, I forgot about how you might be feeling."

She was thoughtful for a moment. "So you didn't call me— because you had a great time with me?"

"In a nutshell, I guess, yeah."

She brushed something off my coat collar, then straightened it.

"Most times, a girl assumes that if a guy had a good time, he'll call. If he doesn't call, it means he's not interested."

"I can see how that would work," I said.

"But you're saying the opposite."

"Yes. I am. I am so interested, in fact, that I didn't call."

"'Cause it scared you."

"Yeah."

"Because you don't know if you're ready to really connect with someone, like we did?"

"I was working through that."

"Are you still working through that?" she asked.

"Your dimples," I said, "have helped tremendously."

She let me see them some more.

"And so?" she asked.

"When we're together, there's nothing to work through. I'm ready to move ahead. I need to go one step at a time, but I'm ready."

"When we're together," she said.

"This week when we were not together, I think I was over-thinking things."

"So together is fine. Apart is a problem, if you start thinking about things."

"I guess."

She swung in front of me, making me stop, and looked up into my eyes. "So let's be together when we can, and you don't think about things when we can't."

"Sounds like a plan," I said. We started walking again. I looked over the lake. I looked back at her.

"Can I think about your dimples when we're apart?"

"You can think about whatever parts of me you like," she said, "as long as you're just admiring God's creation."

CHAPTER 15

We went into one of the small cafés at the waterfront, and sat down for a cup of coffee. I asked her what Eric Berg had been saying on the courthouse steps.

"He said they had caught the man who shot Daniel Spooner. While he sympathizes with anyone who feels rage at Spooner, he says it is vital for the preservation of law and order that we do not allow vigilante killings to go unpunished."

"Wow. You sound like a reporter."

She tossed her hair. "One has a certain experience."

I said, "He meant Doug Norstad, didn't he?"

"Yes, he said they would indict Doug Norstad for the killing."

I shook my head.

"You still think Norstad didn't do it?"

I was quiet.

"Jonah, the man went on the run for a week. When he came back, he lied about his alibi for the killing."

"He came back because I got on TV and urged him to."

She put her hand on my arm. "Is that what's bothering you?"

"Among other things."

"Other things?"

I shook my head again. "I can't really talk about them right now. Someone told me something in confidence. I'm trying to evaluate it."

She smiled slyly. "Do I smell a story?"

"Not right now anyway," I said. "I take pastoral confidence pretty seriously."

She thought about that for a moment. "I guess I'm glad you do." She thought a while longer. "So if you think Norstad is innocent, who did it then?"

"That," I said, "is the question."

"You can't tell me why you think he's innocent."

"Nope," I said.

She looked at me for a bit, then looked at the lake out the windows of the café. "You're pretty good, aren't you?"

"I never got into trouble by saying too little."

There was a pause.

"Well . . ." she said.

"True," I said. "I promise you, I'll call you this time."

CHAPTER 16

After I left Leyla at her minivan, I walked back to the Justice Center. I went the up the steps so recently occupied by Eric Berg. The building was pretty new, built on the taxes generated by the tourist trade. A wide, curved, reception desk sat in the middle of the back of the lobby. Behind it, a board listed various offices. The assistant DA was on the fourth floor.

I went up the stairs and down a clean, dark-paneled hallway, and turned left into a suite of offices. A very heavy-set, dour-faced, middle-aged woman sat at a desk just inside the door, looking at a computer.

"Can I help you?" she asked.

"Yes," I said, "I need to speak with Mr. Berg."

"Whom shall I say wants to see him?"

"I don't know, do you think Mahatma Gandhi? Or would he be more likely to see Hilary Clinton?"

She smiled faintly. You couldn't be employed by the government if you had a sense of humor. I wondered if they all went to some sort of government finishing school where they had the humor removed surgically.

"Your own name, please, sir."

Definitely some sort of humor-restricted finishing school.

"Pastor Jonah Borden."

She clicked on her computer a few times and stared dully at the screen. "Do you have an appointment, Pastor Borden?"

"No." I wanted to add that, since it was an election year, he had given me the impression that he was a close personal friend of mine and I could drop by and see him anytime. I decided not to.

"I'm afraid he's busy right now," said the secretary.

"When could I come back and see him?" I asked.

She did some more clicking.

"He has an opening on July 17th," she said.

"That's more than two months away," I said.

"I'm sorry. The assistant district attorney is a very busy man."

"I'm sure he is," I said. "The matter I want to see him about is time-sensitive."

She looked at me blankly. I returned the look.

After a while I said, "I'll tell you what. I'll write him a note. Could you please deliver this message to him right away?"

"I'll put it in his box."

"I'm sorry," I said. "This is really very urgent. If you could, please take it to him directly. I'm sure he'll be upset if he doesn't get it right away."

"I can take him a note," she said at last.

I borrowed a pen and piece of paper and wrote on it for a bit. I folded it in thirds and handed it to her. She put it down on her desk and looked back at her computer, clicking some more. I stood there, waiting. She looked at me and sighed.

"I have things to do also," she said, pushing herself away from the desk and standing up with effort. "I'll take him the note now, so you can leave."

I didn't move. "I'll wait here. After he reads the note, he may want to rearrange his schedule and see me right away."

She shrugged. "Suit yourself. Wait here, please." She turned and waddled toward a maze of cubicles. I leaned over and glanced at her computer screen. On it was a game of solitaire. She was just walking past the first cubicle. I followed her.

After a few steps, she sensed me behind her and turned.

"You need to wait in the reception area, sir."

"This is very important," I said. "I want to make sure it doesn't end up in the wrong place."

Her moon face registered nothing. At last she turned back and continued walking. We reached a large mahogany door.

"Wait here, please," she said, and knocked at the door. When a voice called from inside, she opened the door, went in, and shut it behind her. I heard murmured voices, and then the secretary came out, again closing the door behind her.

"I gave him the note," she said.

"Thank you," I said, standing aside to let her precede me. After she went past, I turned back to the door, opened it, and went in.

"Hey," she called half-heartedly.

Eric Berg had a large corner office. Dark wood bookshelves filled the wall on either side of the door, as well as the wall immediately to my left. The two remaining walls boasted large plate-glass windows and a beautiful view of the lake and the harbor. Berg himself sat behind a huge, dark-stained mission-oak desk. The desk was clear except for a telephone, a lamp, and my note. Berg was looking out the window at Superior, his nose in a mug. He didn't look busy. He turned with an inquiring look when I came in. The secretary came huffing after me.

"I'm sorry, Mr. Berg," she said. "This man came in making jokes about Mrs. Clinton and then he followed me here and walked in without permission."

Berg waved a hand. "It's okay, Gladys," he said. "I know him. I'll take care of it."

Why were they always named Gladys, or Shirley?

"What can I do for you, Jonah?" Berg said as Gladys left. "I'm pretty busy," he said, looking at his watch, "but I guess I could spare a few minutes for my pastor."

It was technically true. Berg and his family showed up at church just often enough to be kept on the membership rolls. "Speaking of that," I said, "I haven't seen you at church in a while."

He waved his hand airily. "I travel a lot. Is that why you came to see me? Surely you're not doing a stewardship drive in May?"

"Actually, I came to see you about Doug Norstad."

Berg's brow furrowed. He looked at me the way a principal looks at a bright but misguided student. "What about Doug Norstad?"

"Eric, I think you're making a mistake. I don't want to see you prosecute an innocent man."

"Jonah, we all know what the Norstads have been through this year. No one hurts for them more than I." I refrained from snorting while he paused, gathering his words like the careful politician he was.

"Even so, we must have justice in this state. We can't allow people the freedom to kill others, even if the one they kill is a killer himself. I will not compromise justice, even if Doug Norstad was a member of your church." He sat back, as though expecting applause.

"Our church," I said. I knew I was just needling him, but I

couldn't help it.

"Yes, of course," he said hastily. "Our church."

"I agree with you about justice," I said. "Spooner was a scumbag, but he had a right to due process, like every other citizen. The thing is, it wasn't Doug who killed him."

Berg leaned back in his chair and steepled his fingers together. In a moment I expected him to break out a meerschaum pipe. "Jonah," he said pompously, "this is not your province. You are a pastor. I am an officer of the court. It is my job to determine whom to prosecute, and in what manner. It is your job to be a pastor. Now, people don't come to you all the time and tell you how to preach and how to run a church, do they?"

I smiled beatifically. "Every day," I said. This was the first time I'd ever been thankful for it.

Berg looked irritated. "My point is this. You don't have all the information I have. You don't have the responsibilities I have. When someone commits a crime, we get the right man for the right crime and prosecute him in the right way. I'm pretty good at it, actually. My conviction rate is eighty-five percent. I don't know if you know anything about that, but it is an unbelievable number. Prosecution is my calling, like your calling to the ministry."

"So you won't be running for congress in November?" I asked.

He lost his warm, paternal façade, and his eyes snapped at me. "Was there something else you wanted?"

"Eric, I am a pastor, and that's why I'm here. As a pastor, I am privy to information you may not have. And I'm telling you, you are making a mistake."

Berg's manner changed abruptly, and he looked almost worried. I'd be worried too if I had made a grand announcement on television that turned out to be completely wrong. It wouldn't help his chances in November.

"What do you know?" he hissed.

For a moment I was silent. The truth was, I hadn't had a chance to verify what Doug had told me. And even if I had, Doug had not given me permission to share it. Reluctantly, I decided it was time to back off.

"I'm just saying I have a sense about these things sometimes." I knew it sounded lame as I said it. "I'm just asking you, Eric, to look into this a bit more closely."

"Are you saying you have a sense—from God?"

"Something like that," I said.

Berg came back on-balance, and the paternal, warm, political manner came back online.

"I'll tell you what, Jonah," he said, standing up and extending his hand. "I'll look into it. I sure appreciate you stopping by."

I took his hand and then left.

~

That night, I called Leyla on her cell phone.

"Hi," I said. "I had a good time with you today. When I can I see you again?"

"Don't lay it on too thick," she said.

"The thing is," I said, "it's true. How was the rest of your day?"

"It was a pretty ordinary day," she said, "except I'm in Grand Lake instead of at home."

She paused. "How about you? What do pastors do all day, anyway?"

"Funny, I was going to ask the same thing about reporters."

She laughed.

"Well," I said. "I need to be very busy, but always available with hours to spare for whoever needs it. I need to be friendly to everyone and easy to get along with, as well as deep and good at one-on-one interaction. I'm supposed to be full of energy, and also quiet. I should be out visiting folks ten hours a day, but always in my office. I need to be an administrator, people person, scholar, counselor, cheerleader, coach, quarterback and friend."

"Sounds like a tall order," she said.

"Nah," I said. "Mostly I just sit in my office and drink coffee and listen to rock music. You know, I only work for an hour a week."

"Really, Jonah," she said, "I want to know."

"Well," I said, "it's not all that romantic. I spend twenty to thirty hours a week studying and preparing my sermon. I try to keep from being a hypocrite, so I also try to nurture my faith—you know, with prayer and stuff like that. I do a fair amount of counseling and quite a bit of planning. I have already attended enough boring meetings to kill Donald Trump. When I can, I attend ball games and other community events. I visit sick people and people in jail. I do some writing and sit on a community board or two. But I'm not a workaholic. I'm full-time, but I always have enough room in my calendar to date a beautiful reporter."

"Well," she said. "I suppose that's adequate." She paused. "I always thought priests and pastors just spent all their time—you know, being holy or something."

"I've got the 'or something' part down. Still haven't mastered the holy thing, though."

"Have you learned anything more about Doug Norstad?" she

asked.

"I have certain confidentiality guidelines I need to follow. I'm not trying to put you off, but you're going to have to be patient."

We talked for a few more minutes, and then hung up. All in all, it seemed a satisfactory way to end the evening.

CHAPTER 17

I knew I needed to verify Doug's story. He'd already sold me a line once. I wasn't ready to go to bat for him again until I knew for sure that what he'd told me was true. Friday morning, I got up early and finished the bulletin at my home office. I emailed it to Julie. "I'm going fishing," I typed. "I love emailing you, 'cause then I don't have to wait for you to come up with a smart reply." I hit *send*. As I stood up and straightened my office, my computer beeped, telling me I had an email.

"You don't have to wait," Julie had written, "because email is instantaneous."

I decided to pretend I had already left.

I got into my Jetta and drove down the long ridge to 61. I took it southwest, through Grand Lake and along the lake shore. An hour and a half later I stopped in Duluth for some breakfast. We don't have an Embers in Grand Lake, so I went there, just south of Duluth on 35. Nothing in the world like the Andouille sausage skillet, unless maybe it was Irma's totally awesome skillet.

Sufficiently loaded with cholesterol, I got back on the freeway and kept on south toward the Twin Cities. A little less than two hours later, I took 694 west and then went south on Snelling. Across 36, at County B, I turned left. After half a mile I turned left into the parking lot of a tall white office building.

It was warmer down here than up by the Lake, so I left my

jacket in the car and walked into the building's lobby. According to the directory, there was an office for "Freedom Ministries" on the fourth floor.

I took the elevator up and wandered around on the fourth floor for a bit until I found the right door. I knocked, and then walked in.

I was in a small reception area. Across the room from me was one door, closed. To my left, a small middle-aged woman sat at a desk in front of a computer monitor. Her hair was cut blunt and short, a man's haircut. She wore jeans and a button-up, mannish-looking shirt. She wore no jewelry and no makeup on her small delicate face. With different clothes and hair, she would have been very attractive. As it was, she looked like a grown woman trying to be a tomboy.

"Can I help you?" she asked.

"Yes," I said. "I'm here to see Dr. Solberg."

She turned back to the computer. "Do you have an appointment?" she asked.

"I'm afraid not," I said, "but it is extremely important."

She looked at me skeptically. "I'm sorry," she said. "But Dr. Solberg does not see people without an appointment."

"It's an emergency," I said.

"Dr. Solberg is not a physician," she replied.

"A man's life is at stake," I said. "I'm serious. I need to see him. Today."

She glanced at her computer. I wondered if I had interrupted another important game of solitaire. She looked back at me. "We can't normally do this," she said.

"I'm here on a confidential matter," I said, encouragingly, "but believe me, this isn't about losing a job or just feeling blue.

This is truly urgent."

"Hold on a minute, please," she said. She went through the door next to her desk. After a few minutes, she came back.

"What I can do is this," she said. "When Dr. Solberg is finished with his current appointment, I'll see if he can give you five minutes."

"Thank you," I said.

I went and sat down. The waiting room didn't look like a doctor's office. Then again, "Freedom Ministries" wasn't much of a name for a health clinic. There was a *Reader's Digest* and a few *National Geographic* magazines lying around on a coffee table.

I decided to read about how a 72-year-old man had survived a grizzly bear attack. After that, I read about the latest weight-loss fad. There was a mushy story about how a woman had found her daughter, whom she had given up for adoption twenty years previously, when the daughter ended up as a kidney donor for her diabetic, biological mother. Somehow the words diabetic and biological didn't go together with the expected warm fuzzy tone of the story.

I was rather desperately thumbing through every article in order to read the jokes at the end when the secretary spoke on the phone. I looked up.

She hung up and said, "You can go in now. Five minutes."

"Thanks," I said.

I went through the door next to her desk and found myself in a short hallway. A door on the left appeared to lead into a bathroom. On on the right was a good-sized conference room, furnished with about twenty chairs in a semicircle. At the end were two more doors—one leading back out into the hallway of the building, and one to a large roomy office with big windows.

In the big office was a big desk with a big man sitting in front of the big windows. Bookcases lined the walls and a low dark-wood table held a fountain which trickled softly. Peaceful music played quietly in the background. The big man stood up and reached out with a muscular forearm.

"Rich Solberg," he said, his voice unexpectedly high and light. His handshake was firm and steady. He had thinning blond hair and a thick reddish blond beard, highlighted with white.

"Jonah Borden," I said.

"My secretary tells me you were very insistent that you see me," he said. He looked at me through stylish gold-rimmed glasses. His eyes were the eyes of a man who expected to be deceived, and who expected to catch and uncover the deception.

"She said I only had five minutes," I said, "so I'll be brief."

He nodded and leaned forward, still ready to expose my lies.

"I am pastor to a man named Doug Norstad. You may have heard of him on the news. He is accused of killing the man who raped and killed his daughter up in Grand Lake on the North Shore."

Solberg's expression didn't change a bit.

I waited. He waited. Finally I said, "Doug Norstad says that he is a client of yours."

Solberg leaned back. He put his hands together and pointed both index fingers up, as if he was holding a gun with both hands.

I waited. He waited. At last he said, "I'm not at liberty to disclose who my clients are." He pointed the two-handed gun slightly toward me. "You say you're a pastor. You must understand confidentiality." He brought the gun back up to his cheek.

"I do," I said. "That's why I'm here. Doug said he was here, with you, when Daniel Spooner was shot. You are his alibi, only he won't tell anyone about it but me."

"So you want me to tell the police that Doug Norstad—I'm not saying he's my client, you understand—was with me at the time of the murder."

"Actually, no," I said. "Doug doesn't want that. I just need to know for myself if his story is true. Once I know, then I can figure out what to do."

Solberg thought about it. I could feel my five minutes slipping away.

"Do you know what we do here, Pastor Borden?"

"Well, Doug told me in general terms why he was here. The thing is, he has lied to me before, and I'd like to hear it from you, without me making a suggestion."

Solberg thought some more, looking at the ceiling. "Do you have a business card?" he asked.

I dug one out of my wallet and slid it across his glass-topped desk.

He studied it as if it was a piece of ancient pottery. At last he looked at me.

Would you like a cup of coffee, Pastor Borden?" he asked.

"I am," I said, "a Lutheran pastor in northern Minnesota."

A slight smile split Solberg's beard. It wasn't much, but it looked genuine. "I'll take that as a yes. Do you have time to wait while I make it?"

"Fresh is always best anyway," I said.

CHAPTER 18

It must have been gourmet coffee, because it was more than fifteen minutes before Solberg came back. While I waited, I stood and examined some of the books on his shelves. He had Jung, but no Freud. There were a few books by Henri Nouwen, one of which I had read. F. Scott Peck was there. Alongside the psychology, he had some Christian classics: C. S. Lewis, G. K. Chesterton, Andrew Murray, Tozer, and the like.

If I was less scrupulous, I could have searched the office for a file about Doug Norstad. I decided not to.

I was examining the fountain when Solberg finally came back. He seemed a bit out of breath as he came around his desk and sat down in his high-backed, leather, swivel chair.

"All right, Pastor Borden," he said. "Where were we?"

"So I'm assuming this is decaf," I said, pointing to my empty hand.

"The coffee!" he exclaimed. He didn't slap his forehead, but he looked like he wanted to. Without another word, he got up and left. This time he wasn't gone long, and when he returned he held two steaming mugs.

"Cream or sugar?" he asked.

"Neither," I said.

The coffee was good, probably some sort of gourmet vanilla blend. He must have soaked the beans in vanilla himself, with the time it had taken him to make it.

"If you will, Pastor Borden," said Solberg, "let's start over."

I nodded encouragingly.

"I'm clear now for the lunch hour, and I've sent Susan out for Leann Chin. I hope you like Chinese?"

"I love Leann Chin," I said. "Sounds like a great way to start over."

"I'm sorry about all the caginess before," said Solberg. "The fact is, what we do here is not well-received by certain individuals and groups. In fact," he added, "I personally have received several death threats. I don't think they were serious, but in any case, you understand that I want to be careful about talking to unknown individuals about what I do."

"I can see that," I said. "Am I not still an unknown individual?"

"I made a few phone calls," he said. "Susan looked you up on the Internet. In short, you check out."

"So it really didn't take you twenty minutes to make coffee?"

He chuckled. "It didn't."

"You were going to tell me about what you do here."

"Yes. I am a clinical psychiatrist, and I work exclusively with homosexual clients."

I nodded. This is what Doug told me. The door opened and Susan the secretary came in with some white and purple bags from Leann Chin.

"I didn't know what you wanted, so pick from these," she said.

I took the Peking Chicken. "I love this," I said.

We thanked Susan as she left, and began to eat.

After a while I said, "How exactly do you help your homosexual clients?"

"The people who come to me don't want to be gay or lesbian anymore. I help them to change."

"You make them straight?" I asked.

"It's a little more complicated than that," he said, "and I don't have a one-hundred-percent success rate, but yes, a large majority of my clients end up identifying as heterosexual."

I thought for a moment. "I can see why you aren't popular," I said.

"Yes. I get accused of brainwashing and coercing. But all of my clients are working with me voluntarily—in fact, they pay me."

"Insurance doesn't cover this sort of therapy?"

"Unfortunately not," he said. "I've had to move twice. People were coming and trashing my lawn, writing all sorts of obscene graffiti."

"How did they find you?"

"I'm not popular with the press either. Very out of step with modern mores. So they don't treat me very kindly. Nor, I might add, do they address the subject of homosexuality very accurately. Anyway, once they reported my address, right in the *Star-Tribune*. Another time a camera crew followed me home, and people figured it out from the pictures."

"Can gay people really go straight?" I asked. "I thought that was a myth."

"It isn't easy. Most gay people would not have chosen to be gay if they had a say in the matter."

"So are you saying people are born gay? If so, how can they change?"

"It doesn't really matter if they are born gay or not," he said. "Whatever the case is, for many of them, their sexuality is set before they are conscious of any sort of choice in the matter. But the interesting thing is, most of them would rather be heterosexual than gay, if they could."

"I've never wished I wasn't heterosexual," I said.

"Exactly," said Solberg. "There are some folks who, as the saying goes, are just perverted. I don't mean that in the derogatory sense. What I mean is, they have made a choice against their own natural heterosexual impulses—a perversion, if you will. Most people in the gay community acknowledge that there are such people out there. But many of them feel that they were simply born that way, however much they may wish they were different."

"So if it is so deeply ingrained, how can they change?"

"As I said, it is very difficult. But it has been done, by more than a few, and by those who were positive they were born that way and doomed to have homosexual feelings all their lives. I think a relationship with God is key to it. But there is, in fact, a well-established therapy pattern as well, called reparative therapy."

"Doug Norstad was married," I said. "He had a daughter."

"It's not that uncommon," he said. "There was a study that came out a few years ago, proclaiming that about ten percent of the U.S. population is gay. In fact, their definition of 'gay' was very broad. It included anyone who had ever had just a single homosexual encounter—which, in itself, was very broadly defined. The fact is, only a very small percentage of gay men have never been attracted to women at all."

"So under today's definition, a gay person could actually be bisexual."

"Exactly," said Solberg.

"And that was Doug Norstad?"

Solberg thought a minute. "I'm still not quite comfortable disclosing anything about someone who may be a client of mine," he said. He held up his hand. "I've checked you out, and I believe you are who you say you are."

"But it's an ethical thing," I said.

He nodded.

"This really is very important," I said. "Doug could be wrongfully imprisoned for the rest of his life. If he does struggle with homosexual feelings that he wants to overcome, prison probably won't help him."

"I hadn't thought of that angle," said Solberg.

"How about this," I said. "You don't have to tell me if he's your client. But can you tell me if you know him?"

"I know Doug Norstad," said Solberg, watching me closely.

"And where did you meet him?"

Solberg grinned and nodded. "I see. I think, considering the circumstances, I can go with this. I met him for the first time right here."

"And did you and Doug—get together and chat, regularly?"

"Yes, we did," said Solberg. "Most Tuesdays, around this time, in fact."

"And the day Spooner was shot?"

"I was chatting with Doug around that time," said Solberg.

"Do you know for sure it was that time?" I asked.

"I could check and find out," he smiled. "I keep close records of some of my, ah—conversations. But there's another thing," he went on. "Part of what I recommend for—people I chat with, is a group meeting that takes place every Tuesday night at Roseville Community Church. Doug was very faithful in attending that meeting. It's almost certain he was here in the Twin Cities all day."

"Well, if you were chatting with him even as late as eleven, he couldn't have been in Grand Lake in time to shoot Daniel Spooner," I said.

Solberg picked up his phone and called his secretary. "Can you tell me the last time I saw Douglas Norstad?" he asked. He grunted and put down the phone. A minute or two later it beeped and he picked up. "Okay," he said, "thanks." He turned to me. "We finished at noon that Tuesday."

"So," I said, "he's innocent."

Solberg was quiet.

"By the way," I asked, "How was it going? Was he making progress?"

"That's confidential information," said Solberg. "But based on my chats with him, if he was in some sort of therapy, it appeared to be helping."

I thanked Solberg and stood to leave, wiping my face with a Leann Chin napkin.

"Pastor Borden," said Solberg. I looked at him. "I appreciate what you're doing for Doug. Didn't you tell me that he wanted to keep this quiet?"

"Yes, he did," I said. "In fact, what he told me falls under laws regarding religious confession."

"I didn't think Doug was ready for his community—his friends and family and so on—to know about his particular struggle."

"I got that sense when he told me. In fact, he asked me to keep it just between us."

"You came to me."

"I was under the impression you already knew of his problem. And if you remember, I got you to confirm it before I told you about it."

"Clever," admitted Solberg. "So how is all this going to help him?"

"I don't know yet," I said.

CHAPTER 19

I called Leyla once I was back on the freeway. "Hi," I said. "I'm going to the WW tonight. Wanna come along? I could knock off early and we could go someplace quieter after that."

"I'd love to, Jonah, but I'm not sure I'll be in Grand Lake tonight. Nothing much seems to be going on with the Norstad case, and so they may pull us back home."

"Well," I said slowly, "about the Norstad case." I thought about it for a bit. I'd have to tread carefully, but maybe I could help Doug this way.

"What about the Norstad case?" asked Leyla.

An uncomfortable thought popped into my head. "Leyla," I said, "an uncomfortable thought just popped into my head."

"What was it?" she asked.

"It's not terrible," I said. "But I need to think on it a bit. If you go back to Duluth could I pick you up there and take you to the Blackwoods?"

"Well," she said, "it's not the rotating restaurant at the top of the Radisson, but it's a start."

"We'll work our way up to the Radisson," I said. "Besides, it can feel frustrating up there. Everything seems to just go around in circles."

There was a pause. "Many women," she said, "feel that a good sense of humor is important in a man. Thus far you are on probation."

"You sound like my secretary," I said.

"She probably has a good head on her shoulders," said Leyla.

I considered pointing out that Julie's head would certainly not be on her knees, but I remembered that I was on probation. I decided to say nothing.

"I'll call you when I know where I'll be," said Leyla.

"All right," I said.

~

She was, it turned out, in Duluth.

I got directions to her condo, well on the north side—that much closer to Grand Lake, I was pleased to note. They were well appointed buildings done about as tastefully as condominiums can be, and the grounds were nicely kept. I found her building and knocked at the door.

The woman who answered wasn't Leyla, but she was easy on the eyes anyway. Long, straight, Scandinavian-blond hair, blue eyes, and cute smile. She looked to be in her mid-twenties.

"Hi," I said. "I'm Jonah. I'm here to see Leyla." I smiled, friendly but not too friendly.

She smiled back, very friendly.

"Come on in," she said. "Leyla's still getting ready."

I followed her in to a well-furnished living room, cute, but tasteful, and very feminine. Like the occupants.

"I'm Jen." She threw her hair back over her shoulder.

"Nice to meet you," I said.

"Leyla's told me all about you," said Jen, eying me speculatively. "I didn't expect . . ." She paused awkwardly.

"You didn't expect a pastor to look so normal?" I asked.

She laughed self-consciously. "Actually," she said, regaining her composure, "I didn't expect a pastor to be so good-looking."

"Thank you," I said, "and back at you."

She smiled and lowered her eyes demurely. "Thank *you*," she said.

There was a slightly awkward pause. "Would you like something to drink?" she asked. "We've got beer, pop, wine and apple juice."

"How about water?" I said.

"Okay," said Jen. "Do you want ice too?"

"Sure."

Jen came back with the drinks, and we chatted for a few minutes more. Then Leyla came out.

Jen was pretty, but when I saw Leyla I felt a little shock, part familiarity, sort of like returning to the street you grew up on but hadn't seen for years; and part beauty. I could feel it all the way into my feet. Jen and Leyla saw it in me, I'm sure. Jen smiled and looked at me and then at Leyla.

"Wow," I said. "You look gorgeous."

Leyla saw the effect she had on me. She pursed her lips. "Well, maybe there are other things besides the sense of humor." She twirled girlishly. "Do you like it?"

She was wearing a crimson and rust patterned mini-dress with pleats. It showed off her legs and figure admirably. Her dark hair cascaded smoothly down over one shoulder, held in place with silver combs. Little silver, bell-shaped earrings dangled by her neck.

"I love it," I said. "The only thing is, I'm going to have to glare at a lot of other men tonight, to keep them at bay."

She laughed, silver bells tinkling. Jen said, "He'll do."

I held the door for Leyla and we got into my car. After a few blocks, Leyla said, "Is this classical music?"

"'1812 Overture,' by Tchaikovsky," I said. "One of the best ever."

"I thought you were into hard rock," she said.

"I'm into music. The best of all genres."

She peered at me. "Really?"

"Well, not rap. And of course, I like some styles more than others."

"You're a complex person, aren't you?" she said.

"Part of my charm," I said.

~

The Blackwoods was a step above the national bar and grill chains, but probably a step below truly fine dining. You couldn't order ostrich there, but you could drop twenty-five bucks a plate, if you wanted to. I had a steak with potatoes, and chicken wild-rice soup instead of the salad. Leyla had a Caesar chicken salad.

"So," said Leyla while she buttered some bread. "You had a disturbing thought today."

I dipped some bread into the chicken wild-rice soup. Perfecto.

"Don't get me wrong," I said. "It was mostly an excuse to take you to dinner."

"You don't need an excuse," said Leyla. She took a bite of bread.

I nodded. "I'll keep that in mind."

"And your thought?"

I swallowed some soup. It was really more like stew, when you came down to it.

"Well, I don't want to make a big deal of it. I found something out today about Doug Norstad. When I was talking to you, I thought maybe I could tell you a bit about it and use Channel 13 to help Doug Norstad." I took another bite of soup. Leyla was chewing, but she didn't seem to want to say anything.

"It was that word 'use' that caught my attention and disturbed me."

"Oh," said Leyla. Then, "oh," again.

"Yeah," I said. "I started to wonder if I was just using you for this situation. I don't want to do that."

"Do you think you really are?" asked Leyla. She seemed very calm.

"No," I said. "I think I'm really attracted to you because you are beautiful, smart, witty, kind, and sort of vulnerable without being weak."

Her face turned the tiniest bit red. But she smiled and didn't look away as I held her eyes.

"So is there a problem?" she asked at last.

"I don't think so," I said. "I would want to be right here, with you, even if you worked as a janitor. But I don't want to abuse the situation."

She chewed thoughtfully, then took a drink of Coke.

"That's very sweet," she said. "But did you ever think that I could be using you?"

I shrugged. "The other side of the same coin?"

"Yes. You are linked to what's happening up there. I've gotten some decent stories from you, or because of you, already."

"So are you using me?" I asked.

"No," she said. "I think I'm just attracted to you because you are witty, intelligent, good-looking, and deeper than Lake Superior, though not nearly as cold."

"Witty?" I said. "Does that mean I'm off probation?"

"You were never really on it."

She held my eyes. I sensed a deep thrill spreading through me like the slow warmth of a fire.

"This was all very unexpected," I said at last.

"It's going faster than I anticipated," she said. "But I like it. Are you okay?"

"I'm better than okay. I want to stand up and shout yahoo."

"Please don't," she said.

We ate for a bit.

"So how do we handle the Norstad/Spooner stuff?" she said at last.

"I guess we just don't make any assumptions about what we each need to do professionally."

"And we don't let that stuff interfere with what we've got between us." She gestured vaguely around our table.

"Definitely not."

"All right," she said. "Can we give five minutes to work, and then let the rest be about us?"

"Absolutely," I said.

"Okay," she patted her lips with her napkin. "Did you want to tell me about what you learned today, or not?"

"If you don't mind, I'd like to try other channels first. But can I tell you off the record, as your—"

"Sweetheart?" she said, smiling.

"Yes. Can I talk to you as a sweetheart, not a reporter?"

"Of course." She grinned mischievously and reached across

the booth and patted my cheek. "How was your day, honey?"

I laughed, caught her hand, and held it between both of mine on the table. She didn't seem to want it back.

"Well," I said. "I learned for certain that Doug Norstad is innocent."

"How did that happen?" she asked. She began to trace patterns on the back of my hand with her free one.

"He told me something confidential—you know, as his pastor—a few days ago. If it was true, it would clear him. Even so, he didn't want anyone to know about it. I talked to the DA after he told me, but they wouldn't budge. Today, I got the chance to verify what Doug told me, and it is completely true."

"But he doesn't want anyone to know about it."

"Nope. And I can't tell anyone without being unethical."

"Can you ask Doug to let you tell someone?"

"I asked him right after he told me. He said no. I'll ask him again, but nothing's really changed from his perspective."

"What does he expect you to do?"

"Well, he told me to get it off his chest, for starters. That's part of what I do, as a pastor, so that's not so unusual."

Leyla kept tracing her finger on my hand, and sometimes a bit up my forearm. She looked at me from under long eyelashes. "You must have a lot of secrets locked away in your head."

I nodded. "It's a privilege and a burden," I said. "I know the most shameful and private moments of many people's lives. Sometimes it's hard to know what to do with them."

"Anyway," I said after a moment, "now that I know for sure where the land lies, I might be able to convince the DA to back off, or maybe get the police to start looking for the real killer."

"I don't mean this is right," said Leyla, "but in some ways, Doug is the perfect suspect." She shook her head as I started to object. "I believe you when you say he's innocent. But everyone knows the story with his daughter. A jury might be inclined to acquit, or at least there's a good chance it would hang. Or, if they did convict him, the judge would probably go easy on his sentence. I mean, whoever *did* kill Daniel Spooner did us all a favor, and Doug Norstad would get off easier than anyone else."

"That's not justice, though," I said.

"If we lived in a death-penalty state, Spooner probably would have been executed anyway."

"If Minnesota was a death-penalty state, he probably wouldn't have committed the crime here. But in any case, there's a difference between the state taking a life according to carefully conceived laws, and an individual deciding to do it for revenge or something."

"Do you really believe the death-penalty deters crime?" she asked.

"Probably not, the way they do it in most states nowadays. Most death-row inmates wait twenty years or more before they are executed. A lot them die of old age in prison. That's not substantially different than life without parole."

She didn't look bored or shocked.

"I do know this, though," I added, "whether it is a first-time deterrent or not, there are no repeat offenders among those who receive the death penalty."

"I guess that's true enough," she said. "I'd never quite thought of it that way."

The main course arrived and after the waitress left I looked at

Leyla.

"I have a habit that may seem a bit embarrassing to you," I said. "But I pray before meals, even in restaurants."

She looked at me steadily. "Well, at least you are consistent."

I nodded. "I don't show everyone all of my private life, but I do try to keep the public me and the private me in harmony."

"And right now you are the public you?"

"No, I'm the private me now."

"How will I know the difference?"

"Hopefully," I said, "you won't."

She kept hold of my hand, and I said a quick prayer. I'm not embarrassed about it, but private or public, I don't believe in keeping the food waiting for long prayers.

"So, Leyla Bennett," I said, cutting into my steak, "do you have any hobbies?"

She finished chewing some lettuce. She sipped some more Coke. "Actually, I do," she said.

"And?"

"I guess my two biggest ones are hiking and sailing."

I digested this thoughtfully while I finished my own mouthful. "I live about a mile off of the Superior Hiking Trail," I said.

Her eyes widened pleasantly. "Really?"

"Yep. In fact, my property runs nearly all the way up to it. I cut a trail through my woods that hooks up with it."

"How much land do you have?" she asked.

"About a hundred and fifty acres," I said modestly.

"Wow."

"Yeah, it's pretty cool actually. I still pinch myself sometimes."

"So can we go hiking sometime?"

"What about sailing?"

"Well," she said with a smile, "does your property run down to Lake Superior too? To a marina, perhaps?"

"You mock me," I said in mock stiffness.

"Yes," she said, "I do."

"There is a marina a few miles north of Grand Lake. And of course, there's the one in the harbor."

"Do they rent catamarans?"

"I have no idea," I said. "But would you like to find out next week?"

"Why are we talking in questions?" she asked.

"Don't you know?" I said. She laughed.

"All right, no more questions," I said. "I'll pick you up on Thursday morning and we'll find out about the catamarans."

She gave a slight shrug and a grimace. "It may depend on work," she said.

"Okay. Contingent on your work schedule."

"Bring your swimsuit," she said.

"Lake Superior?" I asked. "Are you crazy?"

"Who knows, it may be hot enough to jump into forty-degree water."

"Leyla," I said, "it is never hot enough in Minnesota to jump into forty-degree water."

She shrugged. "You wouldn't want to get shown up by a woman," she said sweetly.

"And by a news babe at that," I said.

"You gotta watch out for the news babes."

"I do," I said. "Lately it has become my favorite thing to watch out for."

CHAPTER 20

It was with some serious regret that I got Leyla home by 7:30 and headed north to Grand Lake and the WW. I had promised some folks I'd be there that night.

Sometimes I hated being a guy you could rely on.

I got there a little after nine. It was crowded as usual. My booth wasn't open anymore. I pushed my way up to the bar and Henry handed me a Coke with a smile. I felt a hand on my arm and turned to find Ally there, her blond hair pulled back into a ponytail. She looked a bit winded but great, flushed cheeks, a strand of hair escaping by her face. She grabbed my hand.

"Come on, Jonah," she said, leading me toward the back of the room. "Your usual booth is taken, but one just opened up here."

I allowed her to lead me back. She didn't let go of my hand until we got to the booth. She turned and pecked me on the cheek.

"Good to see you," she said, laying a hand on my shoulder and trailing it down my arm.

The thing with her hand had gotten to be a habit. I wondered if the kiss on the cheek was going to be too. "Thanks Ally," I said. "You're a honey."

She looked at me from lowered lashes. "You better believe it, stud," she said and left.

The first people to come over were John Dorland and his wife

Kelly. Kelly was short and blond and beaming.

"I don't know what you said to him," she said to me, "but say some more of it."

John grinned sheepishly.

They slid into the booth and we talked for a while.

After that it was a steady stream of visitors until about eleven. The room was still pretty full and loud. A woman at the bar caught my eye. She had long brown hair, straight, and streaked with blond highlights. The line of her chin was clean and firm, and her makeup, from that distance, looked expertly applied. She peered directly into my eyes and smiled. I felt a little heat come into my cheeks, and I wanted to look away but I didn't. Without breaking eye-contact, she swung off her stool, caught her drink, and walked toward me. She wore a tight, short mini-skirt and calf-length boots. Her hips swayed as she walked, showing off great legs clad in black hose. Her blouse filled out very nicely too.

She slid into the booth opposite me. We had never broken eye-contact, and for some reason my heart was pounding.

Now she looked down at her drink and then back up at me.

"Hi," she said. After her walk across the room, it was all she needed to say.

"I'm Jonah," I said. My voice sounded a little hoarse.

"I'm Susie," she said. I noticed that the top two buttons of her blouse were undone, and I could see some cleavage and the edge of a black bra. I got the feeling I was supposed to notice.

"I saw you from over there," she said.

"I saw you seeing me," I said.

"Can I sit next to you?" she asked suddenly, and without waiting for an answer, slid out of the booth and then back in, next to me. I moved toward the wall and she kept coming until her right thigh was pressed against mine. She had on a heavy, musky perfume. There was too much of it, but it still did to me what it was supposed to.

"I've been lonely," she said, "and I was hoping we could talk."

"That's what I do here," I said. "Talk with folks."

"I bet you're good at it," she said and then sipped her drink.

I shrugged, bumping her shoulder accidentally.

"I bet you're good at other things too," she whispered hoarsely, pressing herself against me.

Somehow they hadn't trained me for this at seminary.

"You wanna go somewhere?" she asked.

Since I felt a bit stupid, I decided to play it that way. "Where?" I asked.

"I need someone to take me back to my hotel," she said. Her eyes were burning as they held mine. "I'm a little drunk," she added.

"I never would have guessed."

"Well, sholdier, how 'bout it?" she asked.

I was quiet.

She looked down into her drink. "I could get another guy to take me, I guess," she said.

"I bet you could," I said.

"But I want you," she said. "Right now."

If I took her back, she'd be in good hands, I reasoned. If another guy from the WW took her home, he'd probably take advantage of her.

I swallowed. "Okay," I said.

CHAPTER 21

I held the door of my Jetta for her, and then went around to my side. "A real gentleman," she said as I got in. "I like that." She put her hand on my thigh.

I took her left hand gently with my right one, and put it back in her lap. She held on to my hand, and moved to a region of a woman's body that is usually considered rather personal.

I gently extricated myself. "I need that hand to drive," I said.

She giggled.

She told me which hotel she was at. It was one of those cheap, drive-up-to-your-door outfits. Every room would be sold out on Memorial Day, but right now the parking lot was mostly empty. I pulled up to her room and waited, the car still running.

"Aren't you going to come in?" she said.

"I don't think so," I said.

She leaned over and kissed me on the mouth, hard. Sliding out of her seat, she pressed her body against me. She moved a hand up my thigh and then broke off the kiss, panting.

"I can tell you want to."

I moved her hand. "No, you can tell that I'm a normal healthy male and my body works right. That doesn't mean I want to."

"But you do," she said, her lips brushing mine as she spoke.

I took hold of her shoulders and gently sat her back in her seat.

"No," I said, "I don't."

She looked out the window.

"Don't you like me?" she asked.

"I don't know," I said. "I don't know you enough to know if I like you or not."

"What's the problem?" she said. "I can tell you're attracted to me. It's just a physical act, you know. Like eating or going to the bathroom."

"No," I said. "That's a lie that everyone pretends to believe, but everyone knows, deep down, it isn't true. Sex is never just physical."

She turned and looked at me. She didn't seem nearly so drunk anymore.

"Then I'm really screwed up."

"I'm sorry to hear that. But it's true. You are very attractive. If it was just a physical thing, I'd be in that room with you right now."

She smiled broadly.

"But it's not. Sex is emotional and psychological. And spiritual too."

She was quiet for a bit, looking straight ahead out the window. She didn't appear even tipsy.

"So you aren't coming in there with me?"

"No," I said. "And you should have more respect for yourself than that. You're an attractive woman, and I'm sure you are a beautiful person too. You don't need to go around sleeping with people you randomly meet in bars."

"I didn't meet you randomly," she whispered, almost to herself.

"What?" I asked.

"I was *supposed* to meet you, to seduce you."

That took a moment to settle in for me. She was quiet while I processed it.

"Why?" I asked at last.

Her voice was almost inaudible. "Someone paid me to."

I looked at her. She was still staring straight ahead.

"Are you a prostitute?" I asked.

She started to cry and shake her head. The head shake could have meant "no" or "I don't know" or "what a mess." Belatedly, I realized it wasn't the nicest question to ask.

"I guess that's what I am," she said, still sobbing. "I took money to have sex. I know *you* didn't give me the money, but it's the same thing."

"Who did give you the money?" I asked.

She shook her head. "Some guy," she said.

"Well, we didn't have sex," I said.

She gave a short snort of laughter. "At least I'm not a very good prostitute."

"Do you live in Duluth?" I asked.

She nodded, wiping her eyes.

"So are you on the street there?"

She started to cry again. "No," she said, brokenly. "I work at a bar and I'm a part-time student at UMD. I know I shouldn't sleep with so many people, but I can't help it. I *need* to."

"How many guys have you been with during the last year?" I said.

She kept crying, not the shoulder-shaking kind, but there was plenty of moisture. "I don't know, maybe fifty or a hundred."

"Aren't you afraid of AIDS and stuff?"

"I'm terrified, but I can't seem to stop myself."

"Do you know that you have a disorder?"

She was quiet.

"It's not normal, you know. I'm not trying to make you feel bad, but most people don't need to sleep with so many different partners, so often. What they show you on TV and stuff is a big lie. It's all pretend. Most people don't live like that. And ultimately, it doesn't make you happy does it?"

"I guess if it did, I wouldn't have to keep on doing it," she said quietly.

"It's like an addiction. There's help, you know."

She looked up and met my eyes.

"There is. I know someone in Duluth who can help you, but only if you want it."

She was quiet for a long time. At last she said, "Why are you being so nice to me?"

"God made you," I said. "He loves you and doesn't want to see you destroy yourself. I'd have a hard time facing Him if I just let you go on about your way without seeing if you want help."

She nodded, looking a thousand miles straight ahead.

"I'm not trying to force my religion down your throat. If you like the way you are, it's your choice, you can stay that way."

She was still quiet.

"I'm betting, though," I said after a while, "that you aren't happy. You're scared, you hate yourself for what you do, but you keep doing it anyway. You don't think you're worth a piece of crap, and you've thought about committing suicide before.

She stared at me. "How did you do that?" she whispered.

I shrugged. "It's a gift. A God-thing, I think."

"I want help," she said at last.

I took one of my business cards and wrote a number on the back and handed to her.

"Thank you," she said. She nodded firmly, as if to herself.

"Susie," I said, "can you tell me any more about the guy who paid you to seduce me?"

"Well, a guy I was with once told someone else about me." She shook her head. "If you're easy, word gets around, you know?"

I didn't really want to touch that one, so I was quiet.

"The new guy said he knew someone who would pay me to have a little fun. Not like a prostitute, but sort of like a blind date, you know?"

"Have you ever done that before?"

"No. This was the first time. It was kind of exciting, you know?"

"Yes, and no," I said carefully. "You really don't know who wanted me to sleep with you?"

"No," she said. "I mean, I saw the guy who told me about you and paid me, but I don't know who he is."

"He didn't tell you a name?"

"No. He said it was better if I didn't know."

"Didn't you wonder why he was paying you to sleep with me?"

"Sure. But it was kind of exciting and dangerous feeling, you know? It was actually a turn-on."

I let that one lie also. "Anything else you can tell me?" I asked.

She shook her head. "I'm sorry. You've been so nice to me. I wish I could help you." She paused and looked at me speculatively. "Are you sure you don't want to come in? I could thank you properly."

"No," I said firmly. "And deep down, a little corner of you

doesn't want me to either."

She was crying again. "That just the thing," she said, sniffling. "You are just the kind of man I need. You're not out to just use me."

"There will be someone for you, someday," I said. "A good guy, better than me. But right now, Susie, you need to get some healing."

"Thank you," she said, and leaned over, kissed me gently and then got out of the car.

CHAPTER 22

On Saturday morning I climbed slowly up from the fog of sleep, assisted, as usual, by a cup of dark, aromatic elixir in a clean, white mug. Outside it was cold and gray, the sort of day that made me glad I had a fireplace.

After my first cup I built a fire. I went to the kitchen, put half-stick of butter into a pie plate, and put it into the oven while I pre-heated it. Next, I broke three eggs into a bowl, and beat them with a cup and a half of milk before adding the same measurement of flour. A small handful of sugar, some salt and vanilla followed, and, voila, I had batter for *pannekoeken*. When the butter was melted, I poured the batter over it into the pie dish, set the timer for a half-hour, then took another cup of coffee over to the fire. Breakfast will be served shortly, sir.

The coffee and the fire aroused me sufficiently to recover an appetite by the time the beeper went off. The pannekoeken had puffed out of the pie dish in irregular, slightly crispy bubbles, but the center of it was soft and tender. I had it with blueberries and lite Cool Whip. It was a shame, how my culinary talents were wasted on only myself. Ah well, if the ladies knew, they wouldn't be able to restrain themselves.

Whether they were paid or not.

The last thought intruded like a bad smell. Who would pay a girl to seduce me, and more importantly, why? I considered the possibility of blackmail.

As a young couple, Robyn and I had done the right thing and purchased life insurance. We were young and healthy and it was cheap. The result was that when she died I had received a considerable sum. In the five years since, I'd made some wise property investments and now I had a very comfortable income apart from what the church paid me. It could be that someone wanted to bleed me for money, and so they hired Susie to compromise me. I supposed that most unmarried men wouldn't respond to blackmail demands over that sort of indiscretion, but it is a bit different if you're a pastor. At the very least, I would be certain to lose my job. In all likelihood, it would be hard to find another position as a pastor if I was caught in that sort of situation. Of course, my investments paid me more than what I made as a pastor, so losing my job prospects would hurt my sense of self-worth and dignity, but, not ultimately, my lifestyle. Also, very few people actually knew that I had an outside source of income. I lived moderately, my only indulgence being the cabin and the 150 acres that came with it. And when people asked about that, I told them, truthfully enough, that it came to me through family, in an indirect way. Most polite Minnesotans would not pry further into that statement.

All told, blackmailing a small-town pastor for money didn't seem likely.

Maybe someone wanted me in their pocket for some reason. I couldn't imagine why. I suppose in a town the size of Grand Lake, I had a certain amount of influence. But a pastor's influence is of a certain kind. I mean, what was someone going to say?

"Pastor, you baptize my son, or I'll publish these photos."

Probably not.

The only thought I had, even after all the coffee, was that someone in my congregation had it out for me. It was common enough, unfortunately. There were always complainers, always folks who didn't like the new pastor, even if the "new" pastor had been there eighteen years. My style of ministry didn't always make the status quo feel comfortable. But I couldn't think of anyone in church who would actually go to the length of hiring someone to sleep with me. It was more likely that the thrifty Minnesotans would just start a nasty rumor. Simpler, and much cheaper.

Even so, I reluctantly concluded that someone within the church was the only viable explanation.

I finished my breakfast and cleaned up, and sat in front of the fire again, musing. At last I got up and finished the week's office-work in my pajamas. When I was done I straightened up my study, then threw on some jeans, a t-shirt, and my blue polar fleece. Pulling on my hiking boots, I grabbed my walking stick and headed out for a hike.

The air was cold and damp outside, and tendrils of fog or cloud curled through the trees at the top of the ridge. I moved fast enough to keep warm. I went north, the lake below on my right lying cold and gray like pewter.

As I hiked, I ran through my sermon, for the most part, out loud. Somebody has to preach to the trees. Oddly enough, I've walked up on many wild creatures while preaching. They say St. Francis used to preach to the birds. St. Jonah preaches to the rest of God's creatures.

It was probably fifty degrees out, but I was plenty warm by the time I got back to my log home. Usually, I hike pretty fast, and the ridgeline just northwest of the Superior coastline affords the best hill-climbing opportunities in the state. Coming from the Pacific Northwest, I was inclined to think, the *only* hill-climbing opportunities in the state.

I took a shower and built up the fire again. Nothing like a cup of decaf to go with the fire, I decided, and made it so. I settled in for some reading, studying and letter-writing. David Wilcox was the perfect musical prescription for a gray day, and I made that happen also.

At about three-thirty, the phone rang.

"Borden," I said.

"Jonah," said Chief Jensen. "You got a minute?"

"Sure," I said. "What's up?"

"Could you come down to the station? I'd like to tell you in person."

"That's more than a minute," I said.

"Yeah, I know. Can you come?"

I sighed. "Okay. What's this about, anyway?"

"If you don't mind, I'd rather not tell you until you get here."

"It's not my birthday or anything, Chief. No call for surprise parties."

"When can you get here?" He sounded a bit strained.

"I'll be there in about fifteen minutes," I said.

Shortly after I pulled out of my drive, I noticed a sheriff's car behind me. Curious. At the town line, the patrol car pulled into a gas station, but I noticed a town police car turn out of another lot two cars behind me. More curious.

Precisely fifteen minutes after Jensen's phone call, I pulled into the town police station parking lot. The patrol car that had tailed me slid on by. I walked up the steps into the station. The cop at the desk just inside the door nodded at me.

"He's down the hall there," he said.

"Not in his office?" I asked, to confirm.

"No. Down there in the first interview room. Second door on the right."

I wondered what was up. I walked down the hall, feeling the eyes of the desk cop on me. I reached the door and knocked. Jensen opened for me. Inside was another cop I had seen around town, but didn't know very well.

"Hey, Jonah," said Jensen. "Thanks for coming down."

"Sure," I said, "what's up?"

"This is Tony Grantz,," said Jensen, ignoring my question. "He's from the sheriff's department."

I exchanged greetings with Grantz.

"Have a seat, Jonah," said Jensen," gesturing at a metal folding chair in front of a small wooden table. Jensen sat next to me, on my right. Grantz stayed standing. I looked around. It was like one of those interview rooms you see on TV, where they play good-cop/bad-cop and interview suspects. I half expected to see a one-way window when I glanced over my shoulder.

I did.

Grantz opened a manila folder that lay on the table and extracted a photograph.

"Do you know this woman?" he asked.

It was an extremely unflattering picture, a close face-shot. Her makeup was a bit messed up, as was her hair. Her eyes were closed, almost as if she were asleep. Even so, I saw the resemblance.

"I'm not positive, but it looks like a woman I met last night at the WW," I said.

Jensen and Grantz exchanged looks.

"How about this picture?"

This time I was sure it was Susie from last night.

"Yeah. I'm not sure if the first picture is the same woman or not, but this second one is definitely Susie."

Jensen appeared to relax visibly. Grantz looked frustrated.

"When did you see her last?" he said.

"I don't know, last night at midnight or one a.m., maybe."

"Where was that?" Jensen seemed content to let Grantz ask the questions for now.

"At the Edge-of-Town Motel."

Jensen turned to stare at me.

"It's not like that," I said. "I gave her a ride there. She was tipsy, and I didn't think it was good for some of the other folks to take her back."

Grantz pounced. "So you took her back to her motel."

"Yeah."

"And you went inside, just to make sure she was safe?"

"No," I said calmly. "I never even got out of the car."

Grantz snorted.

The gears in my brain started to grind slowly.

"What's this all about, anyway? Why are you asking me about this lady?"

Grantz's eyes bored into mine.

"'Cause she's dead."

"What?" I exclaimed. "Are you serious?"

"Very serious," said Grantz.

I tried to get my mind around it.

"The first picture we showed you was a blow-up of her face after we found her," said Jensen, reaching for the manila folder. "Here's the whole picture."

She was lying, sprawled across a bed, arms and legs akimbo like she'd been thrown there. There was an ugly purplish line around her neck. It certainly didn't look like she died of natural causes.

"How'd she die?" I asked.

"I'm asking the questions," said Grantz. "Where did you go after you left her?"

He was beginning to irritate me. "I went home," I said. "I live alone, so no one can verify that, of course." I looked at Jensen. "Was she murdered?"

Jensen nodded very slightly.

Grantz shot him an irritated look, and then sat on the edge of the table and looked down at me.

"You get lonely sometimes, living alone, Pastor Borden?"

I looked at Jensen, but he was absorbed with the wood grain of the table.

"What's that got to do with anything?" I asked.

"I'm the one asking the questions here," snapped Grantz.

I stood up. Grantz bristled. Jensen looked up quickly and said, "Jonah."

I pushed my face up to Grantz's. I hoped I had bad coffee-breath.

"I don't know where you went to cop-school," I said, "but you're acting like it was Hollywood, California. You think I slept with this girl and then killed her so no one would find out?"

He didn't back off. I made a mental note to drink more coffee.

"It wouldn't be the first time," he said.

I wanted to slap his face. "It would be the first time for *me*," I grated. "Look, you get out of here, and I'll talk with Dan and tell him whatever I can think of. But if you stay in this room, you'll either have to book me or watch me walk out that door."

I held his eyes. He held mine.

"Tony," said Jensen.

Grantz didn't look away from me.

"Tony," said Jensen more firmly. "Cut it out. We'll do it my way now."

I wasn't going to break eye-contact first. Grantz had to do it. It was juvenile of me, but it gave me satisfaction anyway. He stalked out of the room and slammed the door.

I sat down and blew out a breath.

"You want some coffee?" asked Jensen.

I looked at him without saying anything.

"Sorry," he said, "silly question."

He went to the door too, and came back a minute or two later with two cups. He handed me a white mug that said, "Lutheran Coffee—It's heavenly."

"You two are darn good with the good-cop/bad-cop routine," I said.

Jensen shrugged. "I didn't want to do it that way, but Tony watches too much TV. Thinks he's got a camera on him or something."

"I haven't met him before," I said. "Can't say I was missing anything."

"He'll be all right. He's new here. Came up from Chicago about six months ago."

"Him, and Burton too. Let's not recruit anymore cops from Chicago."

"Hey," said Jensen. "My wife's from Chicago. I was a cop there for four years."

"Sorry," I said.

We sipped our coffee.

"So why did you call me anyway?" I asked after a bit.

"We found one of your business cards in the motel room."

"Is that where she died?" I asked.

"That's right," he said.

"If you looked at the card you would have seen a handwritten phone number on the back."

Jensen nodded.

"Did you check it out?"

He nodded again. "We got a voice-mail. Some sort of counseling service."

"Sex-Addicts Anonymous," I said. "You really think I'd sleep with the girl, and then afterwards give her my church business card with a phone number for where she can go to learn how to stop sleeping with every man she meets?"

Jensen looked uncomfortable. "I never thought you killed her, Jonah," he said. "What I was concerned about was that maybe you—you know, she looked like she was pretty good looking when she was alive."

He looked pained again. "When they're finished with the body, we'll know if she did sleep with anyone—or if she might have been raped. If you did sleep with her, it would be best for you if I hear about it from you, right now."

"I didn't sleep with her," I said. "And, for the record, I didn't kill her."

He nodded. "We haven't had time to check everything out, of course, but I'm sure there will be witnesses who saw you leave the WW together."

"I already told you myself that's what happened."

"Was she coming on to you?" he asked.

"Yes, she was," I said promptly.

He shook his head. "A lot of people aren't going to believe you didn't take the opportunity. You know, widower, living alone, beautiful girl throwing herself at him."

"Doesn't matter what a lot of people believe," I said evenly, "I didn't sleep with her, so there will be no evidence that I did."

"Are you willing to take a DNA test to confirm that?"

I sucked on my lip. "The bottom line is, yes, but only if I absolutely have to. It is humiliating, and I object to giving any governmental authority my DNA, if I can possibly avoid it."

He gave me a quick, tight grin. "I know what you mean. It's already scary, what we know about people."

"Exactly," I said. "But you decide to charge me with murder, I'll take the test in a heartbeat."

He shook his head. "I'm just doing my job, Jonah. I know you didn't kill her. We won't be charging you."

"I won't say that's a relief, 'cause that's the way it should be."

"Is there anything else you can tell me?"

"Yes," I said. "According to her, she was hired to seduce me."

"*What?*"

I told everything I could remember about my encounter with Susie. He asked me a number of questions and repeated several of them. At last he leaned back in his chair and stretched. Then he collapsed back like a deflated balloon.

"Okay, Jonah, I think we're done," he said. "I appreciate you coming down voluntarily and telling us what you know."

"Well, I won't say it was a pleasure. Don't say bye to Tony for me."

"Tony's a good guy. He just doesn't know you, that's all."

"Whatever you say," I said.

We shook hands, and I left.

CHAPTER 23

I was halfway through a humdinger of a sermon on Sunday morning when I noticed Leyla sitting in the congregation, listening attentively. I am a professional, so I didn't stumble over my words, or stop and shout "yahoo!" I gave her a quick wink, and kept right on talking.

After the service, I stood at the door, as usual, shaking hands with people as they left. I could see Leyla hanging back, waiting until most of the folks were gone. Or maybe she was making friends. She was surrounded by a small group of people. After a minute I realized that most of them were the Olsen family – the farmers who gave me my eggs and milk. John and Susan Olsen had four kids, and along with the Olsens were two other couples. They all seemed to be very friendly with Leyla.

At last they filed out together, Leyla first. She gave me a hug and stepped back. She was wearing a very spring-like floral dress made of some sort of gauzy material that stopped just at her knees. As usual, she looked great.

"Hi," I said. I had used all my words during the sermon.

"Hi," she said right back. John Olsen grinned at us. I turned to him.

"I take it you guys have all met Leyla?"

"We have," said Susan.

"She's wonderful!" piped one of the smaller Olsens, a girl

named Mandy.

"When are you getting married?" asked another junior Olsen, this one a five-year-old boy named James.

I looked at Leyla, who was very demurely looking at the ground.

"We haven't discussed it yet, James," I said. "These things take time."

John's grin got wider.

"That's enough out of you," I said.

"I didn't say anything," he protested.

We talked as a group for a while longer about crop prospects and fishing and family. Finally the Olsens and the other two couples departed. That left Leyla and me standing alone in the narthex.

"Well this is quite the surprise," I said.

"I didn't want you to expect me," she said, "but I wanted to come. I've wanted to since I first met you."

"And what did you think?" I asked.

"It was good," she said. "You are a very good preacher, aren't you?"

"I am told so, every six months or so," I said. "But truthfully, I'm not sure how much it has to do with me."

"The whole service was—different."

"Different is what you say when you don't want to hurt someone's feelings by telling them their church service is boring and outlandish."

"No, it really was good," she said. "And it really was different. Remember, I was raised Catholic. I didn't expect a full band and modern music and all that."

"Well, truthfully, a lot of Lutherans don't do it that way yet either. We are a bit different."

"But I liked it," said Leyla. "There was a feeling here—you know? A good feeling. Like family should feel, but even more so, if you know what I mean." She looked off to the corner of the narthex. "I guess you might say it felt like God was here."

I took a deep breath and sighed. "You just made my day."

She looked directly into my eyes and smiled, and made my day again.

"So," I said, "do you have to go back to Duluth right away, or do you have some time?"

"I'm all yours," she said. The way she said it made my heart skip a beat.

"You want to see if we can go sailing today? It's pretty nice out."

Leyla frowned. "I would need a change of clothes and stuff, if we were to do that."

"Oh. I guess that's true. You could wear one of my sweatshirts, but I don't suppose my jeans would fit you."

"Well, then, it's a good thing I brought my stuff with me," she said, her eyes twinkling.

"You vixen! You planned the whole thing!"

"I did," she said smiling.

"Do you have a sailboat lined up?" I asked.

"Actually, no. I was hoping we could improvise."

"We can," I said. "I made some calls. There are no catamarans for rent in the marinas around here. But a member of the church here has one we can borrow."

Leyla walked with me while I returned some of my things to

my office and then locked up the church.

"Let's go to my place and you can change, and I'll call the guy with the boat," I said.

She followed me up the ridge in her car. While she changed, I made the call and secured the boat. I put some smoked trout, Jarlsberg cheese, and rye-crisp crackers in a cooler. I added some soft drinks, chocolate pudding, and a couple pears.

Leyla came out of my hallway wearing khaki shorts, brown hiking boots, and a ratty gray sweatshirt. Her dark hair bounced down to the middle of her back in careless waves and curls.

"What?" she said, putting her hand anxiously to her face. "What's wrong?"

I shook my head. I couldn't seem to speak.

"Do I have something on my face? In my hair? What are you staring at?"

"Just you," I said, somewhat hoarsely, I thought. "You would look great in a paper bag."

She smiled, genuine and brilliant. "Why, thank you, Jonah," she said. She pursed her lips. "I think a paper bag would be impractical for sailing, though."

"So are my church clothes," I said, somewhat normally. "Let me get changed, and then we can go."

After I had changed into jeans and a sweatshirt, we left in my Jetta to go get the catamaran.

"More classical music?" asked Leyla.

"Not exactly," I said. This is the instrumental music from the movie *Forrest Gump*."

She listened. "Oh, I guess you're right. I never noticed before how beautiful it was."

"Alan Silvestri," I said. "One of the best show-biz composers there is."

I drove us over to Mike Slade's place. Mike was a member of our church, and a lawyer, but a decent sort anyway.

"You know, you'll never make partner with a name like Slade," I said to him when we got there.

"Yeah," he said. "Don't see many called "Rupert, Blackthorn, Ginsberg and Slade."

"Shoulda been a hit man," I said. "That would suit the name just fine. 'Pay up, or Slade breaks your kneecaps.'"

"All right," he said. "Leave it alone." He grinned. "Unless you want your kneecaps broken."

"No, I just want your boat."

He looked at my Jetta. "Do you have a hitch?"

"No."

"I didn't think so. I already hooked up to my Jeep."

Leyla and I transferred our stuff to Slade's black Jeep.

"I gotta get one of these," I said. "Be more in keeping with the hunting and fishing culture here."

"This isn't a real Jeep," she said. "It's one of those yuppie models. It's got a CD player."

"It can haul a boat."

"As well as shoes from Nordstrom's."

"Is this our first argument?" I asked.

She thought for a moment. "I don't think so. You're just wrong about the Jeep, that's all."

"Oh. Thanks for straightening that out."

~

We put in at Grand Lake Marina. Leyla knew what she was doing, and it wasn't long before we had the mast and shrouds in place. In very short order we were cruising across the harbor toward the open lake, with Leyla holding the tiller.

It was a good stiff wind, and soon we were heeled over with the right-hand pontoon almost buried in the icy blue water, while the left pontoon barely skimmed the wave tops. It was a beautiful day. It is difficult to be hot out on Lake Superior, and we weren't, but even so, the air was clear, sunny, and almost warm. I watched Leyla as she sat at the tiller, her legs folded gracefully to one side, gazing out to sea as the wind played with her hair.

I didn't need to say anything. Neither did she. We took the cat straight out from the shore, more or less toward Wisconsin in the southeast, though we couldn't see land in that direction. After a while Leyla turned into the wind.

"Watch your head," she said.

The boat came gently round, and then sat, rocking in the small waves, the wind flapping ineffectually against the sails.

"Let's have some lunch," she said.

I opened our cooler and got out my fixings.

"How old are you?" I asked when we started eating.

She sniffed. "It's not polite to ask a lady's age."

"Ah, but you look young enough for it not to be an issue."

She gave me a sidelong glance. "Smooth, very smooth." She took a small bite of smoked trout, cheese and cracker. "Okay then, twenty-six."

I contemplated that for a moment. "How does someone like you—beautiful, smart, fun, intelligent— remain single to age twenty-six?"

She chewed and looked back toward the distant smudge of

Minnesota shore. "I was pretty serious with a guy in college."

"Who is in Omaha now?"

She nodded. "Anyway, we kept dating for a year or so after I graduated. Then, after we broke up, I guess I just sort of focused on my career for a couple years. I saw some people, but—not to be mean—I guess the sort of people I've been working with don't interest me romantically." She took a sip of Coke. "And, I didn't really want to go to bars or something and meet people. I mean, I'm sure some great marriages start in bars, but it didn't seem like the place to meet Mr. Right." She turned and smiled at me. "But of course, that's where we met."

"We were both working," I said.

"Yes."

I bit into a pear.

"And how old are you?" she asked.

"Thirty-two."

"And your wife died when you were . . ."

"Twenty seven. We got married right out of college."

"And how have *you* stayed single for these past five years?"

I knew this was a conversation we had to have. I stayed calm. "Well, it took me a long time to grieve Robyn, you know? It's not something you just get over and move on."

She nodded.

"And, being a pastor isn't really a profession that lends itself to meeting hot chicks."

"Is that what you want? A hot chick?" Her eyes glinted with something that may have been danger or perhaps mischief.

"There's no way I can answer that without getting in trouble, you know."

It was definitely mischief. "I know," she said.

"Anyway, I also liked living alone. I won't say I don't get lonely, but I've been pretty content with my life as it is."

There was a pause. I knew the question was coming.

"How did Robyn die?"

I took a deep breath.

"She was murdered."

I looked at the distant blue horizon.

"Jonah, I am so sorry," she said, and put her hand on my arm.

I nodded. "I think I'm done with the grieving process by now, but it was pretty terrible for a long time."

"You don't need to tell me any more about it, if you don't want to."

I nodded. "Why don't you show me how to sail this tub?"

We finished our meal, while Leyla explained how to use the tiller to steer, and how to loosen or tighten the lines which adjust the angle of the sail. I was surprised to learn that those ropes were in fact called "sheets."

"So this one, here, the one that pulls in the mainsail, is called the main *sheet*?"

"That's right."

"So what do you call the sail?"

"The sail."

"You sailors have such clever jargon."

"People who are four miles from shore shouldn't insult the only experienced sailor onboard."

"Where's the board?"

She punched me in the arm.

"Okay, okay," I said. "How do we get started?"

"Let out the main sheet a bit, so the wind starts to catch sail."

We slowly got moving. I got the hang of manipulating the tiller and the sails fairly quickly, though Leyla had to help with the smaller sail in front, which she called the jib. This far from shore, rocks and reefs were not an issue, so I kept experimenting with ways to move faster. After a while we were slicing through the water with one pontoon well up into the air, and the rigging humming like a meditating Buddhist monk. Leyla climbed out to the high edge to balance us a bit. She whooped with joy.

The wind picked up a bit and we heeled over even farther. I was sitting on an incline.

"How far can this go over?" I asked

"All the way over," she said.

"Very funny." She was grinning. "I meant, how far before we go all the way?"

"About this far."

The wind gusted, and it seemed to me that we passed the fifty-degree mark.

"Nudge her over to starboard a bit," called Leyla, still hanging off the side. She looked slightly anxious.

I moved the tiller and the boat heeled up even farther.

"No!" called Leyla. "The other way!"

I moved it again, but the cat tipped up even more. The water rose up clear and cold at my feet, and I suddenly wished I hadn't been so manly as to leave my life jacket off.

Leyla leaped over to me at the tiller, and the boat, responding to the change in weight distribution, canted crazily, and now I knew we were going in. But she grabbed the main sheet and snapped it out of its cleats, and the sail suddenly flapped free. The catamaran, with the pressure on the sail suddenly released, tumbled back to level with an ungracious smack into the water. I sprawled into Leyla, and we ended up tangled up, lying on the trampoline by the tiller, with me on top. I started to sit up.

"Sorry," I said. "I—"

"The boom!" shouted Leyla, and grabbed the back of my neck, pulling my head down against her shoulder. Overhead, the boom, free from restraint, whistled over my head. We were still for a second while the boat slowly swung around into the wind where it rode placidly on the waves.

"Which way is starboard?" I mumbled into the shoulder of her sweatshirt.

I felt her body begin to shake. Cautiously, I raised my head and saw that she was laughing. I started to laugh too, and soon tears were running down our faces.

The laughter subsided. I was looking into her great dark eyes. In them was an invitation. I bent slowly to her and gently touched her lips with mine. In a few seconds it became less gentle and more passionate. After a moment we came up for air.

"Well," she said, sighing and looking up at the sky, "that was certainly worth waiting for."

"True," I said, "but how do we know the second kiss will be as good as the first one?"

"There's only one way to find out," she said.

It was.

CHAPTER 24

Alex Chan was just shy of medium height, about my age, broad-shouldered, with smooth skin a bit darker than mine. His dark hair was done with plenty of style and gel. He wore a neatly kept blue suit with a conservative blue and gray tie, but his jacket was off and his white sleeves rolled up. His narrow Asian eyes assessed me calmly as I entered his office.

"Jonah Borden," I said, sticking out my hand.

His grip was firm. "Alex Chan," he said.

"Is Chan Norwegian, or Swedish?" I asked.

He grinned, and his face was transformed by warmth and humor. "Not even German, I'm afraid," he said.

"I'll skip the Ole and Sven jokes then."

"My parents would have named me Sven, if they'd have thought I'd end up here," he said. "As it was, Alex seemed to fit in, in California."

He indicated a little sitting area to the side of his desk. I took a comfortable leather chair, and he took the couch kitty-corner from it. From a coffee table in between us, he picked up a pen and yellow legal pad.

"That legal pad is deeply disappointing," I said. "So passé."

"Most lawyers are," he said. He settled himself comfortably. "So what can I do for you, Mr. Borden?"

"Please call me, Jonah," I said.

He nodded. "Call me Alex then."

"All right," I said. "I am Doug Norstad's pastor."

His brow crinkled. "I thought you looked familiar. I think I saw you on TV."

"Probably. Has Doug told you about me?"

"Well, he said his pastor wanted to talk to me. I didn't realize that's who you were until just now."

I crossed my left leg over my right. My ankle rested on my thigh, like most guys. I couldn't seem to sit thigh over thigh, like women do.

I scratched my neck. "I'm not really sure how to begin. How did you get Doug's case? In all honesty, I thought he'd have a public defender."

Chan smiled. "I used to be a public defender. Spent too much time plea-bargaining drug dealers. Now, as you can see, I'm in private practice."

"But, not to be too nosy, I wouldn't expect the Norstads to have the kind of money to pay for a lawyer."

Chan sat back comfortably on his couch. "I'm doing this one pro bono."

"For free? Why?"

"Well, all law firms are supposed to do some pro bono work."

"Sure, but why the Norstad case?"

His shockingly white-toothed smile split his face. "If I'm gonna work for free, might as well get some publicity out of it."

I nodded. "No harm in that, I guess. How's it going?"

Alex's face reverted quickly back to its natural state of stillness. "I can't discuss a client's case with another party. It's the lawyer/client privilege."

"I know about it. There's a pastor/church-member privilege too."

"Right. So how's the state of Doug Norstad's soul?"

"All right, I got your point."

We sat quietly for moment while I thought and Alex Chan waited.

Finally, I said, "Has Doug told you his true alibi?"

Alex just smiled and shook his head.

"All right, client privilege," I said. "Doug told me where he was when Spooner got shot. Not the story he told the police. I checked it out. It's solid, and there's a witness."

"There's another witness says he saw Norstad shoot Spooner."

I felt a cold shock. "A witness? Who says he saw Norstad at the scene?"

"That's right."

My world wheeled around me in a spiral of dizzying possibilities.

"The assistant DA has a witness?"

"That's what I said," replied Alex. "Is there something wrong?"

"Darn right there is. The witness is lying."

"Why would someone lie about something like that?"

"I don't know," I said. "Have you checked him out?"

"The DA's witness?"

"Yes."

Chan tapped his teeth with his thumbnail. "Okay," he said at last. "I'm going to fudge the line a little bit. You're a pastor, and I need this conversation to be confidential."

"It is," I said.

"If it isn't, I could sue your rear end off."

"You don't have to threaten me."

"Sorry," said Alex. "Occupational habit."

He paused. "Okay. I haven't checked out the prosecution's witness yet. In fact, I was trying to get Mr. Norstad to plea bargain. I didn't think we had a chance of winning."

"I'll bet he doesn't want to plead guilty," I said.

"No comment," he said. "But on a completely different subject, you could win some money if you were a betting man."

"You might want to check out this so-called witness to the shooting," I said. "Why didn't he come forward before? After what I've discovered, he can't be genuine."

"So what is Norstad's alibi, the one that makes the prosecutor's witness a perjurer?"

It was my turn to shake my head. "That was told to me in spiritual confidence."

"Hey, what about quid pro quo?"

"You lawyers always throw around these Latin terms. How am I supposed to know what they mean?"

He grinned, seemingly in spite of himself. It faded again and he said, "Seriously. What do you expect me to do without any new information?"

"I can't tell you anything until I have permission from Doug—and he isn't giving it yet. I'm working on him, though. In the meantime, if you check out this witness, I'm guessing you're going to find something wrong with his story. Maybe even something wrong with him as a witness."

"Even if Doug Norstad is innocent, it doesn't mean he'll get off."

"Hey," I said, "don't forget the publicity."

I could see he hadn't. He was tempted. He thought for a bit. "I guess it won't hurt to check him out anyway, interview him, for the unlikely event that we do go to trial."

"That's the spirit!" I said.

"You forgot 'attaboy,'" he said.

"Didn't want you to think it was a racial slur," I said.

"You white devils are all alike," he said.

"Hey, if I could get a tan this close to the North Pole, my skin would be darker than yours."

He grinned. Then his smile faded.

"There's something that bothers me about this," he said. "If we've got a false witness, then someone is trying to cook this thing. Why?"

"I don't know," I said. "That's what's bothering me too."

CHAPTER 25

I didn't sleep well that night. It wasn't the coffee. I could drink a pot of regular and still sleep like a baby. Someone once told me that was because I was addicted, and my tolerance for caffeine was far beyond normal. I didn't care.

But the reason I couldn't sleep was because I kept thinking about the witness for the prosecution. Why would someone set up a false witness against Doug Norstad? The only place to start finding that out would be with the witness himself. Alex Chan would interview him, I was pretty sure. But his position as lawyer prevented him from approaching the witness in a way that may reveal more than an interview. Chan had ethics. So did I, but nothing in my code said I couldn't talk to a witness in a court case where a member of my church was being tried.

Once I had figured out what to do, I fell asleep.

In the morning, I had some chaplain business at the police station. When I was done, I knocked on Chief Jensen's door. He was sitting at his desk, with papers spread everywhere. On one corner was a computer. To his right, behind the desk, next to a window, stood a plain gray metal filing cabinet. On Jensen's nose was perched a pair of half-lens reading glasses.

"Hey, Jonah," he said. "What's up?"

"Not your eyesight, apparently," I said. "You getting old already?"

"You tell anyone about these, I'll throw your butt in jail."

"Good to know," I said.

I sat down and sipped a cup of coffee I had procured elsewhere in the station.

"I was wondering what you could tell me about Eric Berg's witness against Doug Norstad."

Jensen looked at me sharply. With his reading glasses and graying hair, he looked like a principal I'd had in school.

"Nothing," He said shortly.

"Come on, Dan," I said. "What's the problem?"

Jensen sighed and looked out his small window. "There are two problems. The first is, it isn't any of your business anymore. Let the justice system work." He took off his glasses. "The second issue is, it isn't any of my business anymore either. The investigation is over. The prosecutor is satisfied we got the right man. The rest is up to the courts. I'm a police officer, not a lawyer."

"I don't think you got the right man," I said.

"Yeah, just like O. J. Simpson. We need to work to find the *real* killer."

"Look, Dan, this has nothing to do with O. J., and you know it. Are you satisfied you got the right man?"

Jensen turned to look at me directly. "Jonah, I didn't want it to be Doug Norstad. But the man had motive. He had means, the ability to take that shot, and he had opportunity."

"And he has no physical evidence connecting him to the crime."

Jensen was silent.

"And he has a witness who says he wasn't even in Grand Lake

at the time of the killing," I added.

"So you say," said Jensen. "On the other hand, the prosecution has a *real* witness who will testify in court that he saw Norstad at the scene."

"Exactly." I said. "And my question is, *why?*"

The chief shook his head. "Forget it, Jonah. It's over."

He patted his desk aimlessly. "Look, maybe he won't even get convicted. It's up to the courts now." He nodded at me. "It may turn out okay, even now. And if you don't mind," he said, gesturing at his paper-strewn desk, "I've got some work to do."

I got up, said goodbye, and left. I was still getting to know the chief, but he didn't usually strike me as so truculent. Well, Plan A was a dead end. Time for Plan B.

As I stepped toward my car, I flipped open my cell phone and called Alex Chan.

His secretary, inevitably, told me he was unavailable.

I left a message and my number, and headed for the church.

An hour or so later, my cell phone started playing the guitar intro to "Money for Nothin'" by Dire Straights. Cool ring tones amused me.

"Pastor Jonah," I said.

"I thought that was my line," said Alex Chan.

"No, your line is, 'This conversation, and any depictions, descriptions, and appurtenances thereunto are confidential, unavailable and any other legal word I can think of quickly.'"

"Careful, there are as many pastor jokes as there are lawyer jokes," he said.

"True."

"So," he said, "what's up?"

"I was wondering if I could buy you lunch."

"Today?"

"Sure."

"Lawyers are supposed to be too busy for last-minute lunches."

"So are pastors."

"We'll be two-thirds of a joke. If we could just find a rabbi, we'd be complete."

"We may be out of luck in Grand Lake," I said. "But Jesus was a rabbi. I'll bring Him."

"It'll have to do," said Alex.

~

We met at a little coffee shop called Dylan's, across from the waterfront park. I assumed the name was a reference to Bob Dylan, who grew up in Duluth. Duluth was an hour and a half drive away, so I thought it was a bit of a stretch. The owner was probably someone from California.

In spite of the inapt name, Dylan's had a great coffeehouse atmosphere and a truly excellent chicken salad sandwich. Served on a fresh croissant with fresh fruit, and accompanied by excellent coffee, the meal was perfect.

"So," said Alex, "to what do I owe this honor?"

"Well," I said, "I'd like to help you with the Norstad case."

He chewed his ham and swiss on rye thoughtfully.

I chewed some chicken salad and had a bit of cantaloupe.

"I'm not sure that's a good idea," he said at last.

"I can do things you can't, because you're an officer of the court," I said.

"What are you gonna do, break and enter? Come on, Jonah, you're a pastor."

"Listen," I said. "I know Norstad is innocent. I've got some ideas of how to prove it."

"The best way to prove it would be to give me your witness."

"Can't do it," I said.

He snorted. "What are your ideas?"

"I get the feeling it would be better if you didn't know."

Chan swore. "You *are* talking about breaking and entering."

"No," I said. "I won't break the law. But I might do some things that a defense lawyer couldn't."

"And what would this get you?"

"I don't know yet."

Alex ate some more sandwich, and then sipped some ice tea.

"How can you drink that stuff?" I asked. "It's fifty degrees outside."

"It's 'cause I'm Asian," he said. "I drink tea in any weather."

"I see," I said. "And how often do you drink hot tea?"

He grimaced. "Never. Can't stand it."

"You're not Asian," I said. "You're Southern."

"Then how do you explain my evil, shifty eyes?"

"That?" I said. "That's just 'cause you're a lawyer."

"Oh," he said. "I forgot."

We ate a bit more in silence. I was starting to like Alex Chan.

"I've only been in Grand Lake for four months," he said after a while. "I took this case to get publicity for my private practice." He held up his hand. "But I do have ethics. I'll provide the best representation I can for Doug Norstad." He chewed some more. "I don't know what you can do that I can use, but I think I need all the help I can get."

CHAPTER 26

Next morning I did some office work at home. At about eleven, I put on a pair of dark blue dress pants, a white shirt with a blue tie, and a blue blazer.

Chan had given me the name and address of the witness for the prosecution, and I drove to it with a hot, large supreme pizza and a six-pack of beer.

Grand Lake has no very bad areas of town, but there are certainly some areas that are worse than others, places where the houses are old and in disrepair and mostly rentals. The witness for the prosecution was called Larry, and Larry apparently lived in one of these old rentals. It turned out to be a clapboard house in dire need of a paint job. Even in mid-May, the lawn had gone to seed, and there was trash in the yard. The place seemed deserted when I pulled up. If I was right, however, Larry would be there.

The doorbell didn't work, so I pounded on the door with my fist.

A tall, skinny, rough-looking man answered the door. He had a full beard, a bit shaggy, and his head looked shaved. His skin was pale. He had bags and lines under his eyes that told of some hard living. On his bare forearms he had amateur-looking tattoos, and I could smell marijuana in the air. To my experienced nose, he smelled like a prison.

"I didn't order a pizza," he said, looking at me, and starting to close the door.

"Of course you didn't, you moron," I said, and stuck my foot in the door. "You think pizza delivery boys wear ties? *He* sent me down here to check on you."

"Whaddya mean, *he*?" he said.

"You really want me to name names?" I said.

The skinny man grunted.

"You calling yourself Larry, right?" I asked.

He didn't say anything.

"Well, Larry, you gonna let me in, or should I go eat this thing all by myself? I got some beer to go with it."

He struggled with it for a moment, but it was no contest. "I haven't had pizza in a long time," said the man called Larry. He pushed open the door and walked back into the house.

The small living room we walked through was empty, with bare, dusty linoleum floors. The shades were all pulled, and a single electric light bulb was unshaded.

Larry led me into a tiny kitchen, with an old ceramic sink, chipped and yellowed with age. The trash was overflowing with empty boxes of microwave meals. There was a small table and an old, but apparently functioning fridge. There were three folding chairs.

"Hey, man," I said, "could you get me a glass for my beer? I like it from a glass."

He stared at me. "A glass?" he asked incredulously.

"You got a problem with that, man?" I was still holding the pizza in one hand, and the six-pack in the other.

Larry shrugged. "Suit yourself, bro." He reached into one of the small cupboards above the sink and set a glass on the table. I watched him carefully, then set the pizza down next to it. I put the six-pack on the linoleum counter next to the sink.

Larry dived for it. I guessed he hadn't had any real booze for some time. I guessed also that whoever had set him up here didn't let him go out much.

I sat down and took a slice of pizza. Larry was chugging a can of beer.

"So what's he want?" said Larry at last.

"Who?" I said.

"Hollywood, man. You said he sent you down here."

"Yeah," I said. "He wants me to go over your story again."

Larry swore. "I've been going over that friggin' story every day since I got here," he said.

"He wants to see how you'll do with someone you don't know," I said.

Larry crushed the empty beer can, and threw it at the trash. It bounced off an empty box of hungry man and landed on the floor. Neither one of us picked it up. Larry opened a second can. He didn't seem that interested in the pizza.

"I guess that makes sense," he said.

"So let's have it," I said. I was on my second piece of pizza, Larry on his second beer. Perfect symmetry.

"Ain't you gonna ask me questions, the way they done it before?"

"You're supposed to know it backwards and forwards," I said. "It shouldn't matter how I ask you."

He swore again. It didn't seem personal. Just a general sound to fill the silences.

"All right," he said, bouncing the second beer can past the first.

He finally reached for a piece of pizza, but not before he opened a third beer.

"Okay," he said. "Let's see. I was coming up the courthouse steps, and I seen this guy on the roof, like out of the corner of my eye."

"Which roof?" I asked.

"Tommy's," he said promptly.

"Good," I said.

He nodded and took a swig of beer, followed by a bite of pizza. "So I figure this guy, he's just fixing the roof, but it don't look quite right to me, so I looked at him real close."

"What did he look like?"

"I'm not supposed to remember his clothes."

"All right, so what did his face look like?"

He swore again, in a friendly sort of way. "Man, I ain't seen him in real life. In court I'm just supposed to point at the guy."

"What if the lawyer says, 'How can you be sure?'"

Larry crunched his third can, and it joined the others on the floor. "Hollywood ain't got me the picture yet," he said. "When I get it I'll look at it first."

"Guy has red hair or something, doesn't he?"

"S---, man, I don't know," said Larry.

"All right, so you see the guy on the roof, and he's our guy."

"Yeah, that's it."

"So are you supposed to see him take the shot?"

"Naw. I'm just supposed to say I saw a flash or something."

I finished my third piece of pizza. Larry finished his fourth beer. It occurred to me that "Hollywood," whoever he was, was probably keeping Larry away from alcohol. He wasn't going to be happy to find his star witness blasted this afternoon. For that matter, I had no idea when someone else might come to visit Larry.

"Well, Larry," I said, "I gotta run." I looked beyond his shoulder toward the front door. "Is that someone at the door?" I asked. He turned around, and I scooped the glass he had set out for me into my blazer pocket. It bulged. I took the jacket off and hung it over my arm as Larry turned back to me.

"I don't see nothing," he said.

"Guess I was wrong," I said. "Ciao," I said, holding out my fist. Larry bumped it with his, and made no move to leave the beer. I let myself out.

CHAPTER 27

I'm trying not to think of you as a nuisance," said Alex Chan.

"I wouldn't bother if I were you," I said. "It's better to perceive reality as it is."

"This from a professional clergyman? I would have thought you'd prefer faith to cold reality."

I adjusted myself for comfort in one of Chan's client chairs. He sat across from me on his couch, his elbows bent above his shoulders, his hands behind his head.

"Actually, Alex, all worldviews demand a great deal of faith. If you consider the facts, Christianity doesn't require any more faith than any other way of looking at the world, and quite a bit less than, say, atheism."

"How do you figure?" he asked comfortably.

I paused. "Do you really want to get into this?"

"I'm a lawyer," he said. "I love a good argument."

"I'm a preacher," I said. "Ditto."

"We could be at this for the rest of our lives."

"I don't mind," I said. "As long as we don't get upset and personal."

"Go for it," he said. "I'll tell you to stop if it's necessary. You do the same for me."

"Okay. My point is, ninety percent of what any person accepts as fact is accepted on faith."

"You've made the assertion. You've got the burden of proof," said Alex.

"Lawyers," I said. "Okay. Do you believe in the existence of atoms, the assassination of Abraham Lincoln, or the existence of India?"

"India the country?"

"I thought you were supposed to be well-educated."

He flashed a quick grin.

"Yes," I said, "India the country."

"All three of those things are true," said Chan.

"You ever seen an atom?"

Chan shook his head.

"Were you there when Lincoln was assassinated?"

"Of course not, and I've never been to India. But what does that prove? I've met people from India. I've read about Lincoln's assassination. I've read about atoms too. Plus," he said, flashing a quick white grin, "scientists have convincingly demonstrated they can use atoms to blow things up. I'm not going to argue with them about that."

"That's my point, Alex," I said. "Every single thing that is outside the personal experience of your five senses, must be accepted on faith. You believe that the people you met from India are not perpetuating some conspiracy about a made-up nation for geo-political purposes. You trust that those who preserved the memory of Lincoln's death were, in fact, telling the truth. You've never seen an atomic explosion either, I bet, so you trust that when people write or talk about these things, they are, in fact, telling the truth."

"So what's your point, Jonah?"

I shrugged. "You just said that you thought I would prefer faith to cold reality. I'm just saying that 'cold reality' is actually mostly made up of faith."

"Aren't we talking about a different kind of faith here? I mean, isn't it sort of a happy dream to believe that the Supreme Being in all the universe cares about you, personally?"

"Can you think of a logical reason why that is more of a happy dream than the idea that we have no moral responsibility for anything we do?"

Chan looked at his watch.

"Sorry, Alex," I said. "Let's put this to rest now. I respect your views. Just trying to get a little respect for mine."

"We're fine," said Chan. "You even make a pretty good point—maybe you should have been an attorney. But did you come here just to debate with me?"

"You started it," I said. "But yes, I have something for you."

I took a handkerchief and carefully removed the glass from Larry's house from the pocket of my blazer.

"What's this?" asked Alex.

"Fingerprints, hopefully," I said.

"How's that?"

"You're probably better off not knowing the details. Just say that I have reason to believe that on the glass are the fingerprints of the witness against Doug Norstad."

He was silent for some time. He tapped his teeth with a thumbnail.

"You think this guy's a con?"

"If you mean convict, yes. He has 'prison' written all over him in neon."

"And how do you know this?"

"Don't you think you'd be better off if you didn't know where these fingerprints came from?"

"Maybe," he said. "Did you meet him somewhere?"

"It's possible," I said. "It's possible I ran into him, and we started talking, and he gave the overwhelming impression that he was being coached to say certain things on the witness stand."

"Everyone coaches witnesses. If I was calling you to the stand, I'd coach you first."

"Would you coach me to identify a man I hadn't ever seen before?"

Alex looked thoughtful.

"How'd you get him to tell you this?"

"Beer," I said promptly.

We were quiet for a minute.

"Also," I said, "he was under the impression that I was sent to him by his handler, to see if he had his story straight."

Alex leaned forward, elbows on knees and stared at me.

"How'd you do that?" he asked.

"What you don't know, you can't tell."

He snorted. "I'm not going to be tortured."

"Doesn't matter. The point is, do you have enough to start digging and discredit this guy?"

"I'm not sure. Who did he say was coaching him?"

It was my turn to snort. "Hollywood."

"Hollywood?"

"Yeah. Obviously a nickname, or code name, or something."

"I don't know," said Alex. "If his fingerprints are in the system, and he tells the court a fake name, we've probably got them cold.

But I doubt they'd be so stupid. I probably couldn't use the fact that he's an ex-con to discredit him either. The judge usually disallows stuff like that."

"Well, can you use the fingerprints to find out something about him?"

"Yeah. There's a service I can use."

"Will you share the results with me?"

"It's going to cost you another lunch," said Alex.

CHAPTER 28

The next Monday, I went fishing again. It wasn't a nice day. It was raining lightly, and the temperature was in the low fifties. But it was Monday, and it was May, and there is still no better way to spend such a day than in the pursuit of trout.

The Tamarack was a pretty good-sized river, and with a little provocation from the rain, it ran high and muddy. Some folks fished it that way, and claimed it made the brown trout less wary. It also made the deep spots deeper, as well as impossible to see, and it made the river faster and more dangerous for waders. So on rainy days I fished the feeder creeks that ran into the Tamarack, some miles upstream from the Lake. Even in heavy rain, those smaller creeks stayed clear.

As I drove down 13, I noticed a green Honda Accord that had come across the bridge to Superior with me. When I turned off to find the Tamarack and one of my favorite feeder creeks, the Accord came with me. I drove south for a while and turned off into a gravel parking area that served as a trailhead for various fishing points along the river. The Accord drove on by.

I hastily pulled my waders on in the rain, but once I was outfitted, I felt relatively dry, and comfortably warm. I jammed my wide-brimmed hat on my head and hung my sunglasses around my neck. You never know when the sun might break through. Out in the Rain Belt of Western Washington and Oregon people said it'd rain all year and then for one day be sunny. They meant it literally.

Here in northern Minnesota and northwestern Wisconsin, however, you could see the sun more often than that.

I stepped out on the trail that took me to Blue Creek. The stream was about as wide as a rural two-lane highway, but I knew from savored experience that trout thrived in it, especially the beautiful, wild brook trout.

I couldn't suppress a deep sigh as I stepped knee-deep into the beautiful little stream. This was where peace happens and the rest of the world disappears. Trees grew close overhead, and I kept my casts low and short. A ten-inch brookie hit my jig on the third cast. He had a pale orange belly and a beautiful green back with lighter, worm-like spots. I inhaled the scent of fresh water, rain, and live fish. I wanted to kiss the slimy creature in my hands, but I refrained. I set him gently in the water and watched him dart away. I caught three more from the same hole, until I snagged the bottom and scared the remaining fish. I continued on upstream.

The sun did not break through, and the rain kept steady. I was relatively dry in my waders, and my thick wool sweater kept me fairly warm even while it was wet. But the sensation of being wet eventually became uncomfortable enough for me to notice. I wasn't truly cold, but it certainly felt brisk, and I began to think about things like hot sandwiches and coffee and dry clothes.

After just three hours of fishing, I squished up the muddy trail back to my car. The rain wasn't a downpour, but it was steady and hard.

With this weather, on a Monday, mine ought to have been the only car there. But nearby, closer to the trailhead than mine, was parked a green Honda Accord. It looked like the one that had followed me all the way from Duluth. Maybe farther.

As I approached my own car, I looked at the Honda. Through the rain-streaked windshield I saw two figures in the front seats. Just for the heck of it, I started to memorize the license plate. As I passed it, the doors opened and two men got out.

The driver was a big man, maybe six-two, which gave him three inches on me. He had on a ball cap for the Duluth-Superior Dukes, a minor league baseball team which had left the North Shore in 2003. I couldn't see much of his hair under the cap, but it looked sandy blond. He had a thick sandy-colored mustache. The rest of his face made it look like he had been to the wars. He wore a black leather jacket and blue jeans and looked long, lean, and powerful.

The second man was shorter than me and considerably thicker. He had black hair, slicked back over his low forehead. He also wore a black leather jacket, which stretched over what looked like an extra fifty pounds of gut.

"Have any luck?" asked the smaller, thicker man.

They were standing in a considerable amount of rain. It was soaking into their clothes. I stared at him. The taller one noticed my reaction and grinned in a cold way that didn't reach his hazel eyes.

"Did you follow me from Duluth, sit in the car for three hours, and now stand in the pouring rain just to see if I caught some fish?" I said.

"Just trying to be friendly," said the shorter man. He sounded to me as if he might have spent some time in Chicago.

"Friendly, and what else?" I said.

The tall one regarded me with an expression of grudging approval.

"Just get it done, Risotti," he said. "This guy knows

something's up."

The shorter one, apparently called Risotti, turned to glare at his partner. The tall man appeared unperturbed. "I'm handling this, Paul Bunyan. You're just the local color. So do me a favor and shut up."

The bigger man shrugged. "It's your show," he said. But he didn't break off eye-contact with Risotti. At last the shorter man snorted and turned back to me.

"We want to talk to you," he said.

I turned away and walked to the trunk of my car, which I opened. "Then talk fast," I said, "I'm getting out of the rain."

Risotti nodded, as if to himself. He hunched his burly shoulder up against the rain. "All right. I gotta friend who wants you to do him a favor."

"Who?" I asked, putting my rod into the trunk.

"Doesn't matter who," said Risotti. "He's prepared to be very generous."

"For what?" I asked. I stripped my vest off and put it in the trunk next to my rod.

"My friend would like it if you left the Norstad matter alone," said Risotti.

I stopped what I was doing and turned and looked at him. He was blinking his eyes in the rain, trying to look friendly. He looked like a wet thug.

"And what if I don't want to do that?" I asked.

"My friend has a temper," said Risotti. "You could get hurt, accidentally maybe, if you weren't careful."

"I've been hurt before," I said, looking him in the eye.

"It would be a shame," he said, "if you were to be crippled in such a way that you could never again come out here in the beautiful weather and catch fish."

I rubbed my unshaven cheek. "So it's the easy way or the hard way?"

Risotti beamed at me, still blinking water out of his eyes. "You are an intelligent young man."

"And just how 'easy' is the easy way?"

"Ten grand," he said promptly.

"And what if there's a third way? Say, I go to the police?"

He stopped beaming abruptly, and his eyes were cold. "That's the hard way," he said. "You got nothing to take to the cops."

"I bet your friend is willing to pay more than ten grand," I said. "I bet if I take ten grand, you take the difference."

"See?" said Risotti to the tall man. "This guy is smart. I told you he'd be smart." He turned to me. "Okay, since I like you, I'm gonna level with you. I am authorized to offer you fifteen now, and fifteen later."

"What's later?"

"When the Norstad business is all settled."

"How do I get a hold of you when it's over?"

"You don't. I come to you. I did it this time, didn't I? I'll do it again."

"Twenty-five, now," I said.

His eyes narrowed and became unfriendly.

"Look, you got thirty grand to give me, according to you," I said. "I'll take twenty five now, and you can keep the five. That's not bad for standing in the rain for a few minutes."

The tall man chuckled quietly.

"Shut up," Risotti said to him.

I sat down on the trunk and began to unlace my wading boots. "I could always put an ad in the paper," I said. "Something like, 'Thanks, Risotti, for the five grand.' Maybe your friend would see it and wonder what happened to the rest of the money."

"You don't know who you're messing with," he said, his voice low, shaking with rage.

I slipped off a boot, and began to work one leg out of my waders. My dry undergarments were pelted with rain. I pretended to ignore it.

"Just do it, Risotti," said the tall man.

"That's less for you too," replied the black-haired thug.

"We came here to do a job, and this guy's ready to jump. Close the deal and let's get out of here."

Risotti shrugged. "I won't forget this," he said, and walked back to the green Accord.

"He talking to me or you?" I said to the tall man, who hadn't moved.

He shrugged too.

Risotti came back with a little deposit envelope. He counted out twenty thousand dollar bills in front of me, and then slapped them on the roof of my wet car.

"Twenty," he said. "Take it, or take the hard way."

I was shrugging into jeans and hiking boots. I stood up and picked up the damp bills.

"Don't forget now," said Risotti. "No more interference in the Norstad thing."

"I won't forget," I said.

He turned on his heel and stalked back to the Accord like a wet cat. The tall man nodded at me and then turned and joined him. I got into my car, out of the wet and cold, while the Accord pulled

out and disappeared northward into the rain.

CHAPTER 29

I'd appreciate it if you could look up a license plate for me," I said to Dan Jensen, while I sat and sipped coffee with him at Lorraine's. "Thank you so much for the opportunity to serve," he said. "Is there anything else I can do for you? Shine your shoes maybe?"

Plates and silverware clinked in the background. The coffee was hot and good. Outside, it was pouring rain, as it had been for almost a week now.

I took a clear Ziploc bag from my jacket pocket and threw it on the table in front of Jensen. Inside it were nineteen of the twenty one-thousand dollar bills the thugs had given me. He looked at it without expression.

"A bribe, Jonah?"

"Not for you," I said. "For me. On Monday, a couple thugs came and gave this to me to stop me poking my nose into the Norstad case. The license plate number I want was on the car they drove."

He took a sip of coffee. Other than openly expressed emotion, nothing much rattled Chief Dan Jensen.

"How much?"

"Twenty grand. There's only nineteen there, though. I kept one bill for a file I'm building."

He still registered no expression. "That is suggestive of something," he said.

"You still think Norstad is the guy?"

Jensen grimaced.

"I know it's not convenient, but I thought you'd want to know."

He nodded. "I've been pretty much thinking that you were too personally involved with Norstad to see this thing straight. But this is worth musing over."

"Musing? You sound almost educated."

"Your bad influence shows up more every day."

He opened two creamers and poured them into his empty cup. He added a package of sugar, then refilled it with coffee.

"The thing is," he said, "there's not a lot here to help us. If we find these guys, they'll just deny it, and we're at a dead end."

"But if we find out who they are, maybe we can connect them to whomever hired them?"

"Whomever?"

"I don't know," I said, "it sounds educated anyway, doesn't it?"

"It sounds sissy anyway," said Jensen.

"The other thing is," said Jensen, after a pause, "is that it's not Grand Lake's case anyway. County and the DA have it. I'm out of the loop."

"All right, how about this. I suspect that this car was involved in a felony in the town of Grand Lake. I'm a citizen, tipping you off anonymously. No one will blame you for at least running the plates."

"And when I run them?"

"Pass it on to me."

"It'll probably be a rental," said Jensen.

"So, I'll find out," I said.

"Look, Jonah, you aren't an officer. Don't go around acting as if you are."

"I'm a private citizen," I said. "Nothing wrong with trying to track down a benefactor to thank him."

He tapped his thick fingers on the table for a moment. "Whatever else you are, I've never known you to be a liar."

I smiled encouragingly.

"Anything you haven't told me?"

"They also said that I could end up having a bad accident if I chose not to take their advice."

His face darkened. "They threatened you?"

"Well, yeah, I guess that's what it was. They said I could end up crippled."

He sighed. "I think you ought to stay out of this."

"Objection noted. But you've said your hands are somewhat tied."

He nodded, and started tapping his fingers again.

I drank more coffee. It's a profitable way to use up time.

At last Jensen stopped with his fingers. "We'll probably never be able to prove anything, but I can't let this thing slide." He frowned. "I'm not saying I want your help, you understand."

I grinned. "You can't always get want you want," I said.

"But if you try, sometimes you get what you need," he said.

CHAPTER 30

I was at a Little League game on Friday night. Leyla was with me. Little League on the North Shore was considerably colder than it had been in Oregon. It was about forty. At least there was no wind. We both wore down parkas. Leyla's left hand was in the pocket of my coat, entwined with my right. She had on a maroon knit stocking cap. She looked like a fashion model.

"So which one is from Harbor Lutheran again?" she asked.

"Three kids in the yellow and gray are from church families," I said, "and two in the blue and white."

"Like a family feud," she said.

"Actually this is a small town, not the suburbs. We don't take it quite as seriously here. So far, no parents have killed each other over children's sports."

My phone vibrated in my right hand pocket next to our hands. Leyla jumped and squealed, tearing her hand away from me. Several people turned to look at her.

I started to laugh quietly. She joined in, laughing harder and trying desperately to be quiet about it. She dropped her head to my shoulder and shook like she was having a seizure.

"Borden," I said, making a huge effort to keep my voice steady.

"Jonah," said Dan Jensen, "what you up to?"

"Trying to preserve some decorum at a sporting event," I said while Leyla's body erupted with a new series of spasms. "Why?"

"I thought you might like to drive to Duluth with me tomorrow."

"I'll cancel my trip to Disney Land," I said.

"Very funny. I've traced the plates of your thugs. You wanna meet them?"

"I thought you couldn't do that."

"Tomorrow's my day off. I can do what I like with my own time. I'll just be going to Duluth with a friend. It might be better if you drive, though."

"No problem," I said. "Pick you up at eight?"

"Let's have breakfast at Lorraine's first. Make it seven."

I flipped my phone closed and put it in my left-hand pocket.

"Does your hand want to brave the dark scary pocket again?" I asked.

"I couldn't help it. It startled me."

"I noticed."

~

Next morning at Lorraine's I had the western omelet. Variety is the spice of life. I sipped my coffee.

"So what do you know?" I said.

"Strangely, the Accord wasn't rented," said Jensen. "Belongs to a guy named Tom Lund." He paused and stirred cream into his coffee for effect. "He's a private eye."

My coffee spilled onto my shirt. "I thought private eyes were just fictional characters in books and movies." I wiped at my shirt with a napkin.

"Nope. There's plenty of 'em," said Jensen. "Mostly, they do divorce work, sometimes investigative stuff for big corporations, some security. Once in a while they even help out the cops."

"Any private eyes in Grand Lake?"

"Not yet," he said, and sipped his coffee.

"Retirement plan?" I asked.

"Could be. There are worse ways to supplement the income."

"But this guy's dirty," I said.

"That's the funny thing," he said. "I would think so too. But I called some people on the Duluth PD, and they say he's one of the good guys. He's helped them out a few times. He presses his luck, like a lot of them do, but my contact in Duluth was pretty clear that when push comes to shove, he's on the side of the angels."

"So what was he doing, threatening me?"

"That's what we're going to Duluth to find out."

~

Twenty minutes later we were headed down 61 toward Duluth. The Great Blue Lake loomed massively to our left.

"I've been thinking," said Jensen.

"Did it hurt?"

"Very funny. Just 'cause these guys came after you, doesn't prove anything."

"What do you mean?"

"I mean, Norstad could still be the guy who shot Spooner."

"Then why would someone give me twenty grand to quit looking into it?"

"Maybe someone doesn't want any complications. You know, just have a quick simple trial, clear conviction, and move on."

"Who would want that?" Even as I asked it, I knew the answer.

"Only one person I can think of."

I nodded. The DA. On the other hand, I *knew* that Norstad was innocent. I'd verified his alibi. I said as much to Jensen.

He shrugged. "Berg could still be honestly mistaken. He's running for office. Maybe he just wants to make sure that this thing goes well. Make sure he looks good, you know?"

"Seems a pretty shady way of conducting a fair and honest trial," I said.

"You get into politics, you get a lot of shady stuff going on."

"That's the truth, no doubt," I agreed. "You really think that's what this is all about?"

"I don't know. But you've convinced me that something isn't right, anyway."

"I'm glad to hear it," I said.

CHAPTER 31

Tom Lund's office was in the Canal Park district, above a little tourist gift shop in one of the restored brick buildings from the 1800s that sat on the inland side of Lake Avenue South.

Dan and I climbed the stairs next to the tourist stop, and stepped into a corridor with an old wood floor that had been refinished when the building was restored. I knocked on the first door to our left, the one that said "Lund Investigations" on the plaque. A muffled male voice called out something intelligible. I shrugged, and pushed the door open.

We were standing in a bare room with clean white walls and a plain desk in the corner to our right. Two tall gray metal filing cabinets stood in front of the desk against the stark right hand wall. On one of them sat a coffee maker, and three porcelain cups upside down on a clean cloth. Next to the cabinets was a sink with a cupboard above it. There was a partly open door on the left side of the wall we faced.

"Secretary's out," called a laconic voice through the door. "Come on in here." I looked at the bare desk, which had no chair behind it.

"Wonder how long the secretary's been out," I said to Jensen.

He nodded and then jerked his head up to the ceiling. In the corner above the desk was a camera.

I pushed open the door to the inside office. It was large and spare, clearly devoid of a feminine touch. There were no pictures, no colors, and no decorations. A wooden chair in the right hand corner held a stack of file folders and papers. Another one next to it supported a medium-sized cardboard box. Large windows looked across the road toward the harbor, which could be glimpsed between buildings. A big wooden desk sat in front of one window. Behind it, with his feet on the desk and his eyes looking toward the harbor, was the tall man who hadn't said much when the shorter man, Risotti, had given me the twenty-thousand dollars. There was no sign of Risotti.

The tall man, presumably Tom Lund, looked a bit like a blond Tom Selleck back in the days when Selleck played *Magnum P. I.* He even had the same first name. Lund was lean, with curly blond hair and a thick blond mustache. Unlike Selleck back in the day, Lund had a beginning bald spot on the back of his head.

He took his feet off the desk and peered at me closely.

"Where do I know you from?" he asked.

"Do you go around offering twenty thousand dollars to so many people that you forget?" I asked.

He glanced at Jensen and his eyes narrowed. He looked back at me.

"You were wearing a hat and sunglasses and a bunch of fishing gear. But yeah, I see it now. He stood up. "Hold on a sec," he said.

He came around his desk and took the cardboard box off one chair and put it in a corner. The stack of paperwork was moved from the other chair to the top of the box in the corner. He then turned back to us.

"Tom Lund," he said, sticking his hand out to me.

Bemused I took his hand, "Jonah Borden," I said.

Jensen also shook hands and gave his name.

"Have a seat," said Lund, gesturing at the now available wooden chairs. As we sat down, he walked back to the other side of his desk and stretched out again in his chair.

"What can I do for you guys?" he asked.

I glanced at Jensen. "Your show," he said. "I'll jump in as needed."

"Okay," I said, turning to Lund. "Who hired you to bribe and threaten me last week?"

A slow smile spread across Lund's face. In spite of myself, I thought I could almost like him.

"You just made my day, Pastor Borden," he said. "I gotta admit, I expected you to take the money, but I was kinda disappointed anyway when you did. You took the money all right, but you're not going to stay away from this thing, are you?"

I met his blue eyes without blinking. "I never said I would," I said. "And if you're happy for the chance to take a crack at me, you could be disappointed anyway."

Lund cut his eyes to Dan. "Personal protection?"

"I can handle myself," I said. "Who sent you?"

Lund suddenly looked serious. He put both hands on the desk and leaned forward.

"I think we may have a misunderstanding here. Risotti's a thug. I'm not. I quit the job as soon we got back to Duluth."

"Maybe you better start at the beginning," said Jensen in his deep authoritative voice.

Lund glanced at him again, and then at me. I nodded. "I didn't know the deal until we talked to you," said Lund.

"Tell me about it," I said.

"I got a call last week from this Risotti guy. Names a guy I've done work for, and says he'd like to hire me. Well, I know the guy he mentioned, so I say, what kind of work. He tells me he wants someone followed, and he may want to confront the guy at some point. I asked him what kind of confrontation, and he says if it happens at all, he just wants to talk." Lund rubbed the back of his head. "So I ask him why he needs me, and he says he's from out of town. Then he offers me a cash number that was pretty good, but not too good to be true, if you know what I mean."

I nodded, and so did Jensen.

"So we follow you around for a couple days and then on Monday Risotti says, Okay, I wanna talk to the guy." He picked up a pen and started fiddling with it. "By this time I knew a little bit about you—I mean, I'm not bad at my job, and I can't follow you without learning some things. I thought maybe Risotti had some connection to that reporter chick you've been seeing. I get roped into that kind of thing from time to time. And yet at the same time, Risotti didn't seem the type. Seemed more like a thug, you know. But he didn't tell me anything about himself, and in my business, you don't ask until you need to."

He looked out the window and back at us. "So we go out there, and he does his thing with you. As soon as he got into it, I knew what was up, and when we got back to Duluth, I terminated our contract. You can ask around. I don't break legs, threaten, or bribe. I got a license and I'm a professional. I'm good, and I get plenty of referral business, and I got no need to cross the line for a few bucks."

He looked at me. "I really was disappointed when I thought you caved. I'm glad you were just ripping him off."

"So Risotti hired you," I said.

"That's right," he said. "I'm glad you've got more intestinal fortitude than I thought at first. But listen, Risotti and his folks are not people to mess around with. They *will* come and break your legs when they find out you've stiffed them."

"Maybe I'll break their legs instead," I said.

Both Lund and Jensen stared at me. "They teach you that at pastor school?" asked Lund.

"How they gonna find out?" asked Jensen.

Lund looked at him. "Cop?"

Jensen nodded. "Off duty, off the record—for now," said Jensen.

"Duluth?"

"Grand Lake."

Lund nodded. "Okay. I got nothing to hide. I've done nothing illegal. But they aren't gonna find out from me. I may push the line hard sometimes for a client, but push comes to shove, I'm on the same side as you. I've got no love for the likes of Risotti."

"So give him to us," said Jensen.

Lund pursed his lips. "There's the problem," he said. "He was a client. I took his money. I would just as soon send him swimming in the lake in January, but I have standards to maintain."

"You're going to protect him?" I asked.

"I don't like it any more than you," said Lund. "But I'm running a business here, and word gets around. I can't rat on my clients."

"But he threatened me," I said.

Lund nodded. "We both know that, but there's nothing there that will hold up in court. If we had something concrete in terms of criminal activity, I'd do it. But without that, I can't."

Jensen, surprisingly, was nodding in approval. "It's true," he said. "We don't have anything on Risotti yet."

"You know where Risotti came from?" I asked.

Lund leaned back in his chair and looked at me. "I liked you, first time I saw you. I like your style. I like to see a preacher who's got some backbone. But I can't give up a client with no concrete evidence of a crime." He leaned forward and put his hands on his desk.

"I want to double check something, hang on a minute." He stood up and walked to the corner where the file folders were piled up on the cardboard box. He shuffled the folders around and selected one. After looking through the papers in it, he nodded to himself.

"This is my file on that job. It's like I thought. I've got no evidence that would justify giving you any more information."

He threw the folder onto his desk. "Guys," he said, "I'm gonna step out for some coffee. I'll probably go to Starbucks, be back in about a half hour. You can let yourselves out." He nodded at the folder on the desk. "Remember, all these files are confidential. It would a terrible thing if you took advantage of my absence to look at a confidential file without permission or authorization."

Jensen stood up. I could see the gleam of respect in his eye.

I stood up too. "Thanks," I said.

"You've got nothing to thank me for," said Lund, looking me in the eye. "Understand? I can't help you."

"Got it," I said. "Thanks for nothing."

He winked at us and walked out of the office without another word.

CHAPTER 32

Lund's file didn't exactly give us Risotti. Even so, Jensen seemed pleased. "Says here Lund picked up Risotti on the Northwest Shuttle from the Twin Cities."

"All that means," I said sourly, "is that he's either from the Cities, or he flew in from somewhere else and caught the shuttle. He could be from Mumbai."

"Mumbai?"

"Yeah, I think it used to be called Bombay. It's in India."

"I know where Bombay is, Jonah."

"Fine. Anyway, Risotti could have come from there for all we know."

"Actually, that's not true. We have a flight number here. We can call the airline, get Risotti's itinerary. I'm guessing he came from Chicago. That's in America."

"Thanks for the geography lesson. Why Chicago?"

"Didn't you say he sounded like a Chicagoite?"

"Is that how you say it?"

"Do you want to talk about this, or do you want to show off your largely useless education?"

"Okay," I said. "Yeah, I thought he sounded like he was from Chicago."

"All right. There are a couple shuttles between Duluth and the

Cities. And several between there and Chicago. Risotti was on the one you would catch in Minneapolis, if you had flown in on the nine a.m. from Chicago."

"How do you know that?"

"Father-in-law's funeral, six months ago. It was in Chicago. But it doesn't matter. The flight number is all we need." He copied it down in a little black notebook he produced from a pocket in his jacket.

"You think Lund is square?"

"No one says 'square' any more, Jonah."

"So I'm a dinosaur in my mid-thirties. You think he's telling the truth?"

"Basically, yeah. He does have a P.I. license, and what he said pretty much backs up what the Duluth cops said about him. He probably does some borderline stuff now and then, but I'd guess he's got a pretty clear line he won't cross."

"And threatening me was on the other side of that line."

"You got it." Jensen looked at me seriously. "What he said about Risotti and company was true, though. They hear you're still poking around this thing, and you could be in for some pretty serious crap."

"I can handle it," I said.

He looked at me skeptically. "When's the last time you were in a fight, Jonah?"

"Five years ago," I said promptly.

Jensen stared at me, then shook his head. "I don't mean some theologian argument thingy, I mean a real, the-other-guy-is-trying-to-break-you-in-half, knock-down, dirty-fingers-in –your-eyeballs kind of fight."

"Five years ago," I said again.

He looked at me uncertainly. "Fine," he said at last. "But this isn't something to mess around with.

CHAPTER 33

I was coming back home from a hike in the woods when I smelled cigarette smoke. Maybe someone from church had dropped by to see me. Smoking isn't a sin to Lutherans, but there are fewer smokers among churchgoers than the rest of the population. I ran through the list of church members whom I knew smoked. None of them seemed likely to drop by unannounced and then wait for me when they discovered I was gone.

I had made several trails throughout my property. The one I was on approached the cabin from the southeast. The deck of my cabin faces that direction towards the lake. The driveway curves in from the northwest, and ends in my attached garage. The front door is on the southwestern side of the house.

I started to move slowly. The pine needles beneath my feet absorbed most of the sound of my walking.

They were on my deck, two guys, smoking, sitting in my chairs with their feet on my railing. They looked like tough guys, city guys, cut from the same mold as Risotti. One of them wore a black leather Bears jacket. The other had on a plain leather jacket and long black hair gathered in a ponytail. I started to feel mad.

I backed off carefully and when I was fully screened by the trees again, I circled quietly around to the back of the cabin. I stepped into the clearing on the northwestern side of the house, with the whole building between me and the guys on the deck.

There was a black Mercury Sable in the drive in front of the garage. I slowly opened the side door of the garage and slipped inside. No one seemed to have noticed me yet.

From a rack in the garage, I took down my pump-action, twelve-gauge shotgun. I opened the drawer of my workbench and removed a set of keys. First, I unlocked the trigger-lock on the gun. Then I pulled an ammo case out from the corner and unlocked it as well. I slid four shells into the magazine. I thought about it for a moment. Suddenly, as quietly as I could, I ejected all four shells and put them in my jeans pocket.

Taking off my shoes, I padded through the garage and through the inside door into the cabin itself. No one seemed to be in the house. After cautiously reaching the end of the hallway, I walked quickly through the front room and slid back the door to the deck. The two tough guys were scrambling to their feet, startled. I worked the action on the shotgun as if I was jacking a round into the chamber.

"Be still, guys," I said. "I'm a bit nervous." I flicked off the safety, hoping they could hear the little metallic *snick*. I pointed the gun in their general direction.

I expected them to put their hands up, but they didn't. "I wanna talk," I said. "Who are you, and what are you doing here?"

"Hey, man," said the guy in the Bears jacket, "we're just here to see if you're interested in selling this place."

"I'll give you three guesses at my answer," I said, motioning at him with the shotgun. "Let's try this again. Who are you, and why are you here?"

The guy with the ponytail flicked his eyes behind me and started talking rapidly and loudly.

"Don't shoot! Don't shoot! I've got a kid at home, man! Don't kill us!"

Something wasn't right. He didn't really look like he was afraid. His eyes flicked over my right shoulder again. I stepped quickly to my left as I felt something swing down from the right. Something struck my right arm with horrible force, and I dropped the shotgun. A man leaped in from behind me and scooped it up, cradling it in his hands like a submachine gun and pointing it at me.

I looked at him. He was small and wiry, with curly black hair and a dark, hook nosed face.

He spoke to the ponytailed guy without turning his head from me. "I almost missed him, Crockett. You kept looking at me, gave it away."

I took a step towards the curly-headed guy. My arm was numb, but I thought it was still serviceable.

"Easy now," he said. "You picked a nasty weapon to use on us. I'd hate for you to get blown in half with your own gun."

I nodded. "So would I," I said taking another step and closing the gap between us. "I mean, I—"

While I was still speaking, I grabbed the barrel of the gun and jammed it backwards into Curly Head. His grunt of surprise and pain, as it drove into his solar plexus, drowned out the empty click as he tried to shoot me. He involuntarily loosened his hold on the gun, and I whipped it away from him.

I reversed it quickly and pumped it again. The three thugs stood for a second, staring at me. It did not seem to have occurred to them that I would actually approach them with an unloaded gun.

Curly Head snapped at the others: "Run! He won't shoot us in the back!"

And, putting his words into action, he tore around the corner of the house for the car. Hesitating for a second, the other two followed him. As I cleared the corner of the house, they were in their car, engine roaring to life. The last door slammed as the black Mercury spun out and roared up my gravel driveway into the trees.

My right forearm started to ache. I looked around the deck and saw a short thick pine branch. For some reason, it made me even angrier to think that Curly Head had used a branch from one of my own trees to attack me on my own deck.

I rolled up the sleeve of my gray Vikings sweatshirt. My arm was bruising but it didn't look serious. I doubted it was fractured.

I went back into the house and called Jensen.

"Well, they showed up," I said.

"What? Who?"

"Risotti's thugs. At least I assume they were part of the same crew. There were three of them waiting for me here when I got back from a hike."

"What a happened? Are you okay?"

"I've got a banged up arm, but other than that I'm fine."

"What did they want?"

"They were in a hurry to leave. They didn't say."

"Jonah," said Jensen, with exaggerated patience, "tell me what happened."

So I told him.

"You live out in the county, and that means this belongs to the sheriff's department," he said when I was done. "I don't want to step on toes, so I'll call them. They'll send someone up for fingerprints and such. Don't touch anything."

CHAPTER 34

Predictably, Rex Burton was the first sheriff's deputy to show up.

"Ah, my biggest fan," I said.

He looked at me from behind his big square glasses and mustache and said nothing for a moment. Then, still standing just outside his car, he looked all around the clearing that held my cabin. Finally, he turned to me as if it pained him.

"So what's the problem?" he said. "Nobody here." It sounded like it cost him a great deal of effort to say it without spitting on my shoes.

"They ran off." I felt I was being particularly patient.

"And why would they do that?" Rex was obviously also being excruciatingly patient.

"There's no 'would' about it. They did."

"Why."

"Because they were scared." I knew it was juvenile to be so uncooperative, but at the moment I didn't care.

"Why were they scared?" said Burton. It looked like he had started chewing on something. Maybe the inside of his cheek.

"I showed them my shotgun," I said.

Some vague vestige of an expression twitched across his face. I knew he wanted to hear the whole story. It was his *job* to hear the whole story. But he didn't want to ask.

I felt a sudden burst of Christian charity. "You want me to tell you the whole story?"

He shrugged as if it might be a waste of his valuable time. "If you want to."

All the charity went back out of me.

I told him what had happened.

"Why'd you pull a gun on these guys?" He asked when it was over. "That could be a crime."

I stared at him. "Three thugs show up at my place, and you say it's a crime for me to hold a shotgun while I talk with them?"

"You say they're thugs," he said. "What if they really want to buy your place?"

"They don't."

"How do you know?"

I glared at him in frustration. The fact is, I *knew*. But he was right that I had no proof.

"Let me look around a minute," he said. "I wanna start in the garage where you got your shotgun."

I walked over to the garage and punched the button that opens the door for the car. We walked in, and I showed him where I keep my guns.

"Where's the key?"

I showed him.

"Take a hike," he said. "I'll handle it from here."

"I already took a hike," I said. "This is my place, and I'll do what I want."

He ignored me and continued to look around the garage. I went back into the house and opened a bottle of Woodchuck's Hard Apple Cider. I didn't offer any to Deputy Burton.

I went out and sat on the deck. He came out and glanced

around. He flicked a cigarette butt off of the rail and ran his hands over it. I wondered about fingerprints, but I was trying to ignore him, so I didn't say anything.

He turned to me. "Got nothing here says your story is true."

"How 'bout that cigarette butt you just flicked away. I don't smoke."

"Way I figure," he went on, ignoring me, "if your story *is* true, you'll be lucky if those guys don't show up and charge you with assault with a deadly weapon and attempted kidnapping."

"When do the detectives get here?" I asked, pointedly.

"Ain't no detectives coming out here," he said. "No reason. Nothing to see. Just pathetic little preacher sitting on his porch, too afraid to drink real beer."

I took a long pull and smacked my lips. I stood up. "Don't you ever," I said emphatically, "insult my hard apple cider."

He didn't know how to take that. I didn't expect him to.

"So you're the one who decides whether or not to call the detective unit," I said.

"That's right."

I couldn't see his eyes behind the reflection of the thick square lenses. I thought maybe he was glaring balefully at me. I wondered what "balefully" really meant.

"Are you glaring balefully at me?" I asked.

"Just you and me preacher," he said. "You wanna take a swing at me?"

Heck, yeah, I did. But getting into a brawl with a cop probably wouldn't sit very well with those who expect a little more decorum from their servants of God. Like God.

"Get out of here," I said.

He nodded slightly to himself. "Didn't think so. He spat on my deck, a thick slimy wad of phlegm. I held myself still with immense effort. He smiled without mirth, turned on his heel and walked back to his car.

While the tires still crunched on the gravel driveway, I got a rag and some bleach and cleaned off my deck.

CHAPTER 35

A few days later I got a call from Alex Chan.

"Let's have lunch," he said.

"Sure," I said. "Except it's about time you started paying your own way."

"I'll do you one better," he said. "It's on me."

"Where did you want to go? McDonald's?"

"Very funny. How about Dylan's on the waterfront?

Chan ordered an iced tea, as usual and some sort of focaccia bread sandwich. I got another chicken salad on a croissant with fresh fruit. It's good to stick with a winning combination.

"So what's up?" I asked after we had exchanged pleasantries and gotten our food.

"Got our fingerprints back," he said. He took a bite of his sandwich.

"You going to share?"

"You were right," said Alex. "He's a convict. Out on parole right now."

I chewed thoughtfully. "Does this help us at all?"

"It's better to know than not to know," said Chan. "But I'm not sure how much good this does. Usually the fact that a witness is a convict is considered irrelevant." He took another bite. "I could always ask a question aimed at putting the thought that he is a convict into the minds of the jury. But the prosecution will object, and the judge is almost certain to rule in their favor. It isn't much to hang our hopes on."

"But doesn't it at least bring us closer to the truth?"

"I'm not sure what you mean."

"I mean, we know now that they've dragged up a false witness. If they are doing that, then we know that Doug Norstad is innocent. There's got to be a way to prove it."

"I like you, Jonah," said Chan. "I like your style. You are a refreshing antidote to the stereotype of a pastor." He sipped some ice tea. "But, no offense, you've got nothing. If you would give me Norstad's real alibi—or convince him to give it to me—we might have something. But the fact that this witness is an ex-con doesn't mean he's lying."

I started to protest, and he held up his hand.

"And even if he is lying—if he wasn't really there when Spooner was shot—it still doesn't mean that Norstad is innocent."

This sounded a lot like what Chief Jensen had said. But I wanted to make Chan say it.

"How do you figure?" I asked.

"Eric Berg is an ambitious prosecutor," he said. "This is a big-time case. The camera is going to be on him. If he does it right, his face will be all over the state, and his opponents in the election this fall won't have a chance. Maybe he just wants to lock this one up for sure."

"You know, Chief Jensen said something like that," I said. "But it's a pretty big risk too. If he gets exposed, he could lose everything."

"It could be more subtle than that," said Chan. "He could be trying to lure me into court with the idea that there's some sort of hanky-panky going on. Then, when it comes down to it, he won't even call our convict as a witness."

"What do you mean?"

"I mean, Berg probably doesn't even need this witness. He wants this to go to trial. A plea bargain doesn't get him the publicity he wants. If he can use this potential witness to fool me into thinking I've got a chance, the case will go to trial, and he gets more publicity."

"Have you talked to him about a plea bargain yet?" I asked.

"No. Doug Norstad isn't willing to do it yet."

"So you don't really know if Berg really wants the trial or not."

"All I'm saying, Jonah, is that there is a lot of complexity involved here. It may just all be pretrial maneuvering.

"What about Doug's alibi?"

"Berg probably doesn't know that Norstad is truly innocent. Like the good politician he is, he's just using this opportunity to his best advantage." Chan took a sip of ice tea. "For that matter, *I* don't know for sure that Norstad is innocent. You are the only person who has heard this alibi."

"Have you asked Doug to tell you?"

"Yes. He says you are the only person he trusts with that secret."

"So do you think he and I just cooked this up between us? Why would we do that?"

"For all I know, Eric Berg put you up to this to convince me to take the case to trial. Then you convinced Doug you could help him, and here we sit."

I stared at him. "You don't seriously think that, do you?"

He looked at me steadily, and for a moment he seemed very

foreign. Then he shrugged and smiled. "No, I really don't think so. I'm just saying that the situation is quite complex, and even without an eyewitness we have serious obstacles to overcome. Norstad had motive, means, and opportunity, and what's more, he fled immediately after the crime was committed."

"So where does this leave us?"

Chan grinned again. "Well, the thing is, I'm ambitious too. I'm trying to build a business in this town. I know that people here generally sympathize with Norstad, and may like the guy who tries to defend him, whatever the odds. I'll represent his best interests, and I think right now, a plea bargain is the way to go. But as long as he insists on a trial, I'm willing to do that too. I probably come out ahead either way."

I devoted more serious consideration to my excellent sandwich while I thought things over.

"Alex," I said after a bit. "Could you represent me on a matter?"

His eyes brightened. "Sure," he said, "always happy to build that client base. What do you have in mind?"

"Well, I've been getting some threats lately," I said. "I'd like to get my affairs in order. Also, I've been developing a file. I'd like to have that in your keeping, to be opened only in the event of my death."

He looked at me steadily a moment.

"You're serious."

"I am," I said.

"Who has been threatening you? Have you contacted the police?"

"If I knew who, Doug Norstad may be a free man. They've

been telling me to stay away from the Norstad case, 'or else.'"

He thought for a moment. "That could help Doug too. You got any proof?"

"Of course not," I snapped. "The only proof I have of anything is stuff I can't use, or the cops can't use, or you can't use."

"Take it easy," he said. "Listen, Jonah, I think you should consider backing off of this thing. Your life isn't worth it."

"You saying I should let an innocent man spend his life in prison because I'm scared?"

Chan said nothing. We were starting to rehash old territory.

"Look, Alex," I said. "I'm not afraid to die. I have no unfinished business here. I have a lot more waiting for me after death than I do in this life. I'm not suicidal – I would prefer to live here until my proper time. But death doesn't intimidate me. I know someone who died for a guilty man. I'm not afraid to die for an innocent one."

He looked at me with thoughtful eyes. "I almost believe you."

"Doesn't matter whether you believe me or not. Can you help me set up my estate and hold that file?"

He nodded. "We can go back to my office after lunch and draw up the papers."

CHAPTER 36

After I was done with Alex Chan, I went back to my office to think for a while. I got myself a cup of decaf coffee and sat down in my chair. If I pushed it over to the corner of the room I could look out the window and just see a piece of the lake. I did so.

Who benefited from the framing of Doug Norstad?

Obviously, as everyone pointed out, Eric Berg, the Assistant DA, the man who would be a US representative, stood to gain from a public trial and a compassionate victory. A Democrat, he could claim to be tough on crime for prosecuting Norstad. But it was highly unlikely that he had pulled the trigger on Spooner. Berg was one of maybe two men in Grand Lake who did not hunt. He just didn't strike me as the coldblooded killer type.

I sipped some decaf. What if it wasn't Berg, but it was the political machinery surrounding him? Getting a US representative elected was no simple matter. Maybe the shady side of the election machine had shot Spooner and then framed Norstad. Their man Berg might not even know it was them. They just set him for publicity and victory. That could explain the thugs, who smelled a bit like organized crime.

Even so, the political-machinery option seemed a little farfetched. Berg wasn't exactly in trouble in the polls. It was a big risk for a gain that may not even have been necessary.

My phone rang and I ignored it. After a while it stopped. Who benefited from the framing of Doug Norstad?

I thought about Leyla for a while. Things were going well. She was back in Duluth, but we were definitely still an item. Maybe she'd like to have dinner in Two Harbors tonight. I reached for the phone.

Who benefited from the framing of Doug Norstad?

Doug's enemies. I pulled my hand back from the phone. Who were Norstad's enemies? I had no idea. Maybe he had none. I generally didn't.

I shook my head in irritation. The point was probably not to get at Doug. The obvious person who benefited from Doug's plight was the real killer. The benefit was that the real killer got to go free while Norstad took the rap. So the real question was: Who killed Daniel Spooner?

My Dad's police detective maxims came slowly back to me. The first one, which annoyed me, was that usually the obvious suspect was in fact the perpetrator. I dismissed that one. What were the main reasons for murder? Passion, revenge, or gain? A fit of passion often led to murder that was not premeditated. But obviously Spooner's murder was a coldblooded execution. Gain didn't fit, either. Spooner was a pathetic excuse for a man. I wondered briefly, however, if there was some way to check and see if he had life insurance, and who the beneficiary might be. Another motive was revenge or jealously. I couldn't imagine anyone being jealous of Daniel Spooner in any way. Revenge fit Doug Norstad as the murderer, but I knew it wasn't him. Even so, it seemed obvious that revenge was the motive. Spooner had been convicted of three other cases of child-rape before they found Melissa Norstad's bones on his property. Maybe a friend or relative of the other victims killed him. Maybe it was even one the former victims in person—Missy Norstad was the only one Spooner had killed. I doubted the police had looked into those options seriously once they had Norstad in hand.

I picked up the phone and called Alex Chan.

"Can you check and see if Daniel Spooner had any life insurance, and who the beneficiary is?"

"Don't you have a job or something?" said Chan.

"I only work for a half-hour a week," I said blandly. "And I'm single and I live alone. A man must have a hobby."

"Maybe you should take up something more constructive," said Chan. "Like arson."

"I can't take the heat," I said.

Chan sighed. "I guess it couldn't hurt to check into it. I would think the police already did, though."

"That's the spirit," I said. "But I wouldn't be so sure about the cops. Once they've got a prime suspect, they don't tend to waste resources checking out others."

"You're pretty serious about helping Doug Norstad."

I was quiet. "The fact is, I know he's innocent. He's sending himself to prison, I know, but he's put his trust in me to get him out of this without revealing his secret. I've got to do everything I can."

"So why don't *you* find out if Spooner had life insurance."

"My secretary is only part-time," I said. "And I lied about only working for half an hour a week. Besides, you're his attorney."

Chan grunted. "I'll check into it," he said.

CHAPTER 37

A week later, I secured Doug Norstad's freedom.

It was Wednesday, and I was at the church late. I filled in as the youth group leader for the evening, and then hung out and chatted. One of the things I loved about Harbor Lutheran was that nobody ever seemed in a big hurry to leave. They really seemed to like each other. Miracles still happen every day.

At 9:30 or so I drove up the hill to my cabin. As I swung into my driveway, the lights of the car raked the front door.

It was open.

I punched the garage door opener. I stopped the car outside the garage, because there was no room for it inside. The floor was covered with my stuff. Shelves had been pulled over, my workbench emptied and boxes strewn across the floor. It looked like the final battleground between two crazed elephants.

I shut off the engine and got out of the car, leaving the lights on. As I stood for a minute off to one side, I could hear nothing but the rapid cooling of engine in the northern night air. After a moment's thought, I killed the car lights and raced for the house. I reached the front door without incident, snaked my hand through the open space and flipped on the lights, immediately jerking my hand back and standing in the comparative shadow of the wall outside.

Nothing happened.

I knelt down, and then flattened myself on my belly and peered into my home. At first I couldn't tell what I was looking at, and then I realized that the elephants had saved their best work for the inside. I still heard nothing.

I stalked back down the front steps and down the slope and around the corner to the woodpile I kept underneath my deck. I groped for a long piece of pine and then went back to the front door. I entered like a mist drifting on the wind, stepping carefully over the wreckage of my living room. There was no one there.

Slipping like a wraith over to my kitchen, I eased open a cupboard and retrieved a flashlight. It was difficult to move quietly. The floor was almost completely covered with papers, books, smashed furniture, cushion stuffing, and junk I could not immediately identify. I moved carefully from room to room, first sticking my arm in with the flashlight, and then, receiving no response, flipping on the light and entering. Every room had been trashed, but there was no one in the house.

I turned on every light I had, inside and out, and went to check the perimeter. Whoever had done the deed was gone.

Returning to the living room, I noticed for the first time that there were bold letters sprayed in red across the glass of my patio doors. They said:

"Stay out of the Norstad case."

I found the same message, again, spray-painted in red on my bedroom wall.

Shakily, I returned to living room, kicked aside the detritus of my bookcase, turned my couch right-side up, and sat down. I felt violated. I felt scared and angry.

I searched in vain for my telephone. Finally, frustration

beginning to boil, I pulled out my cell phone and made the call that would ultimately spring Doug Norstad.

Leyla answered on the third ring. "Hello?" she said. But the way she said it told me she knew it was me, and she was glad.

"You knew it was me," I said.

"What if I didn't?" she said.

"I just hope you don't answer the phone that way for everyone."

"What, by saying hello?"

"Never mind," I said. "Do you want a scoop? I don't know, but I think it could be big time."

Her response surprised and pleased me. "Is that the only reason you called?"

"I talked to you just this afternoon, and twice yesterday," I said. "But my house has been trashed."

"What do you mean?"

"I mean someone came in and destroyed just about everything I own. The couch I'm sitting on is slashed to ribbons. My silverware is all over the floor. My pictures are smashed, my books scattered and torn. My computer monitor is smashed and there is some sort of liquid on the computer. My buck is on the floor with only one antler and my salmon trophy is ruined. I haven't even seen my trout yet."

"Oh, Jonah, I'm so sorry." All the banter was gone from her voice. "Are you okay? Are you safe?"

"I'm fine. I was gone when it happened. I mean, I'm not fine, but I'm okay physically."

"Do you want me to come up there?"

"Yes I would like that very much. But I think you should also bring a news truck."

"Jonah, this is terrible, and I'm so sorry it happened. But this stuff does happen sometimes. I mean, it's not really very much of a scoop. I want to come up there to be with you. I know it's important to you, but I'm not sure Channel 13 will send a crew just for senseless vandalism."

"They wrote on my door and in my bedroom: 'Stay Away from the Norstad case.'"

There was silence on the line.

"Don't you see?"

"Jonah, I can ask, but I'm still not sure that just mentioning . . ."

"Leyla," I said, "this all but proves he is innocent."

She was quiet again.

"This was a punishment and a warning. Why do this if they have nothing to hide? Something fishy is going on. If Norstad is really guilty, and they've got it sewn up, why warn me to stay away? It means I've touched a nerve somewhere."

"Okay," she said, "give me a minute to catch up." She paused again. "So this was not some random act of vandalism. This was a warning."

"Leyla," I said, I'm sorry I didn't tell you this, but it isn't my first warning. I was bribed and threatened before. Last week, three guys were here waiting for me, but I chased them off."

"You chased off three guys?"

"I had the aid of a fellow named Winchester."

"Who's he?"

"A twelve-gauge shotgun."

"Oh." There was a pause. "Jonah, why didn't you tell me all

this? We just had dinner two days ago."

"I know, I'm sorry. I don't know why. I guess maybe I just didn't want to worry you. I was handling it."

She made an exasperated sound on the other end. "Jonah, this really bothers me. What else are holding back?"

"Listen, Leyla, I'm sure you're right. There's probably something I've got to work on here, relationally. But I'm not really up to it right now. I'm sitting in the middle of a disaster area. This is ground zero. I promise you, we can talk about this subject. But are you open to doing it later?"

She sighed. "Okay, you're right, of course. And, of course, you're right about the news crew too. This could be big."

"In a way, I'd rather you could just come alone. But I know you'd get flak from your news manager if you didn't tell them this. And it could just set Doug Norstad free. If the whole world knows this is going on, they'll have to change their tactics."

"Is that a good thing? That they change tactics?"

"I don't know. I thought so. I haven't been making much headway until now. And if they change tactics, presumably they'll stop threatening me and ruining my stuff."

"Who are 'they,' anyway?"

I sighed. "I have no idea."

"Jonah, what about the police? Will they let us in?"

"I'm giving you an exclusive. I want you to take pictures and everything, before the cops even get here. You guys will just have to be careful not to leave fingerprints anywhere."

"Is that a good idea? Won't the cops be irritated?"

"I hope so," I said. "When those three guys ran off, I called the cops and got a sheriff's deputy called Burton. I don't think he even believed me. I'm not sure he even filed a report. He'll *have* to call the detective team in on this one if the media is already there."

"You have a devious mind, sweetheart."

"Wise as a serpent, but innocent as a dove," I said.

CHAPTER 38

Leyla must have broken the speed limit, because she got to my cabin within an hour and a half. She got out of her car and half ran over to where I stood at the front door. She hugged me, holding me tight for a moment.

"The news truck will be here in about half an hour. Are you okay?" she said.

"Getting better," I said. I kept my arm around her shoulders and steered her into the house.

"Oh, Jonah!"

I had to admit, it looked just as bad as it had two hours ago. It looked like a small bomb had exploded. My stereo was smashed beyond repair. Ashes from my wood stove were sprayed all over on top of the shattered remains of my possessions.

Leyla turned and hugged me again.

"Your beautiful cabin," she mumbled into my shoulder. When she pulled back I could see the tears in her eyes. Suddenly, she went very still. I followed the line of her gaze and saw that she was looking at the spray paint on my sliding glass doors.

"This is serious."

"Yes," I said, "it is. But it also helps us tremendously. This is going to cast serious doubt on the idea that Doug Norstad killed Daniel Spooner."

"How can you even think about stuff like that right now,

Jonah?"

"I've been sitting here for two hours. After a while you get tired of being upset and mad, and you find something else to think about."

She held my hand while we wandered through the wreckage. In my office she bent down and stroked the muzzle of my fourteen-point buck.

"Poor thing," she said.

"I'm the poor thing," I said. "Stroke me."

She stroked my nose. "Poor thing." She laughed, but there were tears in her eyes. "This is horrible," she said, wiping at her face.

The Channel 13 van arrived, as predicted, about a half an hour after Leyla. They maintained their professional decorum for the most part. But the cameraman turned to me when he first entered my front room.

"Man, this sucks," he said.

I agreed with him.

After they had been there less than ten minutes, a sheriff's car pulled into my drive, lights flashing.

A tall square man got out, leaving the lights on and flashing.

"Keep shooting," I said to Leyla and the news crew. "I'll handle this."

As I approached the officer, my suspicions were confirmed. It was Rex Burton. My lucky night.

"What's going on here?" said Burton.

"What's going on is you are on my private property without my invitation, and, I bet, without a search warrant." I couldn't help it. He brought out the worst in me. "You want a better answer than that, start by turning off those lights and using a bit of common courtesy."

"What's the news truck for?"

"Deputy Burton, they are probably filming us right now. But the fact is, it is none of your business. Yet. You are on private property."

Burton was trying to see into my house. I stood right in front of him.

"Don't you ever take a day off? What kind of hours are you putting in anyway?"

He took a step back. "As it happens, I was just driving home, and I saw some activity going on here. I thought I'd check it out, since you seem to have had some trouble lately." His tone and body language mellowed me. A little, anyway.

"All right, the fact is, I did have some trouble. It's all over now. As soon as the news crew is done, you can take a look."

"Look at what? What happened in there?" He started to push past me. I moved in front of him again, and he bumped into me.

"Get out of my way," he grated.

"Get off my property," I said.

"I think you might be interfering in a police investigation," he said.

"I think you might be the most irritating excuse for a human being I've met," I said.

He punched me in the solar plexus. It was a fast, hard punch, and I doubled over, unable to breathe. As I folded my body, he shoved me to the ground and walked up to my open front door.

While I gasped for breath I heard him barking angrily at Leyla and camera crew. I staggered to my feet and tottered over to the door.

"I said turn that thing off!" Burton shouted at the cameraman. His voice shook with rage.

"Is it true that Pastor Borden has been threatened before and the sheriff's department did nothing?" said Leyla quickly, sticking her microphone into Burton's face.

Still recovering from getting the wind knocked out of me, I thought for a hazy moment that he was going to hit Leyla too. He was almost out of control.

"Yeah, Burton," I wheezed from my place at the doorway, "why don't you tell the nice lady all about it."

For just a moment everything was silent while Burton teetered on the edge of a homicidal rampage. Everyone was quiet. He literally shuddered with the physical effort, and then turned back to the news crew.

"Listen, folks," he said, voice still trembling with the effort of suppressing his anger. "This is now officially a crime scene. You folks are stomping all over the evidence and tainting it." He took a deep breath, and the dangerous rage was gone as if it had never existed. "I appreciate your interest in what is going on here. The people have a right to know. But right now, in the interest of justice, you are going to have to step outside this house and stay next to your truck." He breathed in again and then he was locked down, expressionless, once again the hyper-typical cop. "I could lock you folks up for obstructing justice, but I'm not going to do that unless you continue to interfere. Now move!"

Reluctantly, the crew got their stuff together while Burton went back to his patrol car to call for an investigative team.

Leyla didn't seem to notice that I wasn't standing quite straight as I walked her over to her car.

"Did you get enough?" I asked.

"I think so," she said. She was speaking to the others at the same time. "We got some good shots of the mess, and some clear pictures of the spray-painted message. We're exclusive too, so all in all, I think we're in good shape.

She turned to me. "I think we've got our work cut out for us for a while. I'm sure we'll be in Grand Lake for a few days. Right now, I've got to do some voice-over and then a closing segment. I don't think we'll go live at this time of night, but you never know."

"I'm not going anywhere," I said wearily. She reached up and hugged me quickly, and then turned back to her coworkers.

They all appeared to be discussing things and writing them down. I heard Leyla say, "That's true," and she turned back to me.

"Jonah, could we interview you before the rest of the police come? Once they get here, I'm sure they'll want to talk to you."

"Okay," I said.

I wondered for a moment why Burton wasn't interrogating me. I didn't know enough about police procedure to be sure he should do that or not. I supposed that this time, with the detectives called in, they would interview me.

Leyla smiled at me and touched my face. "I know you've already told me everything, but the cameras haven't heard it, so I'm going to act as if I don't know anything, okay?"

"All right," I said. Everyone but me seemed to know what to do and what was going on. I felt vaguely helpless.

With some effort, I pulled myself together to appear collected and professional as I answered Leyla's questions and told the story of coming home to the vandalized house. I wondered whimsically if this would be good press for the church.

I began to remember the silver lining, that this would be sure to put pressure on the DA to consider other angles to the Daniel Spooner slaying. I tried to put some of that into the interview.

"Do you have any idea who might have done this?" said Leyla, for the sake of the camera.

"Not specifically," I said. "But you saw the spray painting. I've been doing a little investigating lately, because I know that Doug Norstad is innocent."

Leyla took over for a second. "Of course, everyone is considered innocent until proven guilty. But why do you think the police have the wrong man in the Daniel Spooner killing?"

"Doug Norstad told me something in confidence, as his pastor. I am bound, as his pastor, to keep it confidential, and the law cannot compel me to reveal it. But what he told me proves he is innocent."

"And you've been trying to prove him innocent without revealing this thing?"

"Yes. Anyway, somewhere in the poking around I've done, I've touched a nerve. I think someone wants this case to simply be done and go away."

"Who do you think would want you to stop looking into this?"

"Of course I can't name names, and I really couldn't say for sure anyway. But obviously, if Doug Norstad is convicted, then whoever actually killed Daniel Spooner gets to go free."

"So you are saying that the person who vandalized your home is the same one who killed Daniel Spooner and now wants to make sure that Doug Norstad is framed for the crime?"

"That seems a likely possibility anyway."

She continued to question me for a few more minutes, and then the producer called "Cut."

"I thought they only did that in the movies," I said.

The producer smiled at me. "Nope. This is real life."

The sheriff's department detectives arrived not long after that. They spent a long time looking around, while the Channel 13 team finished and packed up.

Leyla came and gave me hug.

"We're going to get going now," she said. "Call me in the morning."

~

My luck was running true to form. The lead detective was Tony Grantz, blood brother in spirit to Rex Burton. I wondered idly if they'd known each other in Chicago and taken lessons together on how to deal with pastors.

"So you say your house was just like this when you came home," said Grantz.

I was tired and didn't like him any better than Burton. "Is that a question?" I asked.

"Look, Borden," he said. "I don't like your style. I think you're arrogant, and you abuse the fact that you are a big fish in a small pond. But your buddy Jensen isn't here to protect you. You've got to deal with me, and if I don't like what you say, things will get very unpleasant for you. *Comprende?*"

"What was that last word?" I said admiringly. "That was like a whole 'nother language."

"You want to do this the easy way or the hard way?" he grated. As in my previous encounter, Tony Grantz seemed to be playing "bad cop" for an imaginary camera.

I figured he was too absorbed with himself to benefit from any more needling. But I was still irritated. "Detective Grantz," I said, "I respect your position here. But I am not the suspect. I am the victim."

"I will be the judge of that," said Grantz.

"Fine," I snapped. "I came home, trashed my own place, and called in a news crew. I'm gonna collect big-time insurance money from my ruined deer trophy. I'm also hoping I can go to jail. I intend to press charges against myself."

"Is that your statement?" asked Grantz relentlessly.

"No, it's not my statement!" I took a depth breath and said, more quietly, "That, in certain circles, is known as sarcasm. Do you want my real statement?"

"Whenever you are ready."

I gained enough self-control to start at the beginning and tell Grantz what happened. My eyes were starting to feel gummy and red. Grantz asked several questions, and repeated a few of them.

"Anything missing?" he said, after he was sure he understood how the news crew happened to be there.

I stared at him. "I have no idea," I said. "Have you seen that place?"

"Yes, I have seen it." Fifteen years ago Grantz would have been a cigarette smoker. It would have greatly enhanced his big-screen cop image. As it was, he pulled a toothpick from his shirt pocket and began to chew on it.

"Those things'll kill you," I said. He didn't laugh.

"So you don't know if anything is missing."

"That's correct."

"Did you see anyone?"

"No."

"Did you see anything suspicious?"

"Apart from the fact that my house looks like it's been pillaged by Vikings?"

Grantz chewed on his toothpick, waiting.

I sighed. "No, nothing suspicious—other than the trashed house."

Grantz kept at it for another hour or so. Finally he snapped his notebook shut. I'm gonna have a statement typed up, and then you'll need to sign it."

"Okay," I said.

"Tell you what," he said. "I'll bring the statement by later on this morning, and you can sign it then."

"Okay, thanks," I said. I was feeling bleary.

Gradually, everyone left. I went to the bathroom, but my toothbrush was floating in the toilet. I went back to living room, brushed my hand futility at the mess on the couch, and then laid down. I fell asleep almost immediately.

~

I was awakened by the blare of a horn, and then the brief blast of a siren. It was still dark outside. I got up, wondering vaguely where I was. I tripped on some of the junk lying on my floor. Muttering curses acceptable to my profession, I made my way to the light switch and then the door. Tony Grantz stood there.

"Here's your statement," he said, without preamble.

"I thought you said you'd come by later this morning," I said.

"It is later," he said. "It's almost 5:30."

I could see the eastern sky just blushing gray with the first light of dawn.

"Sign this," he said, thrusting the statement on its clipboard toward me.

My mind was not working well. I tried to read it, but my porch light must have been broken by the vandals. "I can't see it," I said.

He poked a space near the bottom of the page. "Right there," he said. "Doesn't matter exactly where."

I signed, my mind still fuzzy with exhaustion. Grantz took the clipboard, shuffled papers, and pushed it back at me. "This one next."

"Everything in triplicate for the government," I grunted.

"There is a reason for these procedures," he said stiffly.

"Gives paper-pushers something to do," I said.

He gave me three more papers to sign. I just wanted to go back to sleep. Finally, he was done.

"You look tired," said Grantz. "Get some sleep."

They were the sweetest words anyone had ever said to me. I began to think Tony Grantz might be human after all.

CHAPTER 39

When I awoke, it was almost ten. I looked sourly at my messed up house. There really wasn't any way to cook breakfast without doing an hour's worth of cleaning first. I shuffled through the mess to my bedroom and picked up some clothes from the floor. I showered and shaved. I pulled on a pair of blue jeans, a long-sleeved t-shirt, and a blue polar fleece. While I was lacing my hiking boots, the phone rang.

I shoveled through my scattered possessions and found the handset about two seconds after it rang for the last time. Caller ID told me it was the church. I selected the number and the phone dialed it back.

"Good morning, Harbor Lutheran," said Julie.

"Julie, it's Jonah," I said.

"Jonah!" she exclaimed. "Listen, I know we joke about how I have to remind you of everything, but this is serious. Do you even realize that you missed the men's breakfast?"

"Oh, shoot. No, I forgot."

"Seriously, Jonah, you've got to do something. I'm only part-time here."

"Julie," I said, cutting off the coming tirade. "My house was broken into last night. They trashed everything."

There was a brief silence. "What do you mean?"

"I mean, when you called just a minute ago, I couldn't find the phone until I'd moved three broken plates and a pile of books. The place looks like a bomb went off. They sprayed graffiti on my sliding glass doors and on the mirror in my bathroom."

"What? They trashed your house? Who? This is Grand Lake, not the Twin Cities!" Julie's outrage was immediately transferred to the crime.

"I don't know who yet," I said. "I was up until about three with the police, and again at 5:30 this morning. That's why I forgot the men's breakfast."

"I'm sorry, Jonah. Forget about the breakfast—again. I'll cancel all your appointments."

"Thanks. I appreciate it. Maybe you could let some of the guys know why I didn't show this morning."

"Of course. Is there anything else I can do?"

"I can't think of anything right now," I said.

After we hung up I drove into town and went to Lorraine's.

After I had been seated, Lorraine herself came out of the kitchen with a fresh carafe of coffee, which she placed in front of me with a white porcelain mug.

"Drink up," she said. "Everything's on the house this morning."

I looked up at her.

"I saw it on the news this morning. Your girlfriend did a good job."

"Thanks," I said. I looked at the pot of coffee. I looked back at Lorraine. "Thanks."

She patted my shoulder. "It's the least I could do. You enjoy, hear? Order the whole menu if you want."

"Superior Skillet will do," I said.

"Coming right up," she said.

The first cup of coffee went down smooth. It always did. The second and third went down with the skillet. I took my time, enjoying every sip and bite. When I was done eating, I poured a fourth cup of coffee and pulled out my cell phone.

"Hey, how are you?" said Leyla after I dialed.

"I guess as well as I could expect," I said. "I heard you made the morning show."

"Yeah. We scooped—thanks to you. All the other stations are in town already, but we have the inside track. It will be the lead story tonight."

"Any chance you can get away this morning?"

"Oh, Jonah," she said, "I'm so sorry, but I can't. We've got a ton of work to do before we hit the air tonight." She paused. "I might need to interview you again, though. We'd have a few minutes then."

"Whatever," I said. "You know where I live."

"Jonah!"

"Sorry. I'll snap out of it. Just call my cell if you need another interview. I'll probably head back to my house soon to start cleaning up."

"Okay. I'm sorry, Jonah, I know this really stinks."

"You know, it does," I said. "But it could be a lot worse."

Maybe it's a good thing I didn't know at the time that my words were prophetic.

CHAPTER 40

My driveway was a circus. There were three news vans at the side of the road, and a gaggle of cameras and reporters. When I pulled in, I found several cars and trucks parked near my house. I started to get upset. I left my car near the beginning of the drive, which ran through the trees. It was an effective roadblock keeping vehicles both in and out. I ignored the shouting reporters and walked down to my cabin.

Nine or ten people were inside, mostly men but one or two women. I was expecting more reporters or the police, but after a moment I realized with a shock that they were all members of Harbor Lutheran.

They were cleaning my house.

The Olsens were there, along with their grinning home-schooled kids. Mike Slade was there too, and all three elders. Every member of this morning's aborted men's breakfast was there. In the middle of my living room, directing what looked like an amphibious landing under-fire, was Julie. She saw me and grinned impudently.

I opened my mouth, but nothing came out.

She walked over to me and patted me on the cheek. "You're welcome," she said.

I shook my head. I felt some dangerous moisture in the region near my eyes. I coughed. "You guys are awesome," I said. My voice didn't sound quite right.

"You came back too soon," said Julie, taking my arm. She steered me out to the deck and to one of my log-style Adirondack chairs. "Sit," she ordered. "We'll take care of the mess."

I started to protest, but she said, "Jonah, they want to do this for you. *We* want to do this for you. Don't spoil it. Sit here and think or read or drink coffee. Or better yet, go fishing. When you come back, this place will look brand new."

"Are you sure?" I said. I felt sort of stupid and mean saying it. Julie didn't seem to mind.

"We're sure," said Slade, who had come up behind us. "Go fishing, will ya? You might need to replace that trophy trout you had. Might as well get started on it right now."

I went to the garage where two or three men from church were making significant progress on the mess. After greeting and thanking them, I said:

"Did they mess with my fishing gear?"

"Fly rod's snapped," said Dave Shearer, one the church elders. "Sorry about that, Pastor."

"You didn't do it," I said.

Another elder, John Rothberg, held up my neoprene waders. They'd been slashed to ribbons.

"Somebody really doesn't like me," I said.

After we'd searched a bit, we found my main light-tackle graphite rod, none the worse for wear. My vest, with all its lures and tools, was buried under a puddle of foam from a shredded lifejacket, but otherwise it was fine.

I decided to stop at Gander Mountain in Hermantown on my way down to the Tamarack and get some waders. After more thanks and several cheerful admonitions to get out of there, I shut off my cell phone and went fishing.

~

When I got home that night, it was all Julie had promised and more. The cabin was perfectly clean. There was a note from Julie on the table. They had been forced to throw a lot of broken stuff away. There was no sign of my trophy trout. The trophy buck was also gone. But there was new crockery in the kitchen. The spray paint was gone. Everything had been vacuumed, swept, and dusted. I had a new brown leather couch and two new matching chairs. I wandered from room to room and found everything clean, neat and fresh as could be. They had found some of my pictures ruined, and placed them in a cardboard box for me. There was a brand-new laptop computer sitting on my desk.

I opened the fridge—it was completely stocked. I found a chicken breast and threw it into a Ziploc bag with garlic and white wine to marinate. Then I went out on my deck and started my grill. There were fresh greens, and I wasted no time making a salad. I checked the fridge again. To my delight and wonder, there was a six-pack of Woodchuck's Hard Apple Cider. I took out a bottle and sipped it while I threw the chicken on the grill. I went back into my kitchen and made some angel-hair pasta. When the chicken was done, I cut it into chunks and tossed it with the pasta, some butter, garlic and Parmesan cheese. Add the salad, and voila—a perfect meal after a day fishing. Life felt almost normal again.

CHAPTER 41

I didn't check my cell phone until the next morning. I felt badly when I found I had three messages from Leyla.

"Jonah," she said on the first message, "it's me. I'm sorry I couldn't see you earlier. Now I feel bad asking, but we would like to interview you this afternoon if that's all right. Talk to you soon, bye."

The second message was more perfunctory. "Hi, Jonah, it's Leyla. Just checking to see if we could do the interview today."

Listening to the first two messages, I started to feel a sense of distance. Was I just another story to her? She seemed so busy and professional. There was no question that we had hit it off, but the fact that I was also part of her work seemed to make our relationship a bit complicated. I didn't really want that sort of complication.

The third message was a bit better.

"Jonah, are you okay? I haven't heard from you all day, and I'm worried. Just call me, will you?"

I called her. She answered on the second ring. "Hey," I said, "it's me."

"Are you all right?" she asked. The concern seemed genuine. "I couldn't get a hold of you yesterday, and I started to worry that something else had happened."

"I went fishing. Some people from Harbor came over and

cleaned up my house, and they told me to get out of the way. So I went down to the Tamarack." My tone didn't sound quite right, even to me.

"Jonah, are you upset at me for something?"

I thought for a moment. "I don't think so. But I think we should talk about a few things."

"You mean, like why I couldn't find the time to get together with you personally but wanted to interview you?"

"Well, maybe. Something like that."

"Why don't we have lunch?"

"No cameras," I said.

"I didn't deserve that."

"No," I said, "you're right. You didn't. I'm sorry."

"Noon?"

"Noon is good."

I brought the new laptop into my living room and sat in the sun, working on my sermon. At 11:30 I shut it down, got my car keys and drove into town. We met at the coffee shop on the waterfront.

After we got our food, Leyla reached over and touched me on the arm.

"I'm sorry, Jonah."

I shook my head. "No, it's just me being a little sensitive, that's all. I've had a rough few days, and maybe I'm taking it out on you. You were just doing your job."

"Actually, the point is, I'm *not* just doing my job. But it is a little awkward that part of my job right now involves you."

I nodded and ate some of my smoked turkey panini.

Leyla took a sip of Coke and put her cup down. "The truth is, you've probably sensed a little distance in me. I need to tell you, I had a hard time finding out that you'd been pursuing this thing, and been threatened twice, and never told me about it."

"Why was that?" I asked.

"I never told you why I broke up with the guy in Omaha." She took a man-sized bite of her Caesar salad. "I found out I couldn't trust him. He was lying to me."

"He was secretly being threatened while trying to clear an innocent man too?"

She was quiet for a minute, looking out the window.

"Sorry," I said. "Bad timing. Humor is all about timing. Mine is impeccable, but everyone else is a little off lately, which makes it seem like mine is bad."

A smile tugged at the corners of her mouth, and then she clamped it down. "I don't know whether to slap you or laugh out loud," she said.

"Both are probably appropriate. I would prefer to eschew the slap, however."

"Eschew?"

"Hey, I have a master's degree," I said.

She shook her head and the smile was there for real now, though it was sheepish and reluctant.

"Tell me about Omaha," I said. "I really want to know. Sorry about the wisecracks."

She took a deep breath. Maybe it was to control her exasperation with me. On the other hand, maybe it was my cologne.

"It turned out he was a gambler. He had a real problem. He *was* threatened. He was even beaten up once. He wasn't hurt seriously, but it was terrifying."

"So what happened?"

"He promised to get help for his addiction. He did too, for about three months. Then I caught him stealing from me to support his habit. We had a fight—the last of many. I broke it off."

"So when you heard I had been threatened, it brought back a bunch of those feelings for you."

Her eyes brimmed with tears and she nodded. I have often reflected, with awe, on how quickly the female tear ducts can fill.

My eyes caught hers and held them. "I'm sorry that happened to you back then, Leyla. It's not happening right now."

She nodded again and reached for a napkin.

"I know." She sniffed.

"Listen," I said. "I'm not sure what I got into with this Doug Norstad thing. I thought it was just a straightforward case of the police getting the wrong guy, and the DA being stubborn about it. And maybe it was. But there are some kind of rough people involved in trying to keep the lid on it."

I took a sip of coffee, and Leyla waited.

"My point is, I'm not involved in anything you don't already know about. I'm surprised that I got the reaction I did while I was trying to prove Doug was innocent. I'm still not sure what that was all about. But it wasn't about secret gambling debts or drugs or anything other than the Norstad thing."

She smiled at me and repaired the imaginary damage the tears had done to her flawless face. "Thanks, Jonah," she said. She touched my cheek with her hand.

"Anyway," I said, "it's all over now. Doug will get out soon and that will be the end of it."

She nodded. "That's good to know," she said.

CHAPTER 42

That afternoon, Doug Norstad was released from prison. Assistant District Attorney Eric Berg was strangely absent from in front of the TV cameras. He sent an underling out with a prepared statement to the effect that the prosecutor's office had revised its assessment of the case, and Mr. Norstad was no longer a suspect. Other leads were being pursued.

I picked up Lucy Norstad and drove her into town to get Doug. We went into the new county jail. Alex Chan was there at a counter with Doug, who was back in his street clothes. As we walked out into the public area of the building, we were mobbed by reporters.

"Here's your chance," I said to Alex through the noise.

He gave me a tight grin. "You better believe it."

I quickly hustled the Norstads into the Volkswagen while Chan ran interference for us. As I drove past, it looked like he was making the most of his day in the sun.

"I was going to take you out for dinner," I said to Doug and Lucy, "but after that mob back there, I'm thinking maybe it's not such a good idea."

"Aren't you seeing one of those reporters?" said Lucy. Her eyes were cautiously alive, and she clung to Doug's arm in the back seat of the Jetta.

I rubbed my chin with one hand and hesitated. "That's right," I said finally. "She's a good one, though. I'm not sure we could have gotten Doug out without her help."

"You've done so much for us, Pastor," said Doug. He looked kind of like a fish that had just been landed. "I don't know how to thank you."

"I couldn't have let a man I knew to be innocent sit in jail any longer than it took," I said. I thought maybe I sounded a bit pompous. "Anyway, what else did I have to do with my spare time?"

"But you believed him, Pastor," said Lucy. "I wasn't even sure I believed he was innocent sometimes. Heaven knows, I am still glad that man is dead."

I thought it would be prudent not to mention that I had checked Doug's story before I really believed him. And obviously Lucy still did not know her husband's true alibi. I changed the subject.

"Well, I'll have time to get back to fishing again now," I said.

The Norstads were happy to be home, and I was happy to go back to my own. Leyla came over for supper, and that made the evening a smashing success.

On Sunday, in spite of my crazy week, I managed to pitch a pretty good game, and a record low of three people fell asleep. The Norstads were there, and so the church was surrounded by a cordon of reporters. I noted that Leyla was the only one of them who had the courtesy to come in and participate in the worship service. When a pastor becomes jaded about his fellow man, where can the world turn? Nowhere, I decided. Therefore, I badly needed to go fishing in order to straighten myself out.

After church and after she had talked with the Norstads, Leyla came and found me straightening up my office.

"I guess I won't need to be coming up to Grand Lake and

staying here all the time now," she said.

"Not for work anyway," I said.

To my astonished pleasure, she blushed. Very prettily too.

"Well, anyway, I know it wouldn't look right for me to stay with you, and hotels could get expensive."

I looked at her closely. "What are you saying, Leyla?" I asked.

She saw my face and quickly hugged me. "Oh, not that, Jonah. I'm actually happy to get all these professional complications out of our relationship. What I was trying to tell you is that the Norstads have offered me the use of one of their little resort cabins more or less permanently. I have a place to stay here, as often as I like."

I felt my face grinning foolishly. "Well now, that is something." We stood there, both a little embarrassed for some reason. "So you want to have dinner tomorrow in Duluth?"

"In Duluth?"

"Yeah. I'm going fishing over in Wisconsin tomorrow. Can I pick you up at seven?"

"May I ask where you are taking me?"

"The rotating restaurant at the top of the Radisson."

"It's a date," she said.

With everything thus satisfactory I went home to a perfectly lazy Sunday afternoon. A bottle of Woodchuck's, the lazy buzz of afternoon baseball, and homemade spinach pie for supper.

The next morning, by the time the sun began to melt the edge of the blue Superior horizon into gold, I was headed down 61 toward a foretaste of heaven in the form of the Tamarack River. I had seen not a soul on the road. I took a bite of glazed donut, sipped some coffee, and glanced into my rearview mirror.

A police car, probably a sheriff's vehicle, was suddenly on my tail, about half a mile back. I kept driving, as always at about five miles over the speed limit. I finished my donut. When I was almost done with the coffee, I checked to see if the car was still there. It was. Probably my friend Rex Burton. In other generations, Officer R. Burton might have been ribbed a little bit about his Hollywood sound-alike name. *Rex Burton, Richard Burton.* I finished the coffee and reflected that no matter what generation he was in, Rex would not see connection, nor the humor, in any sort of nickname based on that.

A nickname like Hollywood.

I stopped the swerving of my car just in time. My hands felt shaky and cold on the wheel. It all fit too well. Rex Burton—who could resist calling that most un-Richard-Burton-like block of wood 'Hollywood?' It must be.

I looked up. The car was still behind me. The county line was coming up soon, and then we would see. While I waited for the sign that told me I was leaving the county, I tried to think it all through. So what if Burton was indeed Hollywood? The whole thing was over now.

Technically, Daniel Spooner was in Grand Lake police custody when he was transferred from the jail to the courthouse. Even so the sheriff's department had probably been madder than an Idaho liberal when someone took him out. Burton was probably tagged with the job of making sure that everything went smoothly and ensuring that once they had the perpetrator, they nailed the whole thing down airtight. Not a bad sentiment—they just had the wrong perp.

So why was he following me? *If* he was following me? Was

Burton angry because I had screwed everything up for the sheriff's department? Was he trying to get even?

Well, let him try. I was full of coffee and sugar. He wouldn't sucker-punch me again, that was for sure.

At the county line, the police car didn't turn back. It followed me all the way down 61, through Duluth, across the bridge and out onto 13 toward Bayfield. It turned left with me toward the lake and trailed me until I turned into a parking area near the Tamarack. I whipped in quickly so I could be out of the car before Burton was, but as I opened the door and jumped out, the police car slid sedately past without even slowing down. I couldn't see the driver.

After waiting for about twenty minutes and seeing nothing, I decided not to let it ruin the perfectly good day I had waiting for me. I slipped into my new waders and went trout fishing.

CHAPTER 43

I wrapped up an entirely satisfactory day fishing. Man: fifteen. Fish: zero. The fish always scored zero, somehow. Largest size, 20 inches. It was a sporting day, however, so all of the fish lived—the 20-incher wasn't fat enough to mount.

It was 5:30 by the time I pulled myself out of the river and up to my car. I stripped off my waders and stood for a moment, basking in the evening sunshine of the northern summer. Life was good. A perfect day was about to be topped by an enchanting evening with a gorgeous, fun, caring woman. Surely, fish and women were proof that God exists, and loves man.

I stood at the edge of the woods, looking down into the gorge of the Tamarack while I called Leyla on my cell.

"Hey," I said, when she answered, "Can I shower and change at your place before we go out?"

"Oh, Jonah!" she said. This wasn't exactly the response I had been expecting. "Where have you been? There's been another shooting in Grand Lake!"

"What do you mean?" I asked. It's a stupid question, but it's hard to avoid sometimes.

"Another criminal, an accused rapist named James Post, was shot between the jail and courthouse. The same methods were used as with Daniel Spooner."

My head whirled. Was I wrong about Norstad, after all?

"When did this happen?" I asked

"Same time as before, just about lunch time."

"Did they get the perp this time?" Somehow I knew the answer before she said it.

"Not yet, Jonah. I'm up in Grand Lake right now. This story just won't quit."

"What about Doug Norstad? Please tell me they don't think it was him."

"He was in the grocery store when the shots were fired. At least a dozen people saw him. He's clear."

I breathed a deep sigh of relief. "Thank goodness. I mean, it's a terrible thing, but at least that's over." A gull swept over my head and landed next to my car. It hopped toward me beseechingly. "Do they have any other suspects this time?" I asked.

"I think so, but they aren't talking much. I'm sure Berg wants to move on this as fast as he can, though, or it's going to be extremely embarrassing for him."

"It already is."

"Yeah, but more so."

The gull hopped closer. I shooed it away with my hand, and it flew up and landed a few yards further away. Persistent bugger. "So," I said, "I take it we aren't doing dinner at the Radisson tonight."

"No, I'm sorry, I'm staying in Grand Lake tonight. If nothing new develops on the story, we could grab a bite together when you get home."

"All right," I said. "Are you staying at the Norstads?"

"Yes. I have a beautiful little cabin on the point with a deck and a grill and a fireplace and a kitchenette."

"Well, I'll call you when I get home and cleaned up, and we'll see what's going on then," I said.

"Okay," she said. "Jonah?"

"Yeah?"

"At least this is just work. I mean, now you aren't involved in any way. That makes it easier."

"I guess so," I said.

~

So, no fancy dinner, and Grand Lake buzzing again with news, but other than that, there wasn't much to spoil the evening. I settled in to the two-hour drive with Marc Cohn. After I was past Duluth, it was a bit of classic Elton John, some America, and even a few Abba songs. I came in to Grand Lake with David Wilcox, feeling peaceful and mellow.

On the climb up the ridge to my place, a police car slipped into place behind me. It seemed a bit significant, after the car that morning, but Wilcox had me settled and centered, and I gave it no thought. But when I turned into my driveway, the cop car pulled in after me. It stopped in the narrow part of the drive between the trees, effectively blocking the way. Another police vehicle was parked in front of my house. I punched the garage-door opener and the garage door began to close. That meant it had been open. I punched it again to stop the door, and once more to re-open it, and pulled in. The cop in the car that had followed me got out. I had seen him around town but I didn't know his name. The other one by the house got out too. Inevitably, it was Richard Burton.

I sighed. "What can I do for you guys?" I said. Sometimes I wished I wasn't a pastor so I could be less polite.

"Where were you at approximately twelve-noon today?" asked

Burton.

"You know very well where I was," I said. "You followed me there early this morning."

Burton's face was, as always, expressionless. The other sheriff's deputy said, "Deputy Burton was on duty all day. He's been here."

"I was fishing," I said. "And a Lake County sheriff's car followed me from Grand Lake all the way to the Tamarack in Wisconsin."

Burton and the other cop exchanged a look. I couldn't decipher it.

"Did you get the number of the sheriff's car?" asked the other officer. He moved closer and I could see his little gold nameplate said "Neal."

"No," I said.

"Are you sure it was a Lake County car?"

"It followed me from here," I said.

"But did you see the writing? Was it from Lake County?"

"I never saw the writing clearly. It looked like one of your cars."

Neal shrugged. Burton didn't so much as twitch.

"We'll check it out," said Officer Neal to Burton.

Neal turned back to me. "Did you fish all day?"

"Yes," I said.

"Was anyone with you?" Burton seemed content to let Neal do the talking.

"No. What's this about, anyway?"

Burton finally spoke. "Jonah Borden, you are under arrest for the murders of James Post and Daniel Spooner."

"I know you don't like me—Hollywood," I began. Burton's face registered no expression at the nickname. "But you are several sandwiches short of a picnic."

Neal shrugged and recited my Miranda rights while Burton cuffed me. I desperately wanted to resist, or at least spit in his face, but I knew that would only make him feel he had won. I submitted quietly.

"I haven't eaten yet," I said.

"My heart bleeds for you, Father," said Burton. He put his hand on my head to make me duck as he helped me into his car.

On the ride down to the county jail I had no idea what to say. I leaned back and prayed.

At the jail they took me through an externally controlled locking door into a little hallway with another such door on the other end. One wall was thick, wire-reinforced glass. Behind the glass sat a woman in uniform. She operated the door we had come through and it slid slowly shut with a very loud click. She waited almost thirty seconds and then the door on the other side slowly slid open.

We walked into a sort of reception area, almost like an admissions center at a hospital. To my right there was a long counter, almost chest-high, with several people sitting on tall stools behind it. After about thirty feet the counter dropped to hip-height and became indented with little booth-like sections, each of which held a chair on my side of the barrier. To my left were several very secure looking doors, each equipped with a tall narrow window.

Holding my arm, Burton took me to the tall counter, while Neal walked past the whole thing and turned a corner to the left, out of my sight.

Burton snapped the cuffs off my wrists, but stood very close to me. "Empty your pockets," he said. His voice was impassive.

I pulled out my car keys, my clasp knife with the locking blade that I carry when I fish, and my wallet. I also found a gas station receipt. I realized I had left my cell phone in my car at home.

A uniformed lady behind the counter pushed forward a small tray, and I put my things into it. She pulled the tray back towards her and began writing on a small pad attached to a clipboard, occasionally glancing at the tray while she wrote.

She pushed the clipboard toward me. "Sign here, please," she said.

"What am I signing?"

"Your confession, Father," said Burton.

I looked at the sheet.

"You are acknowledging that these are the things we are taking from you, what you arrived with. You'll get them back when you are released," said the woman behind the counter.

"Don't count on getting released, Father," said Burton.

The lady gave him a sharp glance, but said nothing. She looked at me. "Large, I guess," she said. She bent down behind the counter and came up with a small orange bundle. She handed it to Burton. He took my arm and led me to one of the doors in the left-hand, painted, block wall. He glanced back at the counter and waved. There was a loud click and the door opened. He shoved the bundle at me.

"Take your clothes off and put this on," he said, and gave me a little shove into the room.

It was small, maybe ten by eight. The walls were smooth painted cement, and there was a bench on the right, in front of the little window in the door. There was a security-style camera in the upper left-hand corner.

I sat down on the bench and put the bundle beside me. I leaned my head back against the wall. What in the blue planet was happening? How could they possibly suspect me for murder? How could they even expect to make it stick long enough to hold me?

And then, suddenly, I remembered why they could.

A speaker crackled somewhere. "Sir?" said a man's voice in my room. "Sir, you need to change into the jumpsuit."

I jumped in surprise. Glancing out the thin window, I couldn't see anyone observing me.

"I can see you through the camera," said the voice. "Please change into the jumpsuit. Now."

"Close your eyes then," I said. "I'm modest." There was no response. Maybe the camera didn't include a microphone.

Self-consciously glancing at the camera, I moved away from the window and pulled off my sweatshirt, shirt, jeans, and my fishing long-johns. I kept my underwear on, and slipped into the blaze-orange jumpsuit. I felt like a criminal in pajamas. There was a pair of light plastic slippers, sort of like Crocs, that came with the jail uniform. They didn't fit. I folded my clothes neatly and sat down on the bench again.

I began to wonder how much they knew, and how they had found out. I thought the matter had been closed and locked away. It didn't matter, though. Things would be confusing and difficult in the short run, but eventually they would get sorted out.

The door snapped open and a new officer came in. Grand Lake wasn't all that big, and I knew this one. He had cousins who came to Harbor Lutheran. His name was Tim Lane.

"Hey, Tim," I said.

Tim looked embarrassed.

"Sorry about this, Pastor Borden," he said.

"Hey, you're just doing your job," I said. "They'll sort out this mess eventually, and then we'll laugh about it."

"I hope so," said Tim. He didn't look convinced.

Tim had me stand up, and he cuffed my hands together again, in front of me.

"I guess we don't need to hobble you," he said.

"I won't run, I promise," I said.

He shrugged nervously and led me to one of the booths in the reception area. He helped me into an uncomfortable chair. On the other side of the counter was a middle-aged man with a smooth face and silver hair.

"I'm Officer Fuller," he said. "I'll be checking you in." I knew his face from around town, but I'd never met him. Fuller asked me a long string of very personal questions, filling in various forms as I answered. He then went through a detailed list of procedures and explanations. My head was on overload by the time he was done. It was almost nine at night and I was ragingly hungry. Fuller pressed a button off to the side of his booth and shortly Tim reappeared.

He helped me up, and led me along the reception area and then to the right, into the main cellblock of the jail. An imperceptible darkness settled over me. Just as we were leaving the reception area, I caught a glimpse of Tony Grantz coming in from a different door.

I tried to stop and call out, but Tim hustled me along a corridor until we came to a large open area with several doors opening off of it. In the middle was a glassed-in control room that looked vaguely like an airport control tower. A female guard sat inside, watching a bank of TV monitors.

Tim walked over to the control room and knocked on the glass. The guard looked up, pressed a button, and her disembodied voice came through a speaker.

"Where to?" she said.

"Number C. Thanks, Jen," said Tim.

He led me to a door marked C and nodded back at the control room. A buzzer sounded and the door opened. Tim removed my cuffs.

"Go on in, Pastor," he said.

"Thanks, Tim," I said. I didn't feel thankful, but I didn't know what else to say. I stepped into the room and the door clanged shut behind me. The sliding of the automatic latch was like the sound of a shotgun being pumped.

CHAPTER 44

I was in a medium-sized open room with bunks lining the walls. There were surveillance cameras in the ceiling, at every corner. About twenty men in orange jumpsuits milled around the room. About half of them were white, the other half evenly divided between blacks and Hispanics. There were a few lightweight plastic chairs scattered around.

I knew from my jail-ministry days that I needed to be confident and show no signs of weakness. But I didn't know the protocol. Did I claim a bunk? Did I sit down? Did I say, "Hi! I'm the new guy?"

I was pretty sure I shouldn't do the last one so I strode into the room, not swaggering exactly, but maybe with a bit of bravado. I met the eyes of a black guy sitting on a bunk to my left. He seemed familiar somehow. He jerked his head upward as if to say "hey." I mimicked the gesture. Neither of us smiled. I looked around. The bunk next to his seemed to be unoccupied. I went over, looked around again and sat down. I was on the right of the black guy. We didn't look at each other again or speak. Seminary had been thoroughly inadequate preparation for prison protocol.

Over in the corner, three white guys were standing close and talking, looking over at me. After a second, they came up to me. The leader was a big man, well over six feet. He had spider webs tattooed over every visible inch of his body other than his face. He didn't look friendly.

"I bet they call you Spider," I said, trying to seize the initiative.

He stared at me, not saying anything. Behind him, on his left, stood a stocky guy, maybe five-nine and two-hundred pounds, with thick curly black hair. On Spider's right was another man, five-eleven and slender. I stared right into Spider's eyes, waiting.

"You claiming this bunk?" he said at last.

"I was going to," I said.

"I don't want you to," said Spider.

"Why, is it yours?" I asked.

"Everything here is mine," said Spider. "And you don't get a bunk, you sleep on the floor."

I was in uncharted territory. I sat still, staring a thousand miles away.

"You hear me?" said Spider. "Get off that bunk." He stepped closer until he was towering over me. I didn't want to obey him, but I didn't feel quite comfy sitting while he was standing so close. I stood up and shifted to the side away from him.

"We'll talk about it later," I said.

He laughed. It wasn't a pleasant sound, and it didn't seem that he found anything truly funny.

"I heard you was a preacher," he said.

"Word travels awfully fast," I said. "But that's right, I am."

"You in here 'cause you messing with the choirboys," said Spider.

"No, that's not true," I said.

"That's what I heard," he said. "You like them little clean choirboys."

A few other inmates began to drift our way, listening in.

"We don't like fags like you," said the shorter, curly-haired man to Spider's left.

"You heard wrong," I said. "That's not what they're charging me with, and I never did that."

"The hell you didn't," said Spider.

I moved a step back and to the side. Spider came around in front of me. Slim stayed behind me while Curly slipped over to my right. I met Spider's gaze steadily. A few more people drifted over to watch the action. I didn't see any way to change what was about to happen.

"What you lookin' at?" said Spider at last.

"A piece of white-trash scum," I said, "who can't even get his story straight."

Spider flung a straight right punch at my head. As it always seemed to in such circumstances, everything around me seemed to slow down while I stayed the same. I blocked the punch with my left forearm, at the same time slipping my right forearm behind his elbow and pivoting my body. With my left, I drove his arm out, and it bent backwards against my right arm. There was a sickening crunch of cartilage. Even as I completed that, I leaned back on my left foot and snapped a roundhouse kick into his groin with my right. I stepped down and drove my elbow into the side of his temple as he bent over.

Pivoting 180 degrees on both feet, I caught the blow coming from Curly on my left forearm. There was a strange, violent, ripping sensation, and then I hit him in the Adam's apple with my open hand, striking it with the webbing between thumb and forefinger. Something smashed into the side of my head from the right. I drove out a sidekick that caught Slim in the knee. Even as his leg collapsed under him and he began to fall, I leaned back and smashed a roundhouse kick full into the side of his head. He sat down with a grunt. Stepping down and bending my knees I hit him in the face with the back of my right hand.

I straightened up. All three of them were on the ground. Curly was on hands and knees, wheezing for breath, choking and retching. Slim was lying still on his side. Spider was on the ground behind, moaning in agony, holding his arm and retching. The entire episode had taken about seven seconds.

Most of the other inmates were gathered around, but other than the groans of the injured men there was absolute silence in the room for a few seconds. Then someone swore, presumably in admiration. I scanned the group quickly. One of the closest men to me held up his hands, palms outwards.

"We just watching," he said.

"Fast," said the black man on the bunk.

I was starting to feel a strange ache in my left forearm. My head began to throb where Slim had hit me. I looked down at Curly, who was still on the floor. His breathing had eased a bit and he was reaching for something next to him. I stomped on his hand with as much force as I had. He screamed and pulled his hand into his chest. I quickly bent down and picked up the object he had wanted, jerking up and whirling back quickly, but my enemies were still on the ground. I looked at the object in my hand.

It was my own clasp knife, open and bloody.

"That ain't no shank," said somebody.

I looked at my left forearm. The orange jumpsuit was torn, a rent about a foot long, and a dark stain was spreading all around the tear. I pulled the torn sides apart. The outside of my arm was a bloody mess.

Some of the men were looking nervously at the cameras in the ceiling and drifting away. I expected someone to come in at any moment.

There didn't seem to be much to say.

Suddenly the black man on the bunk spoke.

"You fight like that," he said, nodding toward the three men still on the floor. "You really a preacher?"

"That's right," I said. I looked at my forearm again. I needed to stop the bleeding.

"Then I know who you is." The other inmates stopped drifting and turned back toward us.

"I been sitting here thinking I know you. You the dude come down to the jail and talk with me a few weeks back 'cause I ain't had no visitors."

I nodded. Now I knew why his face looked familiar.

"You someone else too," he said.

I waited. My arm was really starting to throb now. I felt a bit lightheaded.

"You that preacher dude done killed the guy that murdered his wife."

I looked at him wearily.

"That's right," I said. "How did you know?"

CHAPTER 45

That man you killed, his name was Charlie Wedge. He my cell dog—my roomie—when I was out west." The black man leaned back against the wall, enjoying the undivided attention he was now getting from everyone in the room.

"Can't remember your name," I said.

"Name's Bronco," he said. "I ain't lookin' for trouble, now."

"Me neither," I said. I took the knife I was still holding and cut some strips from the leg of my jail jumpsuit. My right leg was now bare to the knee. I folded the knife up and sat down on the bunk next to Bronco's. I slipped the knife under my right thigh and awkwardly began to bind up my left arm. No one offered to help.

"What about this Charlie Wedge guy?" asked one of the white inmates.

"He got out 'fore me," said Bronco. "All went down 'fore I got out. All I know is what I heard—gossip, you know, and what I seen on the news."

"Well, what is it?" asked the same man.

Slim was sitting up now, holding his right knee. Curly sat, nursing his injured hand, but listening. Spider was kneeling, bent over, cradling an elbow that was clearly either dislocated or broken. It was a grotesque sight, and he couldn't stop either rocking or moaning softly.

Bronco spoke again. "Well, Charlie Wedge, he in for drugs,

same as everybody else. Think he mighta kill someone on a bad deal or somethin'. Anyway, he gets out, he go right back to it. What I hear is, he come up short of cash. He see this lady goin' in to her apartment, nice looking white chick."

Bronco glanced at me. "I don't mean nothin', Preacher, just telling the story."

There wasn't much to say about that, so I let it pass.

"Anyway, he follow her right in, pull a knife or something. It all go wrong, and she end up dead. He trying to find money or something to sell and her man come home. He a preacher. He see Charlie, they have a fight, and Charlie lose. Preacher-man kill him."

Curly was glaring at Bronco.

"How do you know this is the same dude? That ain't what we heard about him."

"Charlie Wedge was a man, you know? Don't know many dudes could put Charlie down, even if he hopped up on drugs and stuff." Bronco pointed at me with his chin. "But I reckon *he* could. How many preachers you reckon can put you and Spider and another guy on the floor in less than ten seconds?"

Curly didn't respond. As much as it was possible for a man with his low forehead, broad crude face, and one magnificent eyebrow, he looked thoughtful.

"'Sides," said Bronco, "Preacher already told us he the man. Ain't that right, Preacher?"

"I killed Charlie Wedge," I acknowledged. There wasn't much point in pretending. I could still see his face, wild-eyed, high on dope. Robyn on the floor, blood everywhere, it seemed like. Wedge, slightly less startled than me, coming at me with a big knife. I didn't remember the actual fight, really. My Taekwondo black belt had kicked in, boosted to an insane level by fear, rage, and grief. When it was over, Charlie Wedge was on my living room floor, only three feet away from Robyn. Her eyes were looking right at me, but they weren't seeing anything—would never see anything again.

Curly spoke, snapping me out of my painful thoughts. "Hollywood said the preacher was in here for screwing little boys."

He shrank back from my look. "I just saying what Hollywood tole me and Spider."

"What else did Hollywood say?" I asked. I stood up and moved toward Curly.

"Hey, man, I ain't picking a fight no more," he said.

"What did he say?" I took another step.

"He said they was a preacher comin' in who'd been messing with the choirboys. He thought we might want to know. We all hate child molesters. That's why we jumped you."

"When did he tell you?"

"This afternoon sometime."

"Hollywood's a liar," I said. "He's a jerk and idiot too. Question is, why did he tell you that?"

"I dunno," said Curly.

"I reckon Hollywood don't like you none," said Bronco. "Most folks these guys jump is liable to end up in the hospital. Or dead." He paused. "With a knife like that, dead."

"Where'd you get the knife?" I asked Curly.

"Man, we got rules 'bout stuff like that. I ain't sayin' nothin' 'bout that."

I walked closer. "Where did you get the knife?"

He shrank back, but said nothing.

"I could tear you apart like a piece of white bread," I said. "I could take this knife and slice you from your neck to your belly button." I unclasped the knife. I felt like an actor on TV. A bad actor. "Now I'll give you one more chance. Where did you get this knife?"

Curly shook his head. "You really the man that killed Charlie Wedge, you ain't gonna do that to me. You might break a man's bones defending yourself." He glanced at the still moaning Spider. "You might even kill someone in the middle of a fight. But you ain't gonna slice me. You ain't even gonna touch me, 'less I was stupid enough to try and jump you again."

Curly was smarter than I gave him credit for.

I snapped the knife shut and went and sat down. I could feel my arm swell and peak with every heartbeat. "Don't they ever monitor the cameras? I need stitches." My head was starting to hurt worse too. "And a cup of coffee. Can you get coffee in here?"

Bronco shrugged. "They usually in here soon as a fight breaks out. Maybe somethin' wrong with the cameras."

A little pool of blood began to puddle on the floor below me. It wasn't much. If it didn't hurt so bad, the blood on the floor would have made me feel tough.

The good news was, I didn't think any more prisoners would try to jump me. The bad news was that I might be bleeding to death but no one cared, and I was in jail for murder.

CHAPTER 46

Maybe the cameras were broken. At any rate, no one came into the cell. The fight was over, the damage was done, but I was hurting, and so were Curly and Spider. Slim was woozy, and he had a bruise over his left eye, but other than that he was better off than the rest of us.

The other inmates gradually drifted off and left me sitting on my bunk, next to Bronco on his. He looked at me.

"You kill them other dudes too?" he asked.

"You mean Daniel Spooner and that other guy just today, uh—James Post?"

Bronco nodded.

"No." I said. "And I didn't mean to kill Charlie Wedge. Plus, they cleared me of it—they ruled it self-defense. That was five years ago."

"So why you in here?"

"They're accusing me of killing Spooner and Post, but they're wrong."

Bronco glanced at me out of the side of his eyes. "That's a good thing. 'Cause Daniel Spooner not the one who killed that little girl anyhow."

I snapped my head towards him. "What are you saying? Daniel Spooner didn't kill Missy Norstad?"

He shook his head. "Nope." He seemed quite satisfied with the shock he was creating.

"What do you mean? How could you know?"

"I in here with Spooner 'fore he got shot. He weren't no saint, you know, but I'm pretty sure he didn't do that Norstad girl."

I hitched my left arm up, cradling it with my right hand. It was throbbing. "You just think he didn't do it? No reason?"

"Well, I know one thing. All the news and everything said he confessed to it. But he never made no confession. And I don't think they got much evidence without a confession."

"What do you mean, he never confessed? Everyone knew he did."

"You ain't listening. Everyone heard from someone else he confessed. But he didn't do it."

"Bronco," I said, "that's not true. The newspaper and TV people even had quotes from his confession."

"That's the point," said Bronco. "There was a confession, and it had his signature, but he never made it. Someone faked it."

"Well, why didn't he contest it then? Why didn't he tell someone it was false?"

"That's what I'm tellin' you, Preacher. He was on his way to tell that to the judge when he got shot. You understand?"

"You're saying Daniel Spooner didn't kill Missy Norstad. Someone faked a confession, and when Spooner was on his way to reveal that to the Court, he got shot before he could say anything."

Bronco smiled widely. He was missing three teeth. "You got it, Preacher."

"But Spooner had a record. He was convicted of rape before the Norstad case."

"That's just what make it so smart, man. Everyone believe the confession, 'cause everyone know he done something like that before. Only he never had killed no one before."

"You're saying someone picked Spooner deliberately to the take the rap for killing Missy Norstad."

Bronco looked around. No one was paying any attention to us. "That's exactly what I'm saying," he said.

CHAPTER 47

They didn't show up until almost an hour after the fight. It was nine at night. The bleeding had stopped, but I was weak from loss of blood, lack of food and coffee deprivation. The guards came busting in without warning, hustling over to where I lay on the bunk next to Bronco's, and pinned me there, violently ripping the knife from hand. They hauled me up, and one of them pushed me against the wall, pinning me there by holding my arms, reopening the slash on my forearm.

A guard I had never seen before came over to me and got in my face where it was pressed against the cold cement wall.

"Where did you get this?" He brandished the knife in front of me. He sounded like a marine drill instructor. "How did you get this?"

"I got it at Gander Mountain in Hermantown," I said. "For $19.95." It was hard to talk with my face against the wall.

"Very funny," he said. He looked at the legs of my torn jail uniform. "Oh, don't be destroying state property now. You wanna start something with me, you're gonna regret it."

"I had to stop the bleeding," I said mildly.

"Burkus, he's bleeding," said the guard who was holding me.

The guard named Burkus, who was apparently in charge, looked to where blood was again seeping through the already messy sleeve of my left arm. The guard holding me released me.

"That's why we always wear gloves," said Burkus. I noticed

that all the guards were indeed wearing latex gloves.

"Burkus," said one of the others. "We got another one here, hurt pretty bad." He was kneeling over Spider, who hadn't stopped groaning for the entire hour. Curly and Slim were off on their own bunks, but both had obvious bruises, and Curly's hand probably had a few broken bones. Within a few minutes they had separated them from the others. They checked us all over. Burkus spoke into a radio clipped to the shoulder of his uniform.

"Got a medical here," he said. He said some other things that I didn't catch.

He turned to me. "How come the only guy who got cut is the one with the knife?" he asked me.

"I had to take it away from him," I said.

"Who?"

I hesitated. I'd only been in the cell an hour but I knew there was a code here. Prisoners stuck together. They didn't rat each other out.

Burkus turned to the room. "Who was involved here?" He looked at Spider. "Spider finally met his match, huh? Come on, I know whoever did that wants to take credit."

The room was silent.

"I did it," I said.

Burkus whirled on me. "Who are you?"

"Jonah Borden, pastor of Harbor Lutheran in town."

His eyes narrowed. "You the preacher we pulled in for the vigilante killings?"

"I didn't do the killings," I said. "But I'm the guy they pulled in, yes."

He looked at Spider, Curly, and Slim. "Looks like you're doing the vigilante thing in here too. Maybe it's not such a good idea to give you access to more folks who might need killing."

I decided to heck with the code. I was not going to get a prisoner mentality. I was a respected member of the community and I'd done no wrong.

"They jumped me," I said.

"Who?"

"Spider and those two," I said, nodding to Curly and Slim. Their eyes told me they'd get revenge if they could. I tried to tell them with *my* eyes that I'd like to see them try.

"He's got the knife," said Curly. "He's the one who came after us, just like you said. He's a vigi . . . vigee . . . that thing you said. He wants to kill anyone who's locked up."

"Anyone else see it?" asked Burkus again.

It was quiet.

Burkus started to turn away, when reluctantly Bronco stirred.

"I seen it," he said, not looking at Curly. "Spider and them jumped him, just like Preacher say. They just didn't know Preacher the fastest man behind bars."

I nodded at him in thanks. His face was expressionless.

"All right," said Burkus, "let's get these guys outta here."

I was cuffed and leg chained and shuffled out of the cell. They separated us all immediately and took me into a small, bare room that was apparently some sort of infirmary. They left me alone there a long time, proving that visiting the doctor while incarcerated was no different than doing so on the outside.

At last, a man in a white lab coat entered along with a guard. He looked about twenty, with thin blond hair.

"You the doctor?" I asked.

"I'm a nurse," he said. "Let me see your arm."

After he looked at the arm, both men left the room. They returned in about ten minutes with another man in a lab coat, who was quite tall with gray hair and black-rimmed glasses.

"I'm Doctor Munson," said the new man. The guard leaned back against the wall. The blond nurse began to bustle around with some sort of tray he brought into the room with him. Munson examined my arm carefully, and then removed my makeshift bandage.

"Nasty cut you've got here," he said. "What happened?"

"Ah, the kindly healer subtly tricks the prisoner into telling all," I remarked. Munson looked hurt. The guard smiled.

"The thing is, you don't have to trick me, Doctor, I'll tell you right out. Three guys jumped me. The second guy had a knife. After he did this"—I nodded at my arm—"I took it away from him."

"I've looked at the knife. You were lucky. It wasn't an ordinary prison shank. It was actually pretty clean."

I didn't mention to him that I had cleaned it regularly myself, before someone took it away from me and gave it to Curly.

"It's deep, though. Looks like it was driven in with some force."

Assisted by the nurse, Dr. Munson cleaned the laceration and because I was now officially a tough guy, I did not scream. I thought about asking the guard for a bullet to bite, however. Eventually, Munson injected a local anesthetic and sewed me up. There were twenty stitches in all. He gave me some pain medication.

"Anything else I can do for you?" he asked.

"How about some coffee?" I said. "To replace all the blood I lost?"

He looked surprised and then laughed. "I'll see to it myself," he said, and left the room with the others.

CHAPTER 48

Ten minutes later the guard came back with my coffee.

"Come on," he said. He led me down a hall to a smallish room with heavy glass windows that looked on part of the jail complex. It was set up like a boardroom, with a table that was too big for the space, surrounded by chairs. Two men and a woman were sitting in chairs on the far side of the table. They all wore uniforms. The guard seated me, and then stood by the door.

"We want to hear what happened in the cell," said the man to my right. He looked to be about fifty, with iron-gray hair and a matching, neatly trimmed mustache.

"I already told Burkus, the doctor, and anyone else who would listen," I said.

"We need to hear it again," said the lady, who sat facing me from my left. Her tone was not encouraging.

So I told them all again. They took notes and asked an occasional question. Then the gray-haired man spoke.

"I realize that you have never been incarcerated before, Reverend Borden. Different rules apply here."

I gaped at him. "You mean it would be okay to beat people up and knife them if I weren't in jail?"

"We are not amused by your witty comments," he said, though the lady and the younger man beside her were suppressing smiles. "We will enforce the rules and the safety of our inmates."

"You didn't do so well at enforcing my safety," I said. Somehow it sounded like bad grammar. Probably was, but it was the other guy's fault—he was the one talking about enforcing safety.

The gray-haired man wrote something on the pad in front of him. He looked up at the guard. "Give him two days in the hole."

I didn't know what the hole was, but I didn't want to spend two days anywhere in this building.

"I didn't get my phone call," I said.

All three of them looked up at me.

"I never got my phone call," I repeated. "I've seen enough TV to know I should be able to make one phone call."

The lady was checking some papers in front of her.

"It says here that you called your mother at 7:28 p.m. this evening."

"There's some sort of mistake. I didn't get the chance to call anyone."

The three of them exchanged looks. The gray-haired man shuffled his papers into a neat stack and tapped it on the edge of the table.

"All right," he said to the guard. "Take him away."

I allowed the guard to help me up.

"Something's wrong here," I said. "Someone gave Curly that knife."

The gray haired man irritably motioned the guard to stop.

"We know that was your own knife, Reverend Borden. How you smuggled it in, or why you might have given it to one of the other inmates, we don't know. Would you like to enlighten us?"

"I put it in the little tray with my keys and wallet," I said. "It should be noted down on the list of stuff I turned over when they brought me in. Look it up."

The lady looked puzzled. The younger man looked at the older one and shrugged.

"Sleight of hand, maybe?" he said.

"Look it up," I said. "I signed the paper and so did the lady behind the counter. Deputy Burton was there . . ." My voice trailed off.

Rex Burton. *Hollywood.* Hollywood told them I was a child molester. Hollywood told them this afternoon I would be coming in. He set up the fight. He must have slipped the knife to Curly.

"Is something wrong?" asked the woman. "You have a funny look on your face."

"You might want to ask Deputy Burton about all this," I said. "It's no secret that he doesn't like me. Someone told those guys I was a child molester. Someone gave them the knife. In both cases, I'm guessing it was Deputy Burton."

They exchanged quizzical looks. The gray haired man sighed, looked down at his papers, and waved at the guard. He took me out.

We went down two corridors until we came to a steel door with no window. Next to it was a little rectangular tray of the sort used by tellers at drive-thru bank windows. A series of clicks announced the unlocking of the door. It slid slowly back. My guard ushered me in, stepped out, and the door slid shut with a jarring latch. The space was maybe ten by ten. Almost half the room was taken up by a bunk bolted to the cement wall. At the far end of the room was a toilet made entirely of stainless steel. Integrated into the toilet in one piece was a steel sink that sat above the commode part. It all looked very secure and unbreakable. To the right of the door was the little receptacle that was the inside part of the bank-teller tray. I supposed they used this to pass me food.

I sat down on the bunk, and leaned against the bare wall. It actually felt pretty good to be alone. The pain in my arm was dull now, and my headache was almost gone. But for some reason I was not sleepy. I got up and went over to the toilet/sink. I ran the water in the sink. I drank some of it. I flushed the toilet. Everything worked just great.

One can only contemplate a stainless steel toilet for so long, however, before exhausting the possibilities. I looked around the room. Bare, painted, cement walls. Same thing for the floor. Similarly, my bunk failed to yield anything exciting. I decided, finally, to think about what was going on.

Instead, I fell asleep.

I woke up when the lights clicked on in the morning. Someone pounded on my door, and then the little receptacle to the right of the door slid open. In it was a tray of food, with both milk and coffee. I had never seen anyone.

I went over to the tray, manfully restraining myself from diving headfirst for the coffee. With a certain conscious decorum, I lifted the plastic mug. I had read in a book by Agatha Christie that coffee could disguise the taste of several of your more common poisons. I stopped, the steaming cup halfway to my mouth. Where had that thought come from? Well, certainly Rex Burton—AKA: Hollywood—had set me up to be badly hurt or killed. If he could do that, couldn't he put something in my coffee?

I paused, and then shrugged my shoulders. It would be a good way to go. I took a sip. I waited. I didn't die. I took another sip.

On the theory that if someone wanted to poison me, coffee

would be the best choice, I decided that the food would be safe. I ate some. I didn't die, but I did reflect on the meaning of the words *cruel and unusual punishment*.

I finished breakfast and put the tray back into my little exchange window. I washed my hands and face carefully, more for something to do than any other reason.

Time passed. At least I assumed it did, but it was hard to tell in my little four-walled universe. When my door finally clicked and slid open, it startled me badly. A guard stood outside and motioned for me to come out. I was pretty sure it hadn't been two days. I came out.

He escorted me through the jail to the visiting room. Now I was on the other side of the little booths in which I had visited Doug Norstad and Bronco.

The guard led me to the far booth, and on the other side of the glass was Alex Chan and a woman I didn't know. She had a long bony face, pale and expressionless. Her hair was blond and her eyes were dark gray. Alex looked serious.

"How'd you know I was here?" I said to him through the little phone handset. "They didn't let me have my one phone call."

Chan glanced meaningfully at the lady next to him. He turned back to me. "Leyla Bennett called me. When you didn't call her last night, she did some snooping and found out what happened."

"Thanks for coming," I said. "Can you get me out of here?"

"Actually, Jonah, I'm not sure I can," he said. "I represented Doug Norstad in Daniel Spooner's killing. Now you are accused of the same crime. There might be a conflict of interest." He must have seen the dismay on my face. "That's why I've brought Marcy," he said, indicated the woman to his right. "Marcy Torino, meet Jonah Borden."

"Nice to meet you," I said, "though I wish it was in another context."

Marcy nodded gravely without saying anything.

"Marcy will represent you, if you like," said Chan. "She's a good attorney, and she owes me a favor."

Marcy's face was expressionless.

"Okay," I said. "Anyone who owes Alex a favor is a friend of mine." I grinned to show what a funny guy I was. Marcy's face remained expressionless.

"It might be pushing the ethical envelope a little, but Marcy has agreed to let me hang around until she decides I shouldn't be part of the discussion," said Chan.

"Okay," I said. "Where do we start?"

Something seemed to slowly awaken Marcy's face. It would be pure fantasy to say that it became animated.

"Well, the first thing is your plea. We might be able to get by with aggravated manslaughter. But the James Post murder is going to make that very difficult."

I stared at her. I looked over at Chan. His face was serious and intent.

"I'm not sure I understand. Isn't the plea where you say either you agree you did the crime or say you're innocent?"

"That's right," said Marcy, brisk and businesslike. "But in a case like this, where you will plead guilty, there is often some room to negotiate which charges you will accept. Usually in exchange for the guilty plea, the DA will compromise by lowering the severity of the charge and the consequent sentence."

I looked at her through the glass. Her face was reserved and serious. Chan looked gloomy. "What do you mean, when you say this is a case where I will plead guilty?"

"Well," said Marcy, "I wish you had called an attorney before you talked to the police, but now that is really your only option."

"I want to plead 'innocent,'" I said.

"Not guilty," murmured Chan absently.

The first real spark of life appeared in Marcy's eyes. "Pastor Borden, you have already given the police your confession. I am here to advise you of your best options. Given the circumstances, your best option is to agree to a plea bargain. I will be talking to Eric Berg later today. He might be willing to be lenient."

"Wait," I said, touching the glass in front of her. "What do you mean, I've given the police my confession? I haven't done any such thing. They didn't even question me."

Marcy and Chan exchanged looks. "What are you saying, Jonah?" asked Chan.

"Last night they picked me up when I got home from fishing. They brought me here. I didn't get a phone call. They took all my stuff away, dressed me in these orange pajamas, and put me in a big room with other prisoners who attacked me." I held up my left arm. It had bled slightly during the night, and the bandage was gratifyingly macabre. "One of them tried to slice me open. I protested, and three guys got hurt in the protest. Then they put in me in 'the hole'—which I believe might also be called solitary confinement. I was there until they brought me to see you."

Marcy looked at Chan. "That's why we had to make such a fuss to see him," she said. She turned to me.

"So you are saying they never questioned you, never took a statement?"

"Never."

"And you didn't get a phone call?"

"Nope."

"Did they read you your Miranda rights?"

"Yes, they did that."

Marcy looked thoughtful. Chan looked excited. "So you are telling me that you did not confess to the murders of Daniel Spooner and James Post?" asked Marcy.

"That is exactly what I'm telling you," I said. "I am innocent, and I have never said otherwise."

Marcy looked skeptical. "They have a confession," she said. "It has your signature on it."

"It's bogus," I said.

"The confession says you have killed criminals before," she said. "I did some research and found out that is true."

"I killed one criminal before," I said. "And I didn't mean to kill him. Not only that, but I was cleared from all wrongdoing. The court ruled it self-defense."

Marcy pursed her lips. "My job is to advise you as to your best course of action. Let's look at this objectively. In a sense, it doesn't matter whether you are innocent or guilty. The question is, what will be most beneficial to you? Look at it from the side of the prosecution. Your wife was killed by a rapist and murderer. You killed that man. A member of your church is victimized by a rapist and murderer. That man is killed. When the father is accused, you are quite public in declaring the man not guilty, in spite of overwhelming circumstantial evidence. And it turns out, apparently, that you are right. How did you know it wasn't Doug Norstad? Next, a woman you met at the WW and tried to help is raped and killed." Marcy looked a notepad in front of her. "A Susan Scheen. Just a few days ago the police picked up James Post for Scheen's murder. Next, Post gets shot and killed. And then you give the police an explicit confession to both shootings, detailing even some forensic evidence known only to the police. You *might* be able to retract the confession, but it's already been all over the news. Even if you get the confession thrown out *and* we get a jury that hasn't heard about it, when we go to trial, the prosecution will bring up the confession. I will object, of course, and the statement will be struck from the record, but the jury would get the point. It's going to be very tough getting anyone to believe you are innocent."

"I'm a police chaplain," I said. "I've picked up a few things here or there. So I know that one thing they don't have is any physical evidence to tie me to either crime. I know this because I didn't commit the crimes."

Chan looked at me and then looked away. "Jonah," he said gently. "They have your .30-.30 rifle."

"So what?" I said. "I didn't shoot anyone with it."

Marcy looked at me pityingly. "Well," she said, "*someone* used it to shoot James Post."

CHAPTER 49

When the guard took me back to my cell I told him I wanted to talk with Chief Jensen.

"Jensen is town police," he said. "We're county."

"Well who can I talk to about my case?"

"Your lawyer, the judge, or the prosecution."

"Can't I talk to the detectives or something?"

He shrugged. "Their job is pretty much done once you're locked up."

"I got some new evidence to share."

He looked dubious. "I think you might want to talk to your lawyer about that."

"I just did," I said.

He shrugged again. "Okay. I can't make any promises, but I'll see what I can do." He opened the door to my cell and I went in. I sat down on my bunk. Home sweet home.

I was glad now, for the peace and quiet of my solitary confinement. It gave me room to think. I laid everything out in my mind, and all the pieces seemed to fall together. It was time for a day of reckoning with Rex Burton, AKA: Hollywood.

He had been clever—diabolically so. But he lost it when he told the three jailbirds that I was a child molester—the most despicable of all criminals—knowing full well that those three individuals would kill me if they could. They probably wouldn't testify to anything in court, because they'd used the knife he gave them—my knife—and testifying would result in more jail time for them. But I had enough to go on now.

After a few hours of sitting in my cell alone, the door lock snapped open and the big metal sheet slowly slid aside. It was the same guard.

"You still wanna talk to somebody?" he said.

"Yeah."

"Come on, then." He led me through the jail complex to an interview room, much like the room where I had been questioned by Jensen and Tony Grantz.

I waited there alone for a few minutes, then Tony Grantz himself came in.

"Borden," he said to me, nodding curtly. He was full of restless energy, larger than life, still playing to the imaginary cameras.

"Detective Grantz," I said. "I was hoping you could arrange it so I could talk to Chief Jensen. You could be part of the conversation too."

Grantz gave me what was presumably supposed to be a steely-eyed stare. It would have been too, if it hadn't been overdone. "Why should I do that?"

"Because I want to save you both some embarrassment, like I tried to do in the case of Doug Norstad."

Grantz snorted. "Even if I cared about what you have to say—which I don't—you couldn't meet with Jensen. He's out of town. Had to go to Chicago for some sort of emergency with his wife's family."

He dramatically spun a wooden chair around and sat in it backwards, his arms resting on the back. "Why don't you just tell me what's on your mind?"

We've got a big problem," I said.

Grantz waited.

I looked at the big mirror-glass window behind him. "We might want some privacy," I said.

"Let me be the judge of that," he said.

I hesitated. If Burton was behind that window, it could cause me a great deal of trouble. On the other hand, it was unlikely that he was.

"I haven't got all day," said Grantz.

"All right," I said. "Let me tell you a little story." I shifted on my chair. "There's this guy, moves here from down south. A big city in another state. You with me so far?"

Grantz made no move and his expression didn't change.

"Anyway, he moves here" I went on. "He wasn't what everyone thought he was. He has a secret life, a hidden passion, he might call it. A girl gets hurt. She dies. But he knows how to cover it up, because he is a cop."

Grantz got up and stalked dramatically over to me, bent over, and stuck his jaw at my face. "This cop have a name?" he said.

"Let's just call him Hollywood." I said it kind of soft, in case someone was listening.

An unidentifiable emotion flickered across his face, and I thought it was the most real expression I'd ever seen him use. He straightened up.

"I'll be right back," he said, and went out.

Three minutes passed before he came back into the interview room. He sat back down in his reverse-chair position.

"Now, you were telling me a little story," he said.

I nodded. "Well, this city cop from another state, he knows someone he can pin the crime on. Guy who has a record, a nasty, dirty record. Guy by the name of Daniel Spooner."

"Go on," said Grantz softly.

"This Hollywood, he plants a little bit of evidence on Daniel Spooner. He can't really do too much, 'cause it might lead the other cops back to him. So they bring in Spooner, but our guy, the out-of-state cop, he's worried. The evidence probably isn't going to hold up. So he fakes a confession from Spooner. It looks like a winner. Everyone buys it, the media, the DA . . ." Something went off in my head, but I couldn't identify what it was. "Anyway," I said, "things are going swimmingly, but there's one problem. Spooner knows *he* didn't do it. Maybe he starts to suspect our man Hollywood. Maybe not. In any case, Spooner is going to blow the whistle on the fake confession. Our guy can't allow that. He does a little research on who would be likely to kill the man who confessed to killing Missy Norstad. He finds out Doug Norstad is out of town every Tuesday. So he shoots Spooner dead on a Tuesday."

I looked around. "You got any coffee?"

Grantz shrugged. "Maybe later. For now, you are entertaining me."

"So our guy Hollywood is now sitting pretty. Spooner is dead, and everyone believes he went to the grave guilty of killing Melissa Norstad. Doug Norstad is in jail for killing Spooner, and our hero is completely out of the picture."

"If all that's so, how come you suspect him?"

"I didn't, not at first. I just knew that Doug Norstad was innocent."

"How?"

I shook my head. "Can't tell you."

"All right, so how'd you go from knowing Norstad didn't do Spooner, to all this fanciful stuff about this cop?"

"Well, it seemed like maybe someone was trying to hold on to Norstad as the shooter—in an unreasonable way, you know? Like someone didn't really care if it was actually him or not, they were going to make it stick." I looked automatically for my cup of coffee. It wasn't there.

"So I'm working hard to get Doug out, and it occurs to me, who benefits here? At first I thought it might be the DA, you know. Maybe he just wanted a quick easy trial to get famous on." Again I felt the subtle thought in my head. Again it eluded me.

"But the biggest person who benefits from framing Norstad is the guy who actually killed Spooner. Quite a few potential candidates there, but no one who really makes sense. So I'm going along, and someone hires a woman to seduce me—that Susie Scheen you thought I murdered." I paused and looked directly at Grantz. "Did Jensen tell you that, that someone hired her to come on to me?"

Grantz remained motionless. He looked angry.

"Now, why would someone want to do that?" I asked. Grantz was not participating in the conversation, so I went on. "They did it to try and get some leverage on me, to get me to back off investigating the Spooner shooting. It didn't work. So now this guy Hollywood, he has a problem. I know who this lady is. I might trace her back and find him behind it all. I do that and start asking awkward questions, the whole thing might blow up. So he has her killed, by a con called James Post. Or maybe he just has an argument with her, kills her himself, and pins it on Post, like he did with Spooner and the Missy Norstad killing. Doesn't really matter. You with me so far?"

Grantz was nodding slowly. "You're a pretty smart SOB, aren't you?"

I nodded. "I listen to Bach. Anyway, Hollywood has tried the carrot, now he tries the stick. He hires some guys from his hometown—that big city he's from. Probably was a dirty cop for many years. They come and threaten me. That doesn't work either. He's getting desperate. He could have me killed, but that would leave an unsolved murder. He's smart—he specializes in doing murders that are *solved* with the wrong man caught. Next, his guys go too far and vandalize my house. It gets in the media, and virtually proves that Doug Norstad didn't do it. Otherwise, why all the fuss about my investigations?"

Grantz leaned back and stretched. "Then what?" he said. All of a sudden he seemed casual about the whole thing.

"Hollywood figures out how to solve the Jonah Borden problem," I said. "He's been digging into my past to try and find some leverage against me. He finds out I killed the man who broke into my house and murdered my wife. He can paint me as a vigilante and pin Spooner's shooting on me. He got lucky on Spooner's killing, because I was alone that day. He plans to kill James Post, while I'm gone, fishing alone. Half the town knows that's what I do on Mondays. Anyway, the Post killing will be a lock, because Hollywood has stolen my rifle—probably took it the night the vandals hit my house—and he uses that to shoot Post."

"So how is anyone to know you didn't shoot Post?"

"All along the problem is lack of physical evidence. So

Hollywood fakes a confession for me, like he did with Spooner. But then he gets smarter. He knows this confession won't stick either. He tries to have some cons kill me while I'm in here. He tells the meanest guys in the jail that I'm a child molester, and gives them my own knife to kill me with. Only that didn't work out so well."

"Yeah," said Grantz, looking at my bandaged arm. "Who knew a preacher could fight like that?" He stood up. "You got anything else?"

"A few thoughts, some other things that seem to fit in."

"I mean proof, Borden. You got something that law enforcement can't ignore?"

"I'm still working on it," I said. "But we'll find out some things when we look into who was in on the Missy Norstad/Daniel Spooner case. We'll also probably find out who's been digging into my past. I got enough to interest the judge when I go to court tomorrow."

"So why are you telling me?"

"I thought you might want to do something about it before I break this all open tomorrow. It's going to get messy, and I thought I ought to warn you, give you a chance to start making it right."

Grantz stared at me. He seemed to be searching for words. Finally he shook his head. "You are a piece of work," he said. He got up and went to the door. He turned to look at me again, shook his head once more, and left the room.

CHAPTER 50

I wasn't in my cell very long before the door opened again.

"Got a visitor," said the guard.

"This really isn't all that solitary," I said. "Pretty soon I might need to hang a Do Not Disturb sign on the door."

"No knobs," said the guard.

"Good point."

This time the person on the other side of the glass was Leyla. When I sat down in front of her she didn't say anything. Her face was full of tension, and for the first time since I'd known her, I wasn't blown away at the sight of her.

"Hey," I said.

She stirred, and I recognized part of her expression as anger. "Jonah, what is going on?"

"Just taking jail visitation to the next logical level," I said.

She did not appear amused. "I mean it, Jonah, I want the truth this time."

I felt a little stir of heat in my solar plexus. "What do you mean, Leyla—'this time?' I've never lied to you."

She took a deep breath. "Maybe you're right. I never asked you if you had killed the man who murdered your wife, so you never lied about it. I never asked you if you had killed Daniel Spooner, so you never lied about that either. I never got a chance to ask about James Post and Susan Scheen. But you can't call it telling the truth either."

I stared at her. "You seriously think I killed Spooner and Post?"

"You confessed to it, Jonah. I read the confession. I read the court documents about your wife's murder, and how you killed the guy. Do you understand? I found out as a *reporter*. In fact, I heard some of it first from some colleagues. 'By the way, the man you've been dating is a vigilante mass-murderer.'" She shook her head again and wiped at her eyes.

"I can't even believe I came down here. I just wanted something, some explanation, some . . ." She was crying in earnest now. "I don't believe this. I don't even know why I'm here right now."

"Leyla," I said, "the confession is fake. Surely you must have guessed that?"

She met my eyes dead-on through the glass. "Are you saying you didn't kill Charlie Wedge, the man who murdered your wife?"

I looked away. Then I turned back and found her eyes again. "I'm saying I did not kill Daniel Spooner. I'm saying I did not kill James Post. I'm saying I did not confess anything to anybody. I've been framed, don't you get it?"

"What about Charlie Wedge?" She really sounded like a reporter now.

"You already know about that, apparently. Yes, I killed him— in the middle of an intense, confusing, fear-injected, fight for my life, I killed the man. If you did your research, you would know that the court exonerated me of any wrongdoing."

"Why should I have to do any research?" Her voice broke. "Why didn't the man I—why didn't you tell me?"

"Because I thought you would see me differently." I paused. I was angry, and what I said next I said quite deliberately. "Apparently, I was right."

She was quiet and she wasn't crying anymore. When she spoke again, her voice was thick and stiff.

"I see you differently because I can't trust you. I didn't believe you killed Charlie Wedge. But my friends at the station were right about that. They all think you did the other murders as well. It makes sense. I can see how a man like you, going through what you did with your wife, how you might become a vigilante."

"So you think I'm guilty."

"I'm paid to be a reporter, not some stupid girl who starts to fall in love with the murderer in a story she's covering. It's time I acted as I should have all the time. I need to be objective and professional again. To start doing my job."

"So getting involved with me was a mistake."

"It usually is, when you start to fall for a killer."

I bit back a comeback. I had really liked her. I had maybe been on the border of something much stronger than *like*. I wanted to preserve some memory of that.

"Well, as I rule, I don't talk to reporters," I said. I held up my hand before she could reply. "But since you are so keen on being professional and doing your job, I will give you this little lead to work on. Daniel Spooner was on his way to court to claim that his confession was faked by someone in the Lake County Sheriff's Department. Before he could make the claim or corroborate it, he was killed."

She started to talk, but I cut her off.

"Tomorrow, I will try to go to court for exactly the same reason. By tomorrow night, I will be either free or dead. I can't see how you will be happy either way."

I stood up and left the visiting area. I heard Leyla's muffled "Jonah" through the glass as I left. I didn't look back.

CHAPTER 51

It was possibly the longest night of my life. I was supposed to go to court to enter my plea the next morning. It would be my opportunity to tell the judge what I thought was going on—*if* he let me speak.

Some judges just wanted the plea and nothing more, and they got irate when people tried to explain. I had seen a traffic judge like that once. He even had one defendant confined until the guy would just say either "guilty" or "not guilty." Judges were also notorious for not letting anyone railroad them in their own courtroom. So I wasn't at all certain that I would get a chance to talk. My hope was that Tony Grantz had given my words more consideration than he appeared to and would investigate further. Marcy Torino had also said she would talk with Eric Berg, the prosecutor, but I doubted Berg would listen even as well as Grantz. He liked his open-and-shut, slam-dunk convictions, and I had been a thorn in his side about Norstad. So my main chance was either Tony Grantz, or an indulgent judge.

Something tugged at my subconscious. When I'd been talking to Grantz, something I said hadn't seemed quite right. I set my mind to figure it out. I'd been telling Grantz about the lack of evidence against Spooner—at least according to Bronco. I settled on that for a moment. Eric Berg, pompous politician though he was, was indisputably an outstanding prosecutor. For the past six months or so, he had hardly lost a case. Why then, was he so quick to file charges against Spooner, if there was actually very little evidence against him? The same thing held true about Doug Norstad. True, there had been a strong circumstantial case against Norstad, but Berg had proceeded against him as if he had an eyewitness

And he had. The thought hit me like a bolt of lightning—a *fake* eyewitness. Just like he had a *fake* confession from Spooner. For that matter, just like he had a *fake* confession from me. Could it be that Berg had known? Was he in on it? Maybe his conviction rate was not because he was such an outstanding attorney. Maybe he was winning because Hollywood/Burton was manufacturing evidence for him.

And I had convinced Marcy Torino and Alex Chan to tell him my theories about the crimes.

Another thing intruded on my thoughts. If Berg was in on it all, then he must have known that Spooner was not the real killer of Missy Norstad, and that Doug Norstad wasn't the one who shot Spooner. If he was in on it, then he knew Burton was the real killer, and he was not only letting him go, but also cooperating with him in covering up major felonies. I didn't like Berg very much, but I had to admit it was a pretty big stretch that even Eric Berg would do such a thing just to pad his conviction record. Even if you believed that Berg could actually be that despicable, it wouldn't make sense—the risks to his career and personal life far outweighed the gains. Something wasn't right with the assistant DA—I could see that now—but I still didn't understand it.

I chewed on all these thoughts well into the night. Then I lay on my bunk, numb with exhaustion, feeling the throbbing of my arm, the refrain of Jackson Browne's "Late for the Sky" running through my brain while I thought of Leyla. Sometime close to morning, I finally dropped off.

The click of my little food receptacle woke me up. Mercifully there was coffee—I was getting up to a quart less than usual while incarcerated. The food lived up to the terrible standard set the day before. I'd had better in my high school cafeteria, and I couldn't think of a culinary insult worse than that.

Time dragged slowly. Lunch came. I was not delighted, but there was coffee again. I started to feel jittery and then finally the door slid open.

Two guards stood there. One of them was Tim Lane. "Time for your plea appearance," he said. We'll take you over to the courthouse."

They cuffed my hands in front of me with some sort of plastic or vinyl restraints. They let me keep my feet free. "He's not a flight risk," said Lane to the other guard, whose name tag read "D. Johnson."

Johnson helped me into a heavy flak-type jacket.

"Wasn't Spooner wearing one of these when he was shot?" I asked.

"That's true," said Tim Lane. "They won't stop a rifle bullet. But they'll stop pistols and explosions."

"So I'm just as safe as Spooner was," I said.

"Don't know why you're worried," said Johnson genially. He was of medium height, slightly overweight, with thin blond hair and a red complexion. "I think we got the guy who was shooting criminals."

"Innocent until proven guilty," I said. "And all that aside, I am worried. You know those three guys jumped me in the cell. Someone here wants me dead."

"We understand," said Tim. "Actually, we have posted guards all around the area. We even have a guy with a sniper rifle up on top of Tommy's, where you . . . where the guy was when he shot Spooner."

They were leading me through the jail as we talked and we were coming up to the door that led outside to the sidewalk between the jail and the courthouse. The sidewalk where Spooner had lost his life.

I stopped in front of the door. "Who've they got up on that roof?" I asked, fearing the answer. "Do you know?"

"Sure we know," said Johnson. "He's a good guy, and he'll keep you safe."

"Who is it?" I asked. "Not Rex Burton?"

"Detective Grantz," said Lane. "He's a crack shot, and he volunteered for the duty himself."

I breathed a sigh of relief. Grantz had listened enough to at least take precautions. I felt much more lighthearted as Johnson opened the door and Lane guided me through.

"Tony Grantz," I said. "That'll be just fine, as long he doesn't forget and think he's on *CSI: Miami* or something."

Johnson chuckled. "That's our Detective Grantz all right," he said. "Good ol' Hollywood."

And we stepped out into the sunshine.

CHAPTER 52

I took three steps before my feet froze, trapping my body in the open, a clear shot from the roof of Tommy's to my left. To my right was a police SUV. My mind was screaming at me, but my body was stuck in cement.

"What?" I asked. I could hear the tremble in my voice. "What did you say?"

Lane looked at me curiously. "We said Detective Grantz is on the roof. Come, on, keep moving."

I wanted more than anything to move, but I couldn't. "No," I said, even while my mind continued to shriek at me. "What did you call him?"

"Who, Detective Grantz?" said Johnson, still smiling. "We call him Hollywood. 'Cause he always acts like he's the star on a cop show or something."

"Plus he *is* like a cop-show star," said Lane. "Seems like every arrest he makes turns into a conviction."

"Rex Burton, he isn't Hollywood?"

Lane was really puzzled now. "Why would we call Deputy Burton 'Hollywood?'"

Johnson took my left arm firmly. "Come on now, we can talk about nicknames later on. Let's get to court." He moved to my left, took one step and then bumped into me, sending us both sprawling on the ground. Even as we fell, I heard the boom of a rifle.

I rolled over, my body finally released from its stasis. I lurched to my knees even while part of me noted that Johnson was still on the ground with a dark red puddle forming under him. I got my feet under me, while my brain chanted frantically at me. My handcuffs betrayed me and I stumbled, just as I heard another boom. A microsecond later, a much louder explosion burst the air beside me, and I went cartwheeling through the air, landing on my side just beyond the curb, on the street.

I couldn't hear. For a moment, I couldn't think. Red flames danced in front of my eyes, and with agonizing slowness I realized that the second shot had penetrated the gas tank of the police Blazer. Johnson was still on the ground a few feet away from me, but he was crawling away from the flames toward the pitiful shelter of a fire-hydrant. I couldn't see Lane anywhere.

Ears ringing, blood pounding, I stumbled to my feet again. To my surprise, my hands were free. Maybe something in the explosion had sliced through the plastic cuffs. There was blood on both arms, but I didn't stop to examine myself.

Progressively, control of my body returned to me. I darted back toward the door of the jail, but it was smooth, with no handle, and it was apparently locked. A brick splintered next to my right hand as I pushed off the building and dove to put the burning Blazer between me and the roof of Tommy's.

If any more shots were fired, I didn't hear them through the roar of the flames. Something tugged at my leg, but I ignored it. Beyond the fire now, I darted around the corner of the courthouse, and leaned into the safety of the wall, slowly sliding down until I was sitting among the bushes of the landscaping.

Sirens wailed. I began to examine myself. My forearms were

sliced up a bit, but nothing looked serious. There was metal—presumably from the Blazer—embedded in my flak jacket. My right calf looked kind of messed up with blood and flesh, but I told myself it couldn't be that serious since it hadn't stopped me from running.

A cop came tearing around the far corner of the courthouse to my left. I waved my hand at her. "Don't go around this corner," I yelled. "He can't get you back here."

The cop ran over to me. She stopped ten yards away, with her pistol up and trained on me. I wearily put my hands on my head. Blood began to drip on my face from my arms.

"Don't move," she said. She shifted the grip on her pistol and reached up with her left hand to the radio on her shoulder. "I am at the southeast corner of the courthouse. I have a prisoner in custody, white male, sandy hair, green eyes. Looks like he's been hurt. Send someone out here."

She released the radio and dropped her hand back to steady her gun on me. The static crackled to life. "Hold tight, Sam," said the dispatcher's voice. "We don't know what's going on yet. Looks like we might have multiple officers down, and a hostage situation."

Over the roaring of the flames a few yards to my right, I heard the whine of an engine racing by at high speed. Sirens wailed after it. The officer in front of me did not look relaxed.

"The dispatcher called you Sam," I said. "You look much prettier than most Sam's I know."

She smiled in spite of herself. "Samantha," she said. Her radio crackled again and she turned it down, bending her ear to it. Maybe she didn't like me listening in. She turned back to me, her gun still out but pointed away from me now.

"All right, I want to get you safe and secure," she said.

"Sounds good to me."

"I want you to sit there, just like you are, with your hands on your head. I'm going to put my gun away and put on some gloves. You sit still until I come over there.

The truth was, I was quite happy to sit still. The shock of the explosion was beginning to set in on my body. I felt cold and shaky. Officer Samantha holstered her gun and pulled out a pair of latex gloves. She moved rapidly over to me.

"Watch the flowers," I said. "Summer is so short here."

She smiled. She was petite, blond, and pretty. She could not have passed the police height requirement by much.

"Can you stand up?" she asked.

"I think so," I said. "But I might need to use my hands."

She nodded. "That's okay."

I put my hands down and pushed myself to my feet. What blood I had left went rushing out of my head. I swayed, and Sam steadied me.

"Are you okay?" she asked.

The world was returning. I nodded, took a step on my right leg, and fell down. I was in the presence of a female, so I did not scream in agony. I felt more like whimpering than screaming anyway.

"I think maybe I got shot in the leg," I said.

"Stay put for a moment," she said. She knelt down and checked me over, quickly but thoroughly. She paused when she came to my left arm. "Was someone here? How did this get bandaged already?"

"Different incident," I said. "I've been getting around lately."

She examined my injured leg. "Looks like a bullet passed through the flesh of your calf. You have some cuts on your head and your arms, but everything seems superficial.

"Hey, when you're a superficial guy like me, that stuff hurts."

Office Sam smiled easily. Where were all the Officer Sams when I was being hauled in for murder?

"Do you want to try again?" she asked.

I nodded. "I just wasn't ready for it last time," I said. "If I can lean on you, I think I'll be okay."

She helped me up and put her shoulder under my right arm. We made our way to a back entrance to the courtroom. The door opened onto a corridor that led through the narrow width of the building to the front lobby. Several EMTs were in the lobby, as well as what seemed like dozens of police officers, both county and sheriff. The area was buzzing with radios and orders and people talking. Sirens still wailed nearby outside. Officer Sam sat me down on some stairs and went to get an EMT.

She returned with a guy I knew by the name of Peter Shore.

"Hey, Pete," I said. "Busy day?"

He shook his head, knelt down and started to examine me. "Why am I not surprised to find you in the middle of all this?" he said.

"Wasn't my choice," I said.

Officer Sam continued to stand there while Pete worked on me, so once more I was forced to abstain from expressing my true feelings.

"You've got a piece of shrapnel in your right arm," he said after a while.

"It was a Chevy Blazer, not a grenade," I said.

"Doesn't matter where it came from," said Pete. "Shrapnel is shrapnel."

"You gonna take it out?" I asked.

"Better let you see a doctor," he said. "Other than the bullet wound, some bruises, and twelve lacerations of varying severity, you are in great shape."

"Feel like it too," I said.

Sam had been talking to another officer nearby. They came over. Radios shuffled on and off in the background, and groups of cops and civilians were talking to each other. I could still hear sirens outside.

"Do you feel good enough to tell us what happened?" she asked. She had a notebook out.

"Pretty straightforward," I said. They were taking me from the jail to the courthouse," I said.

"Who is 'they?'"

"Tim Lane and a guard named Johnson. They had just told me that Tony Grantz was on the roof of Tommy's when a shot was fired. I'm pretty sure Johnson was hit. I think the next shot hit the gas tank in the Blazer, and it blew up. I was thrown to the street. I think the guy was still shooting. I got up and ran for the jail, but I couldn't get in. I turned around and got into the shelter of the courthouse. Sometime in there, I think I got hit in the leg. Then you came along."

"Did you see who was shooting?" asked Sam.

"I assume it was Detective Grantz," I said. "But I didn't see."

For the first time, it hit me—I was alive. Hollywood had finally screwed up. I was safe, and soon the whole town—the whole North Shore—would know the truth.

"Why would Detective Grantz shoot at you?"

"That is a very long story," I said.

Sam shrugged. "We've got all day."

So I told them about my theories. My mind wasn't very sharp, and I may have left several important things out.

"That's quite the tale, Mr. Borden," said Sam.

"Call me, Jonah," I said, "It will make it more pleasant if you should need to arrest me some time in the future. But I think you'll find out any minute now that Tony Grantz—Hollywood—is missing."

"Actually, we already have. Witnesses saw him coming down the fire escape in the alley with another person. They got into his squad car and drove away very quickly."

"I'll bet you'll find out the other person is the assistant district attorney," I said.

"Mr. Berg?" She frowned. "Actually, I think that they said it was a woman with dark hair."

Out of the milling crowd in the lobby, Alex Chan suddenly appeared. He strode easily over to me. "Jonah!" he said, his smooth face creased with concern. "You look terrible." He looked at Pete Shore, who was packing up his medical equipment. "Is he all right?"

"He needs rest, antibiotics, stitches, burn treatments, and minor surgery," said Shore. "But other than that, he's just fine. Nothing life-threatening, if that's what you mean."

"Why isn't he in the hospital?" said Chan.

"We're still waiting for the all-clear," said Officer Samantha. No one goes anywhere until we know it's safe."

"Well, how long is that going to take?" I asked. "What's the hold up?"

They all looked at me. "It's only been about ten minutes since the first shot," said Sam gently.

"Wow," I said. "Time always goes by so slowly when you're being shot at, and blown up."

Chan eyed me with disfavor. "He's going to be just fine, unfortunately."

CHAPTER 53

I want to go after Grantz." I said.

Officer Sam, her partner Pete Shore, and Alex Chan all stared at me. "Did you check him for head injuries?" asked Chan.

Just then there was a loud hollow thump from outside and the whole building shook. A moment later, two paramedics entered the lobby bearing Officer Johnson on a stretcher.

"There's been another explosion," said one of the paramedics.

"Need some help over here," said the other one.

"One more officer down," said another voice.

Suddenly the lobby was busier and noisier than it had yet been. I sank back on the steps for a moment. Sam and her fellow officer were talking with some attorneys. Chan was drawn into the conversation.

I began to wonder what had happened to Eric Berg. If, indeed, he was not with Grantz, then where was he? I looked around. No one was paying any attention to me. I got to my feet and hobbled around the edges of the crowd. No one noticed me. I slipped into a side corridor. Or I would have slipped, but what I did in reality was more like stumbling. My lack of grace was not observed by anyone else.

The building I was in was called the Superior Justice Center. It held several courtrooms, administrative city and county offices, and on the fourth floor, the offices of the district attorney. I found a stairway. At the next floor, I stumbled into the hallway and sat down. Three more flights of stairs, and Grantz wouldn't need to shoot me again. I heaved myself up and shuffled down the hall until I found the elevator. Ah, modern technology. I made the most of the rest on the way to the fourth floor.

The building seemed almost deserted. The shootings and explosions had brought almost everyone into the lobby area where I had been.

But not Eric Berg.

Gladys, the dour-faced secretary, was nowhere to be seen when I went into the DA's suite of offices. I negotiated the maze of cubicles, and opened Berg's office door without knocking.

He must have been looking out the window, but when I entered, his chair swiveled back to his desk. His face was white and strained.

"Jonah," he said. I could barely hear him. He cleared his throat. "Jonah," he said again. He didn't seem to know what else to say.

"Eric," I said. I hobbled over to one of the leather-upholstered chairs across from his desk. I eased into it with a grunt. "Why didn't you join the party down in the lobby?"

"Jonah," he said again. "Why are you here? How . . . ?"

"'How' is a long story. I think you know why. But *I* want to know why from *you*. Why Spooner? Why me?"

He looked down at his hands, out of sight, in his lap. "You know."

"I believe I do," I said. "But not everything. I don't know why."

He looked up again, and he was holding a gun, a chunky-looking black automatic. It was pointed more or less at me.

I shrugged. "You really think that's going to solve anything?"

He shook his head sadly. "You talked to Chan and Torino, didn't you? Set them onto me?"

"Eric," I said. "You don't have to do this."

He shook his head. "You have no idea."

"Then enlighten me. Why would you protect a man like Grantz?"

Berg's eyes were dull. "I knew him when I worked for the DA down in Chicago. He was with the Chicago PD."

"I think I heard that," I said.

Berg did not appear to notice my comment. "One night, I . . ." He swallowed. "One night, I was out late. I had too much to drink. There was an accident. The lady with me was killed."

"The lady with you?" I asked.

He nodded. "That kind of lady."

"Let me guess," I said. "Officer Grantz was the first one to arrive at the scene."

Berg nodded. "I was terrified of going to jail. I was terrified of losing my job, my marriage, my political career. I just wanted the accident, the girl—I wanted it to all go away."

"And Grantz made it all go away."

Berg nodded. "For a price."

"That you would protect him."

"Protect him?" Berg snorted. "Does a cobra need protection? He made me help him. I had to cover his little drug operation in Chicago. I sent two good, honest, officers to prison for Grantz's crimes."

"Then what?" I was looking at Berg's gun. The more he talked, the less he would think about shooting me. That was the theory anyway.

"I had to get out. The price was too high. So I came back here. I was born and raised in Duluth, you know."

He took a long and shuddering breath. "But about eight months ago, Grantz found me again. He made me get him a transfer up here. He wasn't here a month before he got involved with that Norstad girl. I don't know what happened, other than that she ended up dead. He made me cover that up. Spooner was the ideal fall guy—he had very bad history, you know." Berg looked me in the eye for the first time. "It wouldn't have been so bad, you know. Spooner deserved more time." He looked away again. "But something went wrong. We couldn't work up enough real evidence. In desperation, Grantz made up the confession. I knew we couldn't make that stick, but he told me not to worry. Then you know what happened after that."

"So what now?" I said.

"Grantz has gone crazy. Missy Norstad, Spooner, that other girl—Susan something—James Post, and now you."

"He didn't quite get me," I said.

"Yes. You've been very resilient, haven't you?" He looked at me again. His eyes were cold, dull, and dead looking. "The whole thing started to come apart when you got involved."

"Actually, I think the whole thing started to come apart the day you decided you could make moral choices with no moral consequences. At the very latest, the day you got into that car, three sheets to the wind."

Berg shrugged. "It doesn't matter much anyway. My career is ruined."

I stared at him. His career was the very least of the things he had ruined.

He raised the gun. "I won't go to jail, Jonah. I've sent too many people there myself. That path is not suitable for me. I'm not a convict. I won't wear that jumpsuit you've got on."

"Shooting me won't change what will happen to you," I said.

The gun held steady.

"Eric," I said, "it's over."

"Yes," he said. "It is."

He turned the gun on himself and pulled the trigger.

CHAPTER 54

I limped back through the empty hallways of the Superior Justice Center to the lobby. Chan saw me coming and came over. "Jonah," he said. "Where were you?"

"You don't want to know," I said. If I told either an attorney or police officer that I had been there when Berg killed himself, I would never get out of there.

Chan frowned. But all he said was, "Things are calming down a bit."

And they were. The people were starting to drift out of the lobby, and things looked less hectic and confused. The paramedics were gone, and Johnson with them.

"We've been looking for you to get you to a hospital," said Chan.

I opened my mouth, and Dan Jensen burst in the door.

He spotted us immediately and came over. "Jonah," he said. "I ought to have known you'd be in the middle of this." He paused. "You look like crap," he added.

"Thanks, Chief," I said. "You look pretty good yourself. I thought you were in Chicago."

"That's why I'm here," he said.

"Let's have that again," said Chan. Jensen looked at him with raised eyebrows.

"Chief Dan Jensen, meet Alex Chan, attorney at law."

Jensen took Chan's hand and grinned tightly.

"So, Chief," I said. "Chicago?"

"It was a ploy to get me out of the way, while Grantz took you down," said Jensen. "I guess we knew he was from there. We just didn't know what kind of character he really was."

At that moment, Jensen's radio startled to life. He turned away from us, listened and then turned back.

"Come on, Jonah," he said. "We gotta move."

"Hold on," said Chan. "He's still officially a prisoner. He's injured too."

"He's also the chaplain for Grand Lake Police, and Superior County too. We got a hostage situation, and we need him. There's no one else this close to the scene."

Less than a minute later, I was in the Grand Lake Police Department's unmarked SUV. Jensen had the siren on, and he was moving about as fast as I'd ever experienced in an automobile.

"Grantz is cornered down at Split Rock Lighthouse," said Jensen. "Got a hostage with him."

We were silent for a moment. I started to think I might know who the hostage was.

"So what happened in Chicago?" I said.

"Our boy Hollywood hired some thugs through his connections down there—guess they were part of the same crowd you came across a few weeks ago. They threatened Janie's family. I went down there to sort it out, and in the process I learned some pretty interesting things. Anyway, your arrest was all over the news— even down there. I know a bit now about how Grantz operates, and I caught the next flight up here. I guess I woulda been too late to save you."

"I think Officer Johnson at the jail saved me, though maybe he didn't mean to. I hope he's okay."

Jensen nodded. "Jonah," he said. "She sold you out."

"Who?" I knew who. I just didn't know what else to say.

"Leyla Bennett. She broke the story of your arrest. They all pretend to be objective, you know, but you can tell from the tone of voice and stuff what any reporter thinks. She slanted the story against you."

We were quiet. "When was this?" I said finally.

"Both the night you were arrested—she got a scoop on that— and also yesterday. Yesterday, she did a piece on you, claimed to be the only reporter to have had an interview with you. She gave your side, but made it sound as if you were crazy, you know? 'Jonah Borden *says* he and three other people were framed, but in an interview, declined to reveal who exactly was behind it all, and why.'" He glanced over at me.

"Watch the road," I snapped. "Dammit, you're going a hundred miles an hour."

"You swore," he said gently.

"Yeah," I said. "I did."

"I'm sorry, Jonah."

I nodded my head. There didn't seem to be much to say.

~

We made record time. Following the instructions of the dispatcher, Jensen climbed the hill and swung into the turnoff that led to the top of the cliff where the lighthouse stood. The lake spread out below us on either side and in front, like a rumpled blue carpet. It had turned into a beautiful June day.

We got out. There were two other police cars there. One of

them presumably had been driven by Tony Grantz. Jensen had his gun out. We skirted the right edge of the lighthouse itself. And then we saw them, out beyond the protective fence, at the very edge of the 160-foot cliffs.

Tony Grantz stood at the brink of the precipice, his left arm lightly around Leyla Bennett, holding her in front of him, with a gun pressed into her side.

CHAPTER 55

Rex Burton stood slightly to the left of Grantz and Leyla, his gun up and trained on them. He was unable to get around to either side for a clear shot at Grantz because of the drop-off. Hollywood had chosen well.

Jensen moved to cover Grantz from the right, but he too was hindered by the cliffs. He also kept his gun up, his eyes trained on Grantz, and spoke to me without looking back.

"Jonah, you up for this?"

"You bet," I said.

"You sure?"

"Yes." I said. I moved toward Grantz and Leyla, midway between Burton and Jensen. I moved slowly but steadily.

"Hey, Tony," I called.

"Back off, Borden," he said. He didn't sound friendly.

"It's over, Tony," I said. "End of the road. You don't want to do this anymore." I took another step.

Grantz was not looking at me, but moving his eyes between Burton and Jensen.

"Are you kidding me?" he said. "They're sending *you* to talk me in?"

"Yeah, it's a bit ironic," I said. "But listen, it's over now. There's no point in going on."

"Want your girlfriend to end up in the lake?" he said.

"Jonah," said Leyla. Her voice was just short of a scream. I took another step.

"Tell you what, Grantz," I said. "Let's trade. Take me instead of her."

He snorted. "I heard what you did to Spider and the boys. No, thanks. Besides, your beauty queen here is more fun." His eyes continued to dart between Jensen and Burton.

"Grantz," I said. "Those boys hurt me. Then you shot me. Then I got caught in the explosion. I'm not in any shape to take you on."

"What do I get out of it?" he said. "I like the girl." He still wasn't looking at me, and I took two quick steps and was beside him.

His head snapped toward me, and then back to Burton, then Jensen. He looked to me again, cursed, and shoved Leyla away from him, back toward the lighthouse and safety. He reached out and grabbed my prisoner's shirt, jerking me over and ramming his gun under my chin.

"Nice move, Borden," he said. "Very tricky. So you got what you wanted. Now what?"

"Tony," I said. "This is the end of your lies and your crime, but it doesn't have to be the end of you."

I could feel his breath, heavy on my neck. "What do you know about it?"

I kept my voice steady. "The night they killed Jesus, there were two people who betrayed him, turned their backs on him."

"Don't friggin' preach to me, Borden." He was snarling now.

"Judas betrayed Jesus," I said. "Sold him out for money."

"I don't care, Preacher," he said. "Shut up."

"Peter betrayed him too," I said. "Sold him out to save his own miserable skin."

"I said shut up," rasped Grantz.

"Judas knew he'd blown it. He went later and hanged himself. Peter knew he'd blown it. He went on to become one of the most influential and positive people in world history."

Grantz was silent.

"You know what the difference was between Peter and Judas?"

"I don't care," said Grantz.

I looked around. Burton and Jensen were still tense, like pointing dogs waiting for the prey to move.

"Peter believed he could be forgiven," I said, "no matter what he had done."

The pressure of Grantz's automatic against my neck eased a little.

"No one is past redemption," I said. "The only thing that can stop it is you, yourself. But if you want it, it is there for you. Even you."

The pressure eased some more. Then, incredibly, Grantz dropped his arm, releasing me. I took one smooth, slow step away and turned back to him. His face was working and twitching strangely.

"Are you saying God can forgive me?" he said.

"I am saying God *will* forgive you. All you have to do is ask."

He hesitated a moment. Then he raised his gun and pointed it directly at my head.

"Go to hell, Borden," he said.

There was a loud boom with a popping overtone, and I stumbled back, my ears ringing. Leyla screamed.

Grantz stared at me. A little blood came out the corner of his mouth. Then his body sagged and tumbled over the cliff into the still dark waters of Lake Superior.

CHAPTER 56

I turned to Rex Burton. There was still a little wisp of smoke coming out of the end of his gun.

"Nice shot," said Jensen, holstering his weapon. He walked over to Leyla. "Ma'am, are you okay?"

She nodded, but didn't say anything. I could feel the force of her eyes on my face. There was an awkward silence.

"Thanks," I said at last to Burton. "I think you saved my life."

Burton's face twisted. It was one of the first real expressions I'd seen him use. He checked his weapon, and then holstered it.

"I think I was wrong about you," he said finally.

"Yeah," I said. "There's been a lot of that going around."

I turned and walked back to Jensen's car.

~

I sat there alone while the parking lot quickly filled up with more cop cars, ambulances and reporters. I saw Leyla being escorted to a news van by a bunch of Channel 13 people. She looked toward the car where I sat, but then someone stepped into her line of sight. I didn't move.

Dan Jensen was pretty busy at the scene, so eventually I got a ride back to Grand Lake in an ambulance, and I spent the night in the hospital. I got the hospital to let me go after they ensured my rapid recovery by giving me a terrible breakfast and a worse lunch. The rest of the day I spent with police and attorneys, and finally, at about six in the evening, they gave me my own clothes back, along with my keys. As I was leaving, Rex Burton found me.

"Borden," he said gruffly.

"Look," I said. "We don't have to pretend we like each other now. But you saved my life, and I am grateful for that."

He nodded and looked almost relieved. "I gotta thing about priests," he said. "But I let it get in the way of good police work. That was wrong." He looked at his shoes, and then back at me. "It won't happen again."

I nodded. He nodded too, one man to another. I turned away.

"Borden," he said. I turned back. He sent a small object sailing in an arc toward me. I reached out and caught it. It was my knife.

"You're okay," he said, "for a priest."

I pointed my finger at him, turned and left the jail.

CHAPTER 57

On Sunday, I preached a heck of a sermon. Someone even suggested afterward that I spend more time in jail, if this was the sort of message that came of my experiences. I went home, changed out of my church clothes into jeans and a gray Vikings sweatshirt. I found some leftover roast chicken in my fridge and chopped it up, mixing it with celery, apples, walnuts, and mayo. I threw in a bit of curry, and in a fit of creativity, even a few halved grapes. I filled a croissant with the chicken salad, grabbed an orange and a bottle of Woodchuck's, and sat on my deck in the sun. I listened to "Maggie May" by Rod Stewart, and thought of Leyla.

After Robyn was killed, I had felt lonely all the time for almost two years. But in the years since, I had been quite content to be alone. After all, I lived with a gourmet cook and witty conversationalist.

But for some reason I was lonely now.

The Lake was spread out below me like some obscenely beautiful, three-dimensional work of art. The sun was warm. The food was good. I sighed. The afternoon hung heavy on my hands, and I went to bed early.

On Monday morning, I decided the universal specific was to go fishing. When I stopped at the SuperAmerica on my way out of town, the clerk wouldn't let me pay for gas, donuts, or coffee.

"You gotta make a living," I said. "Your boss will be mad."

"All paid for," he said. "That cop—the new sheriff's deputy from Chicago—you know, the one who killed the murderer last week? He came in here, put down two hundred dollars and said it was for you, and to call me when it was used up."

I shook my head, thinking of Burton. Softie.

It is impossible to remain blue or lonely when you are drinking coffee, eating donuts, and driving through beautiful scenery on your way to a world-class trout stream. I could feel life stirring in me again. Or maybe it was the coffee and sugar. Either way, it was good.

I fished all day. Man: 12. Fish: 0. I didn't want the bother of cleaning any, so I let them all go with a warning. At around five, I climbed up the bluff from the Tamarack to the parking area.

Leyla was on the hood of my car, leaning back against the windshield with her eyes closed. There were no other cars in the lot.

She heard me and opened her eyes, sitting up a little bit. I kept on until I was a few feet in front of her. I stopped. I wished in that moment that she was not so beautiful. Seeing her there was like the smell of flowers in the middle of winter.

I turned and looked down at the river, stained gold with the westering sun.

"I heard someone say once that no one was past redemption," said Leyla.

I nodded, still turned away from her.

"He said forgiveness was always available, for the asking."

I nodded again, still watching the river. A bird sailed the air currents far overhead.

Leyla got down from the car and walked around me until she

could see my eyes.

"And I'm asking, Jonah," she said.

I looked back to the river. "I was talking about God," I said. She flinched but her eyes stayed on my face. I turned and met them. "It hurt Leyla. It was . . . I can't even describe how bad it felt. It was a betrayal."

"Like you said, Peter betrayed Jesus."

I was quiet. I still looked out at the view. Finally, I said, "Yeah, like Peter." I turned and met her eyes. "Not like Judas."

She smiled a little uncertainly. Her eyes looked kind of wet. "So now what?"

I turned away from the sun, and, popping the trunk of my car, started getting out of my fishing gear.

"Where's your car?" I asked. I took off my vest.

She fluttered her hand awkwardly. "I . . . I had Jen drop me off here. I was hoping you could give me a ride, and we could, you know, spend some time together."

"Aren't you working today?"

"I'm on sick-leave—you know, to recover emotionally from everything. But I'm not sure I'll go back. I heard about a position opening up at a small-town newspaper on the North Shore. It's kind of a step backwards, but I think I might take it anyway. TV news— well, it did something to me, made me into a person I didn't like very much."

I pulled my waders off, slipped into my shoes, and put the waders in the trunk. "Where's the paper?" I asked.

"Little town called Grand Lake," she said. It's a small community, but there are some wonderful folks there. I think I've found a pretty neat church up there too."

I looked at her. Her smile was an impossibly winsome mixture of mischief and appeal. I slammed the trunk shut.

"So you've got no ride?"

She shook her head, her hair flying gently around her cheeks.

"Do you have your cell phone?"

She nodded, her eyes clouding. "I'll call Jen," she said, almost whispering. "She can pick me up."

"You don't need to call Jen," I said, irritably. "God made you too cute to need to be left looking for a ride."

Her dimples made an appearance. "Why, Jonah," she said, "you *have* forgiven me."

I looked back to the river.

"I guess at one level, maybe so. But the feelings don't all go away as easily as that."

She nodded. She seemed to have her composure back, but she was serious. "You've forgiven me for the betrayal, but it still hurts."

"Yeah. And it makes me cautious."

"Funny thing," she said, also looking at western sky. "I was cautious before. I was too ready to believe you would let me down. But now, *I'm* the one that let *you* down."

I nodded. "I won't lie to you. That's how it feels."

"So you've forgiven me, but . . ."

I was quiet.

"I want the chance to earn your trust back, Jonah."

I looked at her. The golden evening light streaked her dark hair. The curve of her high cheekbones was delicate, framing her deep, dark, almond-shaped eyes. She watched me closely, her eyes moving from my left eye to my right.

"You aren't the easiest person in the world to just leave behind and forget about," I said.

"Neither are you," she said softly.

I looked back at the sunset.

"Do you think maybe we could just start over?" she asked. Her voice was timid. "You know, sort of go back to the beginning and take it more slowly this time?"

I turned back to her. "I think that's worth a try anyway," I said.

She nodded and looked away. Then she met my eyes and grinned.

"Hi," she said, "I'm Leyla Bennett" She offered me her hand.

I felt a slow smile spread across my face. "Hi, Leyla," I said. "I'm Jonah Borden."

She tossed her hair. "So, Jonah, what's a nice guy like you doing in a place like this?"

"Picking up beautiful chicks," I said.

"I thought we were going to take it slow," she said.

"We are," I said. "But we don't need to over-analyze."

She breathed in. "All right then. Would it be okay for us to have dinner together tonight?"

"I think that would be okay," I said. "Did you have something particular in mind?"

She smiled at me, her eyes twinkling, her dimples irresistible.

"We have reservations at the Radisson in an hour," she said.

Did you enjoy this book?
Would you like to see more like it?
You can help!

- Post about the book, and link to it on Facebook, Twitter, LinkedIN and other social networking sites
- Review it on Amazon, GoodReads and anywhere else people talk about books
- Tell your friends and family about it. Blog about it.
- Check out the other books in the series!

The *Lake Superior Mystery* series depends upon you, and others like you, to keep it going and growing!

Follow Tom Hilpert on Facebook, and on his webpage: www.tomhilpert.com, and his blog http://fictionwritersblog.wordpress.com

Acknowledgments

First, my deep gratitude goes out to Eric Wilson, staunch friend, unfailing encourager of my writing. Out of his own free will, Eric edited hundreds of little errors out of this book. Those that remain are my fault alone. Readers would do well to check out Eric's own books – he is a NY Times best-selling author. Learn more about him at wilsonwriter.com.

My wife Kari also deserves my thanks for putting up with the many hours when I lived in the world of Jonah Borden, only vaguely aware of our home and family.

Lisa Anderson is the cover designer. As you can see, she does world-class work. Learn more about her at opinedesign.com. Many thanks to Lisa for patience with my questions and changes.

My deepest gratitude also goes out to you, my readers. Without you, Jonah and his compatriots would exist only in my own imagination.

A Jonah Borden Playlist

"Partita for Solo Violin No. 2 in D minor"—Bach

"Dust in the Wind"—Kansas

"The Chain"—Fleetwood Mac

"Rest for the Weary"—Marc Cohn

"Maggie May"—Rod Stewart

"Joy to the World"—3 Dog Night

"Unwavering"—Matt Maher

"Late for the Sky"—Jackson Browne

"From the Station"—Marc Cohn

A Jonah Borden Recipe

Pannekoeken

A great recipe to serve guests for breakfast. It leaves you time to visit while it bakes. It can be easily doubled or trebled.

Place ¼ cup butter in a small baking dish or pie plate.
Place in the oven and pre-heat oven to 400.
MIX TOGETHER:
1 ½ cups of flour
½ tsp salt
handful of sugar
1 ½ cups of milk
3-4 eggs
dash vanilla

By the time oven is pre-heated, butter should be melted in pan. Pour the mixture into the pan with the butter. Bake at 400 for about 25 minutes. It will puff up as it bakes. Serve with maple syrup, or fruit and whipped cream, or lemon juice and powdered sugar.

Made in the USA
San Bernardino, CA
28 February 2014